DECKER CARRIES AROUND A B̶E̶E̶R̶ H
HIS BOSS, A CHIP
HORRORS FROM
AND THE NEED FOR

Ex-marine and ex-con Tom Decker, paint clerk at Decker's Hardware, keeps his secret life from everyone except O'Neil, his ex-con pal and owner of the local bar. In his spare time, Decker robs banks, with the goal of building up enough cash to buy the hardware store from his despised boss whose family cheated his father out of it during the depression. Things are moving along nicely until he hooks up with the ex-wife of a NY City mob boss. It's not long until Decker is in way over his head.

"All the other writers of crime fiction who can write this well are dead." — *Robert Sabbag, best selling author of Snow Blind: A Brief Career in the Cocaine Trade.*

" Very Cinematic." — *Linda Biagi, Biagi Rights Management.*

i

DECKER

Kevin Roberts

Moonshine Cove Publishing, LLC
Abbeville, South Carolina U.S.A.

This book is a work of fiction. Names, characters, places and incidents are products of the author's imagination or are used fictitiously. Any resemblance to actual events, locales or persons, living or dead, is entirely coincidental.

ISBN: 978-1-945181-01-6
Library of Congress Control Number: 2016917489
Copyright 2016 by Kevin Roberts

Front cover design by the author; interior design by Moonshine Cove staff, cover images public domain.

ABOUT THE AUTHOR

Kevin Roberts is a U.S. Marine Corps combat veteran with a rather intimate knowledge of crime developed while  taking some missteps in his youth. He's had several Op-Eds published in the *New York Times*. He is currently working on a follow up to Decker for an anti-hero series while maintaining constant weekly snarkings in the Letters to the Editor of his local newspaper. Mr. Roberts has had many careers including but not limited to: cabbie, bank teller, Good Humor sales, demolition, lab technician, construction and import/exporter. He is not much of a volunteer and has never entered a writing contest. Decker is his first published novel.

ACKNOWLEDGMENT

If this book is in your hands it's in no small part because of the support, mentoring and friendship of, Robert Sabbag. Thanks Bob, see you at the weekly.

A great thanks also goes to: Tara Day Roberts, Kevin Roberts, Jr., Mary Roberts, Douglas Roberts, Karen Bucci, Christine Natlo, George Roberts, Cecelia Passabet, Jeremiah Roberts, Dianne Ripley, Linda Roberts, Gibson Craig, Peter Sherer, Chuck Nuccio, Bruce Figler, Peter Maine, Juan Sanchez, Joanne Carroll-Homlish, Joanna Cirasella, Chris Cox Miles, Benjamin Roye, Kristin Michaelsen Roye, Peter Rogovin, Michael Smatt, Marcus Trower, Sarah Biggs Hoyt, Jim Kreindler, Commandos: Charles M. Young and Bo Bryan. And the baristas at the Black Cow Coffeehouse.

DEDICATION

In loving memory of the self-proclaimed poet and comic—
"Comedy is my life." Elizabeth Ripley Roberts.

DECKER

ONE

If I had been a writer I could've written an entire book just on this customer's legs. They were long and her shoes with heels like ten-penny nails added to their length, and I was staring at them like they were about to speak to me. And she didn't seem to mind my staring either, the way she watched my eyes and kept twirling her hair with her blazing red–nailed finger. She had long black hair that she wore long and black. Her face was north of cute several blocks into the pretty neighborhood. Her lips were full but not too, nose ever so slightly tilted up, and eyelashes that fluttered seductively. But the most dramatic features on her face were her eyes, which were a pale green, the color of the Depression glass in my grandmother's china cabinet.

It was a warm day in October and she was wearing short shorts even though she looked a little older than the style really permits, but I guess in these days of Elvis and rock and roll a girl can get away with whatever she wants. I put her approaching the playful side of thirty. She had on a man's white dress shirt, with a few splashes of fresh paint on it. Just above the top of her shorts, which she wore without a belt, the shirttails were tied in a knot, revealing a perfectly formed innie navel on a tan, flat stomach. She had everything needed to make someone leave home without leaving a note.

But I wasn't a writer; I was a clerk in Decker's Hardware Store in Syosset, NY, a town on Long Island that, along with other parts of what used to be the hinterlands of NYC, was now called a "bedroom community." Long Island is a flat, forlorn slab of land that on a map sticks out into the Atlantic like an erection.

9

And in the decade after World War II it had become one large neighborhood of veterans, who had spilled out of Brooklyn, the Bronx and Queens, all of whom were working jobs in the city, raising families and investing a lot of time and energy on growing their lawns.

The hardware store was a one-storied white stucco building with fourteen thousand square feet of merchandise inside. It kept forty-four people employed and was the only hardware store within a thirty-mile radius. It was a cash cow. I worked in the paint department mixing colors for housewives so bored with suburban life that all they could find to do to entertain themselves, besides throwing Tupperware and mah-jongg parties, was to paint their living rooms every six months. This babe with the legs was waiting for me to mix her some Coral Essence in a latex, flat.

"It's for my guest room," she informed me, as if I had shown an interest.

Interest, in anything, was something I'd had little of ever since getting back from Korea four years ago. You take enough crap from commie North Koreans trying to kill you and a sergeant hell-bent on risking the lives of all the Marines in his platoon trying to kill every commie North Korean, and you start to look at your precious little time here in the cosmos a little differently.

When she had put up with my leg-gazing for long enough, she came up close to the counter I was working behind and asked, with some direct eye contact, "Has anyone ever told you that you look like one of those guys on the TV show *Maverick*?"

Her voice was soft, but the words had hard edges to them.

I knew the show; it was one of the few TV shows I watched. I enjoyed the antics of the two gambling brothers.

"Which one?" I said.

"The handsome one," she said. "Bret."

"Can't say as anyone has. What is it about me that reminds you? My full head of thick black wavy hair? My sharp, devilish blue eyes? The square jaw on my handsome face? Or is it just my overall boyish charm?"

"Well, it's certainly not your humility, that's for sure," she said, leaning over the counter, shrugging her shoulders and giving me an eyeful of red lace down her shirt in a move as calculated as any play in the NFL.

When a woman stands close enough to me that I can smell her hair rinse, the first thing I want to do is check her left hand for a wedding ring. And this girl's hand had five thin, wrinkle-free, naked fingers. Of course that could have been for any number of reasons. Could be she was married to some lug ain't got enough scratch to buy her a decent rock. But this woman's looks and shape suggested otherwise. What she had on the shelf wasn't going on no half-price sale.

"Humility's overrated," I told her.

"I think you're right there."

She did the shoulder shrug again; only this time our eyes didn't leave each other's. Something right there and then was telling me, *Tom, this is trouble waiting to happen.* But I went deaf to the little voice of reason that can guide a person in certain situations, like when to pull out of a poker game when you're ahead, or how to keep your mouth shut when a cop pulls you over. But then there are times when you just know you're feeling lucky, or you're sure the cop will take a bribe. And that's when you end up broke or with a fifty-dollar speeding ticket.

"You be needing anything else then, Miss, uh—"

"McKenna," she said. If the "Miss" wasn't right, she didn't bother to correct it.

"Irene McKenna," she added.

She looked around at the stock behind the counter as if looking for something that wasn't there.

"I'll need a drop cloth. A big one."

I looked behind me, and on the shelf where the nine-by-twelve drop cloths should have been was an empty space.

"Looks like we're out right now. But actually there's a shipment coming in a little later today, if you can come back."

There wasn't any shipment coming in, and I knew there were plenty of nine by twelves in the back room. I detected a tiny smile being hidden around her eyes and cheekbones.

"Oh darn," she said, almost childlike, like she was Shirley Temple missing a dance step. "I have other errands I have to get to. Maybe someone can deliver it to my house later today."

It didn't take a master chess player to figure out my next move.

"Yeah, I could probably drop it off for you after I get off."

"That would be sweet. Could you?"

"Sure, where do you live?"

She gave me an address in Oyster Bay, which didn't surprise me; there's all kinds of money in that town, old and new, and plenty of women like Irene McKenna to go around spending it. I told her I'd be there around five thirty.

"Oh, thank you so much, uh — "

"Tom, Tom Decker."

"Oh. Are you the owner?"

Which is what everyone thinks when first hearing my last name.

"No. I just work here. It's a long story."

The short version of which is that my family had owned the business for three generations, until my father had to give it up during the Depression. He had to sell it all — the building, the inventory, even the name — for

12

just enough cash to keep my mother, him and me out of Hooverville.

McKenna held her hand out to shake and I took it. The warmth and softness traveled right up my arm, across my chest and rattled around there for a moment. She turned, and I watched those legs take her to the front of the store to the register, where she stopped and turned to look back and see me smiling right at her.

Soon after she left, the Connolly brothers walked in, needing paint. The two brothers, Ned and Billy, have been in the painting business for as long as I've known them, which is ever since I worked with them during summers in high school. They are older than me by nine or ten years. Billy, the older brother, is a towering man with a big face and a red nose in the middle of it. He likes to keep his hair crew-cut short and flat enough on top to balance any brimming stemware. He carries a big chest of good nature and speaks with a small, friendly roar. He always refers to me as "Tommy me boy," revealing his second generation closeness to the Potato Famine, and is as well meaning as he is large. Ned, born eleven months after Billy, has hair that was once red and a voice that has been shredded by cigarettes and whisky, making his words comes out with more air than meaning. He is a paler, thinner version of his older brother but clearly the head of the business.

Both men are World War II veterans and always eager to swap war adventures. Ned, a cook on a troop carrier in the Pacific, never tires of telling me how revolting it was to watch Marines eat, and I've lost count of the number of times Billy has showed me the scar on his neck from when he was literally clothes-lined chasing Germans through the backyards of some tiny, nameless village in Sicily. Billy always ends one of his stories with, "But

13

heck, war is hell, ain't it, Tommy me boy?" waiting for me to reciprocate with a harrowing exploit of my own.

I never do.

"Two gallons of your finest Linen White exterior paint, Tommy me boy," Billy said, sounding like thunder one county over.

"Comin' up. You guys still working outside? Gettin' a little cold out there, isn't it?"

"A wee bit. But I'm sure it's nothin' like the cold Korea was, eh Tommy?" He opened up a grin on his rugged face, revealing the big gap between his two front teeth, and stood there like he had just hollered into the Grand Canyon and was waiting for his echo. He would have been delighted if I had told him of one of the moments that has been frozen into my memory since one frosty morning of December 1950 when I was on a squad-sized patrol walking point and the blankness of the snow-filled woods got to me and I became disoriented. The whiteness was all around, three feet deep on the ground, a white sunless sky above, tree branches bent over coated in ice, and the air all around me was filled with big, falling white flakes. I couldn't tell north from south, east from west. And if it hadn't been for the black tree trunks running perpendicular, I wouldn't have known up from down. The only thing heavier than the snow was the silence. The only sounds that came through to me were my own breathing and my footsteps crunching through the snow, which fortunately did not announce my coming, when I found myself twenty yards behind a machine-gun nest with three commie residents. I had stumbled behind enemy lines. *Now what?*

I finally started hearing something in the distance some hundred yards beyond the nest. I could make out the green forms of my squad approaching the kill zone of the Koreans' machine gun. The enemy saw my guys and went into action; the gunner slowly and as quietly as he could pulled back the cocking handle and chambered the first round. The feeder held the belt gently at the ready, and the third man took aim with his rifle on one of my buddies.

I got to a tree and like moss found the side to stay alive on as I drew a bead on the rifleman; I figured I would kill him first, then the belt man and then the gunner. And I had to do it all quickly, before my Marines mistakenly returned fire on me. I took a deep breath. The first two men were dead before I exhaled. When I squeezed one off for the gunner my rifle jammed. The gunner had turned and stood up by then and had his pistol out of his holster. I made a dash for him, the snow keeping my run in slow motion. Two steps from him he was fumbling taking the safety off his pistol. I took my jammed M-1 by the muzzle like a baseball bat and swung at the gun, sending it like a rip down the third base line for extra bases. He then came at me with a bayonet before I could get to mine. Fortunately he was a little squirt and I could hold him off by grabbing his weapon hand while I somehow got out my bayonet with frozen fingers. By then incoming rounds from my squad were snapping into the sandbags of the nest. I got the little guy to the ground for my own cover, and that's when it all turned quiet and personal. The little bastard tried to hold my wrist but I was stronger, hungrier for blood and had 172 years of US Marine Corps behind me. I was on top of him inches from his face; his pupils were the size of quarters, black with terror, and I could see straight through them to his very soul and beyond. As the tip of my bayonet touched his throat, the pleading in his eyes was deafening. He got out one or two foreign words before his part in the war came to an end, and my misery began.

"Yeah," I said to Billy, "it was cold all right."

Billy's face still had expectation on it, and Ned tilted his head to one side, gave a brief smirk and just stood there, a masterpiece of indifference.

***

Closing time finally came and I got to my apartment in ten minutes. I needed a quick shower before attempting to cross the border into Oyster Bay; they have standards in that town.

I lived above a three-car garage on a small estate owned by an old high school friend, Freddy DeFrancenzo, who went to college instead of war and then put his degree to use working for his old man, who owns a business that has something to do with plastic. Freddy works somewhere in the city, travels a lot and came home once in a while to make sure the pool was kept clean. He let me use one of the garage bays, where I had a little gym set up. I had a speed bag and a heavy bag hanging from a rafter, and a weight bench facing a full-length mirror on the wall. I kept my car outside. I put a few minutes on the speed bag and another couple on the heavy before going upstairs for a shower.

The apartment consisted of one large room that was my living room, a dining room and kitchen all in one, and a short hallway to the bathroom and the bedroom. The walls were painted a standard ultrawhite with a flat finish, and all the woodwork was coated in cheap, white, glossy acrylic enamel. Typical landlord decorating instincts, a fresh coat of some cut-rate product over everything — including window locks, doorknobs and hinges — and they think someone will pay more than its worth for this sparkling place. None of the surfaces had been painted professionally; the walls had rough patches of spackle that were not sanded smooth and were rolled right over. The windowsills had gouges and loose peeling paint that was just painted over as well. Most of the room was taken up by littered floor space. A worn, corduroy-covered couch was the largest piece of furniture I owned and in front of it was an empty Con Edison wooden wire spool that was my coffee table, and three feet beyond the table was my TV sitting on top of a stack of milk crates. I picked up the empty pack of Luckies and a full ashtray off the coffee table and dumped both in the kitchen trash can, and then proceeded down the short hall to the bathroom, where I entered for a shower. Later, as I stood in the middle of my bedroom getting dressed, I looked around to see if anything needed straightening out. The bed was a bunched pile of blanket and sheets, like it is twenty-four hours a day. Across from the bed my collection of paperback books, about the size of a cord of firewood, were just stacked up against the wall. The clock radio had the correct time and sat next to a small lamp on the rough surface of an unpainted nightstand. The only thing that needed my attention was another full ashtray located on the floor right next to the bed.

After emptying the tray I walked out of the apartment door wearing a clean shirt and jeans, jumped into my '51 Ford Custom and rolled down the graveled driveway. I made my way to Route 106 and headed north toward the Long Island Sound. Two miles later I crossed Hempstead Turnpike into East Norwich, where the air became flush with privilege, where people live by different rules, where they're guided by the strange religion of money and power after being born entitled and baptized in the river of wealth.

After I passed the second golf course I was in the town of Oyster Bay and I could see the black water of the sound. The sun was on its way to meet the horizon, bestowing sparkle on the water between the dozens of cabin cruisers anchored offshore. I found the road where Irene McKenna lived and was not surprised that it traveled right along the coast. The gate to her driveway was right across from a large cove that was filled with small craft. Being mid-October, most of the larger sailboats were in people's backyards by now or tucked away in some nearby marina to ride out the cold fury of a Long Island north-shore winter. The driveway ended in a circle in front of a house that was not in the least bit modest. It was a three-storied brick structure with the obligatory tall, freshly painted white columns holding up a portico over the front double door of darkly stained oak. I went about three-quarters of the way around the circle and parked at about eight o'clock, from where a quick getaway could be made if necessary. I grabbed the drop cloth and made my way up the four twenty-foot-wide marble steps to the door. I lifted the large, heavy anchor-shaped bronze knocker, which probably could actually have anchored down a forty-foot sloop, and let it fall against the brass strike plate. The door vibrated and I waited.

Irene McKenna opened the door as wide as the smile on her pretty face. She showed her small even teeth and said, "Oh, Mr. Decker, thank you so much for bringing that," pointing at the drop cloth.

"Tom," I said.

"Tom."

She was a little shorter than earlier in the store, which I attributed to a change in footwear to white tennis sneakers.

"Please, come in."

As I walked past her she still had on the short shorts and the man's shirt and had added a red Rosie the Riveter handkerchief on her head. Two black braids came out from under the red material down from behind her ears over her shoulders, reaching down to rest gently on the tops of her breasts. The way she reached up and twirled one of the braids made me wonder if I'd got caught leering.

She pointed to a bench against the hall wall and said, "You can put the cloth over there. Would you like a drink?"

She was looking at me with only the green in those eyes of hers. I looked back with my blue.

"Bourbon and soda?"

"Sure. C'mon."

I followed her down the hall a few steps and through a large doorway into the first room on the left. It wasn't a large room. There were white bookshelves on three of the four walls, all covered with a few coats of quality oil enamel with a stately soft gloss finish. All the shelves were crowded with books and elegantly framed photographs. On the last wall, a brick fireplace occupied most of the space, and a bar stood silent in the corner. The couch and two armchairs were leather; the rest of the furniture was wood — dark, antique and expensive looking. Her back was to me as she clinked some ice into two glasses and poured the liquor. I couldn't help but stare at the entire assemblage of womanhood before me.

When she turned around I quickly looked up at the ceiling as if admiring the plaster relief medallion in the center. With a rock glass in each hand she said, "Please," pointing to the couch with one of the drinks.

As I sat down she handed me one of the glasses, then sat herself down on the edge of one of the armchairs across from the couch. She crossed her legs and held out her glass in front of her, resting her elbow on her knee. I took a slug and swallowed almost half the booze, which was smooth of course and went down like silk. She matched me with a good belt of her own.

"So what's the long story about you and the hardware store?"

She settled back in her chair as if waiting to be entertained. I told her the story of how the Smiths, the Boston Smiths, had come to own Decker's Hardware, and of how John Smith, the swindling bastard who had bought — some say stole — the business from my father at the height of the Depression, gave it to his spoiled son Frank, who now owned and ran the place and was my thorn of a boss. I left out the part about how I would like to see Frank dead and how I had made, half seriously, some detailed plans to accomplish this.

She swirled the ice around in her drink with a finger as she listened. When it was my turn to move I took out a pack of Luckies from my shirt pocket and offered her one. She took it, and I lit it with my Zippo. As I went to put the lighter away in my pocket after lighting my own, she touched my hand and asked, "What's that?"

I held out the lighter in my palm with the Marine Corps eagle, globe and anchor emblem facing up. Her face became soft, and her green eyes seemed to glisten a little.

"The Marine Corps," she said. The words came out gentle and with regard.

She took a drag on her cigarette and blew the smoke straight toward the ceiling as she sat back again and looked at me as if I had just turned into Daffy Duck.

"When were you—?"

"I got out four years ago."

"Were you—?"

"Korea."

She nodded slowly. Behind those fetching eyes she was somewhere else for a moment.

"My dad was in the Pacific," she said.

The way her voice just turned cold and emotionless I knew the rest of the story. Some worthless little spec of sand in the middle of the Pacific Ocean with postcard-white beaches turned forever red with the blood of thousands of dead Marines. Her eyes followed my hand as I put the lighter back in my shirt pocket.

"I was twelve when a uniformed Marine came up the walk to our house. At first I thought it was my dad and yelled for my mom. But when my mom saw him from the window she started to cry. I remember being very confused."

"I'm sorry."

We both smoked and drank in silence for a few moments.

Searching for harmless small talk I managed, "Where did you grow up?"

"Well, all around the world, really. My father was a career Marine."

"An officer?"

"Oh no. He was a gunnery sergeant by the time he—" She trailed off and ended the sentence with a swig of whisky.

A new picture of this rich girl was coming into focus. In my four years in the Corps, I had caught only short glimpses of the children of Marines. They mostly kept them pretty sheltered from the enlisted riffraff. I imagined it a fairly rough way to grow up though — no neighborhood or regular friends through your childhood and a constant atmosphere of war and killing hovering over the household.

Finally she got up, took my glass and went to the bar to refill both our drinks. With her back to me she said, "And you, you've been here all your life I'm guessing."

She could guess from then until Ford goes out of business and she would never get me exactly right.

"Well, no, mostly I grew up in Brooklyn before coming to Syosset when I was seventeen."

I told her a little about the nuns in grade school and some high school hijinks. But I left out great big chunks about arrests, misdemeanors, reform school and basically my court-ordered military service.

"I was in Brooklyn once," she said. "My father took me to see the Dodgers at Ebbets Field."

I knew the place well. From the time I was seven years old until I was twelve my father would walk me to school in the morning. On opening day each spring he would take me, unbeknownst to my mother, to the ballpark, instead of Saint Anselm's School on Eighty-Third Street, to watch the Dodgers play their first home game. This was a special secret time of ours, when he would say things like, "How're those damn nuns treating you?" From pride or something I wouldn't let on about the severity of the beatings, but he made it known that he knew that I hated them. "But your mother, you know..." he'd say, like his hands were tied. But it was enough just to know that he was in my corner. Maybe he wasn't the best cut man, but he was at least there with a towel to fan me off.

"Oh yeah, been there many times," I said.

I took a slug of booze and thought it was time to ask the question of the evening. "So, is uh, there a Mr. McKenna?"

The quick smile on her face gave me the answer I needed, no matter what she was about to say.

"There is. But he's out of the country—" She paused for a sip of her drink, then continued, "And out of my life."

"Oh?"

"We've been divorced for a few years."

She put her cigarette out in the crystal ashtray on the coffee table between us. I took a final drag on mine and put it out next to hers. Any other time this would have been when I made a play, a move to something superficial and cheap. But something in the way that she suddenly appeared to be small and awkward in the air of comfort all around us made me pause, reassess. I sensed she felt as out of place as I did. The vague plan I first had in my head of carnal annihilation was melting away and in its place was an emotion that hadn't visited me in quite a while. I didn't even know what it was called; I just knew that this woman seemed deserving of someone's respect.

"I should be going," I said.

She picked up the two glasses, walked over and put them on the bar.

"Well, thank you so much for bringing over the drop cloth."

I told her it was nothing as we walked toward the front door. Outside, on the marble steps, I turned and said, "You available for a date sometime?"

"I'm in the book."

TWO

On Wednesday, my half-day, I was out the door and in the Ford by 12:05, and an hour later I was in Westchester County, some twenty miles north of the city. On the Taconic Parkway, before I slipped the '51 into third gear, I was doing well over fifty mph. The new Holley four-barrel carb that I had just put in last week was already paying me back like a Vegas slot coughing out nickels. With the Everly Brothers on the radio singing "Wake Up Little Susie," I was driving north to the job up in Nelsonville, NY, a small village along the Hudson River on Route 9. In third gear I asked that sweet V-8 to take us up to sixty-five and then settled back to forty-five, a respectable speed that wouldn't attract any cops. The car was six years old and a color that was once called Mexicali Maroon, but after sitting in a junkyard for four years while Mother Nature had her way with it, it looked more like old brick dust. And that was just the way I wanted it to look. I didn't want nobody thinking it was a hot rod all souped up for the drag strip.

The Taconic goes north straight up New York State, about ten miles east of, and parallel with, the Hudson River. I passed through Westchester County, with its soil the color of money, and entered into Putnam County farmland where the soil is rich and the people poor. The countryside was passing by me on both sides in a lush stream. To my right was a bank of rock where the road was carved into the mountainside. The top of the bank was lined with a mix of trees — elm, maple, birch — all turning a hard light green just before the fall color change. To my left was a stone wall and a steep drop hundreds of feet down to a valley below checkered with crops.

24

I got off the Taconic and traveled west on Route 301 toward the Hudson and Nelsonville, through fields of corn and cows, taking note of every telephone pole, every tree and every break in the white line on the road. The blue sky up ahead just above the horizon was inviting, the sun was bright and pleasantly warm, a perfect day for a drive. I rolled down the driver-side window and took in the warm, clear country air of October with its smell of harvest. I got to Nelsonville and proceeded to the far north end of town. From the Taconic to the job was eleven minutes.

The setup for this job was perfect. The cornfield that bordered the back of the rear parking lot was what finally sold me. It was a stretch of seven-foot-high full green leafy stalks that were about fifty yards deep, forming a wall that someone could take two steps into and disappear. Inside the building it even got better. I had been inside the week before looking for a notary public that I knew wasn't there through a little research in the local phone book. The place was completely run by women — even the boss was a broad. That meant that everyone was either a mother or someone about to be a mother, or a girl who had Mr. Wonderful on a hook and was about to reel him in to a life of marital bliss, and you know they don't want to screw that up. From the side-door exit to the cornfield were only a few steps — seventeen, or nine seconds, to be exact. I had this place cased solid.

It was late afternoon when I pulled off 301 onto a dirt road, which was a green corridor between two cornfields, went about a hundred yards, made a U-turn and parked the car on the side of the road. I grabbed the baseball cap from the backseat, put it on and got out of the car. I locked the door and placed the key under a nearby rock, not wanting to take the chance of losing it on the way back to the car. The walk back to Route 301 took two minutes. On the corner there was a drug store. I went in and made a call from the phone booth and then came back outside.

Mostly empty storefronts, warehouses, two-story wooden homes and a few brick structures occupied my side of the street. Across the street was a sad-looking three-story clapboard box with "Lane Plumbing Supply" painted on the front and two trucks parked outside. It was not a bustling concern. I looked up and down the street and found that I was the only pedestrian within sight. My building was a one-story concrete affair at the end the block. From my pocket I took out a pair of sunglasses and a Band-Aid, put on the shades and stuck the Band-Aid on my right cheek. I pulled down my hat to my eyebrows and walked through the front double glass doors.

"This is a stickup!" I shouted.

I liked the old-style phrase; I thought it brought to mind the good-guy folk hero type of gangster like my idol John Dillinger. By then I had my heater out, the TT-33 automatic pistol I had taken from that commie bastard I killed so many years ago, and I made a semicircle sweep with the gun pointing just above the heads of everyone in the bank. The two customers in line I asked not so pleasantly to kiss the floor, and I waved the bank manager and the two officers out of their cubicles over to where I could see them.

"Back away from the drawers two steps," I told the three tellers. That would keep them away from the alarm button. I went up to the first teller, a young blonde of twenty something, and took out the brown paper shopping bag I had folded up under my sweatshirt. I pushed it across the counter.

"Everything in there," I said.

I kept the gun close to my chest, pointing away but still in sight. Her eyes were darting between the gun and the Band-Aid, just where I wanted them to be and not on any facial features. She picked up the money with shaking hands. I noticed a small diamond on her left ring finger. I nodded toward the ring.

"You married?"

"Engaged."

"Just be calm and you'll have a great story to tell at the wedding."

She offered the slightest of nods my way and stopped filling the bag.

"That everything?"

She nodded with more effort.

"Pass it over,"

The next teller was the oldest of the three; her nameplate said "Florence Manning." Her hair color was twenty years younger than the lines on her face and her sweater's plunging neckline should have stopped plunging a decade ago. I stepped in front of her world and felt a cold stare coming my way.

"Everything," I said.

"You want the change too?" she said, pursing her lips, bringing the sarcasm front and center.

"I want you to change that damn attitude." I tapped her nameplate with the business end of my gun and added, "Florence."

As her eyes narrowed I said, "And step on it."

She continued putting money in the bag without a noticeable change in speed. I didn't like the way she looked at me with such contempt. She didn't know me. Something made me ask, "You have any sons, Florence?"

She looked at me without any surprise in her countenance. She said nothing.

"Any of them cops?"

She stopped transferring the cash and said, "You'll get caught, you know." She paused. "One day."

"But not today, doll."

I nodded sideways to the next teller. Florence handed the bag over to one Emily Peterson. Emily was a tall, thin woman about the age of Irene McKenna. She had long hair a chestnut color that reminded me of some of the nags at Belmont I've lost money on. She wore it in a ponytail, which along with her tortoise-rimmed glasses, gave her that classic librarian look, and with money in her hands she looked out of place. She appeared smart and ready to follow any orders given. With her long fingers she transferred the cash like a smooth blackjack dealer. She looked up at me once and quickly looked back down to her task, being nervous, shy and frightened all at once.

"You're doing fine. In a minute I'll be gone and you'll be having every handsome cop in town asking you out for a date."

A smile about the size of a dime brushed by her cheeks. She handed me the bag without eye contact, like she was following the how-to-stay-alive-in-a-bank-robbery manual. I backed my way to the windowless side-door exit.

"Okay, folks," I looked down at my watch. "Two minutes thirty-two seconds," I said with a nod of approval. "A new record."

My eye corner caught a deep smirk on the face of Florence, just what I was aiming for. I pushed the door open a bit behind me, keeping the group under the rule of the automatic.

"Please don't step outside this door. It might be your last step."

I pushed the door open a little wider and stuck my head out.

"Bring the car. Let's go!" I hollered to my imaginary accomplice and then turned back to the bank people.

"I'm five foot eleven." I told them and I walked out the door. I had to push the door closed behind me; the hinges were gummed up with so many years of paint.

I heard distant sirens and horns blaring on the far side of town — the police and fire trucks looking for the burning car that I had phoned in from the drug store. I walked through the rear parking lot not quickly but with long strides and reached the cornfield, stepped in and disappeared. Three or four steps in the only sound I heard was a crow's caw, and the air was shady and green, speckled with yellow corn silk, and the fat leaves brushed my cheeks as I crossed each row of plants. I tossed the hat and sweatshirt, which were recent purchases from the Salvation Army on the Bowery in Manhattan and completely untraceable. I pulled the Band-Aid off and in a minute I was on the other side of the field a few feet from the Ford. Before coming out of the corn I heard the roar of some machine approaching. Through the leaves I could see it was a farmer on a tractor. I put down the money bag and emerged from the vegetation zipping up my fly. The farmer gave me a salute as if thanking me for the fertilizer. I nodded, watched him go by, and then went back for the dough. Back outside I reached down for the key under the rock, got in the Ford, fired her up, and in eleven minutes I was back on the Taconic heading south and thinking about which fine restaurant I would take Irene McKenna to.

THREE

The next morning I set up the coffee percolator in the kitchen, washed up and got dressed for work. In ten minutes I poured the coffee, black and hot, and sipped it as I looked inside the bag of greenbacks. It appeared to be the biggest of my last four scores. I'd be late for work, but I stopped to count it anyway.

Three thousand seven hundred dollars.

That put the total at twenty-five grand. Another couple of jobs and I'd have enough to buy back the hardware store and never have to be worried about being late again. I knew Frank would take any offer I made; he'd whined about his bourgeois job ever since I'd known him. His old man only bought the business to give his lazy ne'er-do-well son something to do. Frank had told me any number of times how he couldn't wait to get his hands on the family cash so he could take on the full-time job of playboy.

I walked into the store through the back door ten minutes late and was greeted by Frank Smith and his face full of annoyance. He looked down at his watch and back to me, with a wrinkle on one side of his mouth.

"Tom, this won't do."

I tried to make my mug look as plain as boiled potatoes, devoid of any emotion or reaction to his admonition.

"Yeah, I'll try not to let it happen again," I said and took a step toward the time clock.

He stopped me with a finger in my chest. I looked down at the digit and deployed a cold stare that said,

Remove it or lose it. He did a quick read and dropped his hand.

"Do more than try. Next time I'll be docking your pay."

The arrogance in his eyes matched the contempt behind mine. I nodded, punched the clock and walked by his handsome face and gym-toned stature wondering what it was like to be that immune to the hardships of real life. He was an attractive guy — tall; sandy blond hair; blue eyes; charming when he wanted, or needed to be. College educated and smart, he'd been running a decent-sized business successfully probably using only a small portion of gray matter. And as God often does in bestowing upon the rich more than they need, He made Frank an adroit shortstop on the company softball team, and at the Christmas party Frank played piano and sang like Nat King Cole. He was single, with a different babe sitting next to him in his Corvette each week, and as an insurance policy for all this to continue, he was the only heir waiting for the family fortune to be dumped in his lap when the old man kicked. The only thing he didn't have was, a likable personality.

Frank would've loved to have me hit the bricks, but it would've been too much of a pain in the ass for him to have to find someone to replace me and then have to train him to run the paint department. Plus I think he liked the fact that he was in the position that should have rightfully been mine. He was right too; I wore the resentment like a plaid shirt. And the fact that he was ten years my junior filled my head with images of him pulling pranks at his private prep school while I was marching around the Chosin Reservoir with blocks of ice for feet. This guy needed a slab of reality to land on his big toe, and I couldn't wait to be the one to drop it.

There were two Dotties who worked in the store. There's the older, original Dottie, a fifty-year-old, who worked in the office, and the younger one was Dottie Gibbs, who had just started working at the store and whom everyone called Dottie G. When I got to the paint department I found Dottie G. helping some lady find some 220 sandpaper.

"Just a light sanding between coats and it should look great," Dottie was saying as I went behind the counter. "And if you need any more help, just call Mr. Decker here. He's here all the time."

The woman turned and walked toward the front of the store. Behind her Dottie wrinkled up her face and stuck her tongue out at me.

"Yep," I called out to the customer. "Allll thaaa time."

Dottie took a step toward me. "A little grumpy, Mr. Decker?"

I came back up from down behind the counter, where I was pulling out my apron. I said, "First of all, Dottie, enough with the 'Mister.' How many times do I have to tell you?" I was fumbling with the apron strings behind my back. "Mr. Decker was my father. And he's dead." The knot behind me was taking evasive maneuvers. "Damn!" I said. With that Dottie put her head down and made with the slow walk in the sulks.

"No, not you Dottie G." I turned my back to her. "It's this...f-f-f-fouled-up string."

She laughed. "You can swear in front of me, Mmm...Tom." She walked over, tied the strings and patted the middle of my back. "Does that make you feel all better?" she said, like a mommy to a toddler who just got his boo-boo kissed.

I turned and grinned down at her; I must have had a foot on her. I looked into her twenty-three-year-old eyes the color blue like on an airmail envelope, from there to the sprinkle of cinnamon freckles on her cheeks, on to a small, narrow nose and finally to her bubble gum–colored lips and the slight overbite that I found absolutely adorable.

"Thank you, sorry if I was a little—" I looked up at the clock.

"A little late, were you? And Mr. Toad Face gave you an earful, right?"

"Something like that."

Neither of us had stepped back after the knot-tying ceremony and I started to take in more of her. Her hair was jet black, very short. She was wearing a black sweatshirt a little baggy, black slacks very tight, and on her feet a pair of black flats. She wore silver earrings that dangled and on her fingers were silver rings — about two or three too many.

"Well, you can always come cry on my shoulder."

With that came a wink and then she turned and walked out of the department as if she were listening to some cool jazz somewhere in her head.

At coffee time I went into the break room before anyone else got there. I lit up a smoke and picked up the phone to call Irene McKenna.

A dry, gravelly male voice answered, "McKenna residence."

I wasn't exactly ready for that. I took a deep drag on the cigarette and got out "Tom Decker for Irene McKenna," trying to sound a little businesslike for some reason.

"Hold on" came back at me, neither polite nor rude.

The silence gave me some time to put some suave into my voice. Finally, "Hello, Tom" came across the line. It sounded like a friendly greeting, so I grabbed it to go.

"Hey, Irene," I said with as much cool as I could muster, "how's the painting project going?"

"Oh yuck," she said. "I had to turn it over to Sally, my handyman."

We talked small for a few minutes. Sally was Salvatore, an acquaintance of her ex's. It was he who answered the phone. He had come over to drain the pool and close up the pool house, but she talked him into helping with the painting. I wouldn't think it took a lot of talk.

As we moved on to the weather, Dottie G. bopped into the room. I turned to face the wall and got serious with my phone call.

"So I was wondering if you'd like to grab a bite Friday night."

"Friiiday." She said, stretching out the word, going through her mental calendar. "Yeah, I'd love to," she said, sounding warm.

"Great. Pick you up at seven?"

"It's a date."

As I hung up the phone and turned around, my eyes were greeted by Dottie G. standing in the middle of the room, slowly stirring a cup of coffee and staring right through me. I stepped toward her and waved my hand across her face as if checking how deep a spell she was in. She blinked and assembled a mild frown around her mouth.

"Big date, *Tom*?" The words crawled slowly out of her mouth.

I walked past her, took a last drag on my cigarette and put it out in the empty coffee can on the table.

"Dinner with a new friend," I said, trying to keep her as uninformed as a substitute teacher.

When I got back to the paint department I could see the side of a familiar face I hadn't seen in a long time standing there looking lost.

"Can I help you, knucklehead?" I said.

The face turned and smiled broadly. "Tommy Decker!" it said.

"Dave Sands. What the hell're you doing around here?"

We shook hands and stood in silence for a moment. He was probably thinking, as I was, *how the hell did we both survive our felonious Brooklyn childhood?* We had lived next door to each other and committed many prosecutable acts together. The only one, yet glaring, difference between us is that Dave never got caught, due in part to his Olympic-caliber running speed, but mostly because when I got nabbed, I never ratted him out.

"Jeez," he said. "How long's it been?"

I shrugged about ten years' worth.

"You live around here?" he said.

"Here in Syosset."

He wagged a double take. "No kidding. I just moved in to a place right outside of town. I've set up a veterinarian business."

"You're a vet?"

"I'm a vet. Can you believe it?"

Somehow I could. He was a good student, went home when his mom called. During our minor league crime days, Dave had to be talked into most of the capers. He could have stayed out of trouble indefinitely if it hadn't been for me. Me, however, I couldn't keep a nontrouble streak going for more than a few weeks, no matter how many slaps from the nuns or wait-till-your-father-gets-home threats from my mother. Once Dave was onboard though, we worked pretty well as a team, except for the last one, the one that landed me two years in stir.

"Christ, Dave, we haven't seen each other since—" I let it trail off. We both knew exactly when that time was, and when I saw the color abandon his face I quickly added water under the bridge. "We were some crazy, wild kids, uh?"

With that a little life came back to his cheeks, which were as shallow as the last time I had seen them just below his frightened eyes some thirteen years ago, when two coppers had grabbed us climbing out of the candy store window in that Brooklyn alley. One cop had Dave by the collar, the other had me by the arm. Dave's captor was a heavy cop with a schnoz the color of a Red Hot Jawbreaker. Dave sized him up and made a break for it. A quick jerk and he was free of the cop's grasp; in two seconds he was down the alley making the turn onto the boulevard. The cop gave chase for about three steps and gave up.

"Crazy wild," Dave said, shaking his head.

"A lifetime ago."

I asked him what I could do for him, and he gave me an order for some off-white paint to paint his examining rooms. I suggested a few sundries, and as I made up his order we compared our recent pasts. He gave me the rundown on the education needed to become a doctor of animals and I gave him some of my story, post jail. Of course I left out the part about my quiet double life of crime and apparent addiction to robbing banks.

"I heard you went into the army or something, you got medals too, right?"

"The Marine Corps. The medals are bullshit."

He gave me a slight stare with a question mark at the end of it.

"People shouldn't get medals just for trying to stay alive."

"Yeah, I guess." He looked to the floor, realizing it was something to be let go.

I handed over the gallons of paint, brushes, rollers and a drop cloth.

"We should get together," I said and meant it. "What're you doing later today, around five thirty?"

"Probably looking to take a break from painting."

"Great, let's get a drink. You know where Mitch O'Neill's is, over on Jackson?"

"I'll find it."

"Good. If you get there early, tell Mitch you're waiting for me. He'll put out a bowl of peanuts for you."

"I'll do that. See you later."

"Yeah."

At noon I went across the street for lunch at the silver blimp that was the diner in town. Inside, I was greeted by Willie the owner and the smell of pea soup. I heard "Tom" to my right and saw Dottie G. waving me over to the booth where she was eating alone.

"Please join me." She paused, and then added, "*Tom.*" She stretched out my name, giving me a good ribbing for my being so short with her in the morning. It worked.

"Okay. But only if you say we're friends again."

She held her triangle sandwich half with two hands almost touching her lips. "You'll never lose me as a friend that easy, Tom," she said and then took a bite in the middle of what looked like chicken salad on whole-wheat toast.

Angie Holmes appeared, pad and pencil at the ready, for my order. Angie is mother to Teddy Holmes, a high school kid who worked part-time in the hardware store. I think Angie has been at the diner since when they poured the footings.

"Special's meatloaf today, Tom. You want it?"

"Yeah."

"Mashed, peas and gravy, right hon?"

"Yep. And a Coke."

"What a surprise," she said and hurried off into the kitchen.

"No variety in your life, Tom?" Dottie said. "A little spice once in a while?"

"I've got plenty of spice," I said with a little complaint glazed on it.

"Yeah, I guess you got some comin' this Friday, huh?" She looked up at me with a mad flutter of eyelash.

"We'll see."

"Well, make sure I get a full report," she said and started making that straw-sucking sound on the bottom of her malt.

In a few minutes my food came. I picked up my knife and fork and told Dottie I would be unavailable for about ten minutes. She waited patiently, and when I wiped up the last of the gravy and took a long swallow of Coke, she started up again.

"At least tell me her name," she said.

"Not that it's any of your business, Dottie, but I know you're not going to let this go until you pick me clean. So I'll tell you what I'm gonna do. I'm giving you three questions and then that's it. Deal?"

With this she unslouched herself and sat bolt upright. "Okay. I'll take that deal."

"All right. Go."

She licked her lips and took a deep breath. "Okay. What's her name?"

"Irene."

"Irene what?"

"That will be question number two." I didn't want any appeals.

"Okay, Okay. Where did you meet her?"

I nodded toward the window.

"At the store?" Her tone was a cross between surprise and disappointment. "But wait, that's not my next question."

I signaled Angie for a check. She came over and put the two bills on the table.

"God," Dottie said, addressing the space between us. "Irene, who could—"

Suddenly her eyes and mouth opened wide, bringing out blue and her two cute front teeth.

"No, no. Not that rich bit — "

"Yes. And that's your last question."

I felt a little bad about leaving her in such a dumbfounded condition, so I picked up both checks and headed toward Willie at the cash register. I looked back to find Dottie's eyes steady on me as she shook her head slowly back and forth, her face riddled with disfavor.

FOUR

When I got to O'Neill's to meet Dave Sands it was a little after five. I found two patrons at either end of the bar, one by the front door end, and one at the men's room end. Both were drinking shots. O'Neill was behind the bar up against the register with his foot up on the sink. He was reading the Racing Form. I took a seat midbar in front of the Schaefer and Rheingold taps.

Only after O'Neill stepped forward, mixed me a bourbon and soda, put a coaster down in front of me and placed the glass on it while I took out a smoke, lit it, picked up the highball and swallowed about half of it did one of us say "Hey."

He went immediately into his daily did-you-hear-the-one-about, after which I gave him a well-deserved "That's a good one."

He had about a week's worth more beard than usual, a sure sign that he was getting ready for a side job. I made no comment on it to him.

"I'm meeting a guy here," I said. "Any strangers show up lately?"

"Not inna last ten minutes. What kinda guy?"

"Just a friend from the old neighborhood. Guy I used to run with. He showed up in the store this morning."

I took a lungful of Lucky and blew the smoke toward the end of the bar.

"Run with?" O'Neill said, like a parent wanting to know what time you got in last night.

"Small-time stuff when we were kids. He managed to go straight. He's a vet now, has a place set up somewhere just outside of town."

"What's he know about your present, uh, situation?"

"He thinks I work in a hardware store."

"Good," he said settling back into the Racing Form, "keep it that way."

I took a last drag from my smoke and put the butt out in a nearby plastic ashtray and lit up another. I thought about how this beautiful relationship with O'Neill had come about. It probably started in the summer of 1947 when I left high school and found I was finally out from under any law that said I had to be somewhere I didn't want to be or had to do something I didn't want to do. It was then that I got the idea to go into a full-time serious life of crime. With that goal and a complete lack of training, I decided the first thing I needed to do was to get a gun, and of course that meant stealing one.

At two a.m. one morning, the breaking and entering into Big Bob's Guns and Ammo did not start off well. The minute my elbow crashed through the establishment's back window, alarms went off, dogs barked and the ranks of the Syosset police force were sent out and had me surrounded in no time. A benevolent judge gave me a choice of two to ten in the state pen or a stint in the armed forces, which I found ironic, but I took the military deal. Part of my sentence included that I had to report to a probation officer for six months after my discharge, should I make it through the service without incident. I did, if you don't count government-sanctioned killing and marauding, and reported to one officer Nicky Brendano, a retired cop who was overweight, overworked and couldn't give a crap less about any of his parolees getting on the straight and narrow.

But it was in Brendano's waiting room where I met Mitch O'Neill. Ten years my senior, O'Neill was about five foot seven but didn't look short. He had black wavy hair and always looked like he was two or three days away from a needed haircut. His face had the same unattended look, with his jaw the color of soot below a nose that unimaginative people would call pug, but was really just the victim of twenty or so punches too many. His eyes, the main event of his physical makeup, were that deep Irish blue that perfectly complemented the daily bloodshot in them.

O'Neill had just gotten out of Sing Sing after serving a five-year stretch for armed robbery. This was a man I wanted to get to know. I waited until my six-month probation was over though, so I could associate with any "known felon" I wanted to without fear of being sent back to prison.

After some dedicated pestering, O'Neill, a little less enthusiastically than I would have hoped, took me under his wing and gave me a few pointers on crime. "It's all about beating the odds of getting caught," he told me, "relative to diminishing returns of course."

Of course, I said to myself at the time, and after a trip to the library I understood and agreed fully. He told me you wanted the score to be big enough to be worth your while, but not too big where too many men were needed to pull off the job.

"Too many guys is too many potential snitches," he would say. "On the other hand, one-man operations are risky. Too many moving parts to a successful robbery."

Armored cars were high risk, high reward but possibly deadly. Credit unions and check-cashing joints were Okay but took a good deal of casing. The perfect capers were where two guys who trusted each other could rob enough dough to satisfy an acceptable level of greed. Small bank branches with no guards were the best targets to address most aspects of the perfect crime. Nothing was perfect of course, he told me, but "ya just don't wanna go against the odds."

After a few years of these classroom lessons, O'Neill finally invited me on a job. There was a mail truck with a friendly driver in Jersey delivering a payroll to some small shipping company on the docks of Bayonne. O'Neill got this information from his often-mentioned "uncle" in the city. This was mob business that I didn't want to know about, and O'Neill never went any further in identifying his uncle other than saying he lived in Hell's Kitchen and "ran things."

Mitch O'Neill's Bar & Grill was a one-story building on one of the main drags in Syosset. It was bordered by a gas station on either side and had a small parking lot in the back. The interior was overrun with dark mahogany and the lighting was minimal, due in part to there being only two windows in the joint, and one of those was in the ladies' room. The said mahogany had collected from over the years about an inch-thick layer of combined varnish, shellac, and either lacquer or some of this new poly stuff from DuPont. The building has housed a bar ever since it was built in '37 the same year Earhart went missing, which was also the last time the inside walls had seen a new coat of paint. Johnny Mills, rumored at the time as being a surviving member of the Dutch Schultz gang, was its first owner, and the place has been in the hands of some level of gangster ever since. I wasn't clear on who currently owned the place and didn't care. O'Neill took over management around the time I met him in '53.

On the morning of the robbery I met O'Neill in the lot behind his place at six a.m. sharp. We drove to Newark airport. It was during a depressing mid-July heat wave and along the way O'Neill briefed me on what was going to happen and my part in it.

"The job should be easy enough with the driver on our side," he said. "But there *will* be an armed guard who is not our friend."

"What do we do about him?"

"*We* don't do anything. *I'll* take care of him. You move mailbags. From the truck to the trunk of our car."

43

"That's all?"

"Well, that and look like a mean son of a bitch."

We got to a lot at the airport and parked O'Neill's car right next to a black Chevy sedan. He nodded toward the Chevy, handed me a pair of gloves and said, "Get behind the wheel. The key's under the mat."

As I walked the two steps to the car, I felt the increasing heat of the day coming up from the asphalt. I got in the driver seat and O'Neill put on his gloves and got in on the passenger side.

"Whose car's this?" I said.

"Dunno. Some poor sucker who's walking to work this morning, I guess. My uncle put it here for us."

We drove toward Bayonne with the windows wide open so the airflow could give us a minimal break from the ninety something degrees of humid fire outside. On a stretch of Route 440 about a mile short of the mail truck's destination was a long curve in the road behind oil tanks on one side and about five square acres of weeds on the other.

"Pull over here," O'Neill said. "Leave two wheels on the road."

He pulled out a pair of sunglasses from his shirt pocket and put them on. I guess I looked at him with a question on my face. He said, "Your mug isn't that memorable; you'll be fine. Next time though, a fake moustache, something."

I nodded and he stepped out of the car, went to the front and lifted up the hood. "You stay behind the wheel and leave your door open," he said.

We waited like that for about ten minutes. Three cars passed; one asked if we needed help. O'Neill said we were okay, just waiting for "this hunk-a-junk Chevy to cool down."

Finally the mail truck came around the bend. O'Neill stepped out into the road just far enough so the truck had to stop or run him over. The open passenger window of the truck came right up to O'Neill's face. He pulled out a snub-nose Colt, put it up against the guard's cheek and gave him a dimple he wasn't born with.

"Out," he said.

The guard stepped out of the truck, hesitated for a moment, but when O'Neill raised his gun as if to clobber the guy, the guard thought better and O'Neill motioned me over with a head jerk. "Take his gun, throw it in the car."

O'Neill had a shirtfull of guard, who was taller than him by a head, and backed the guy up against the side of the truck while I took the revolver out of the holster on his hip and tossed it onto the backseat of the Chevy. O'Neill nodded toward the back of the truck and said, "Go."

I opened the back double doors and said to the driver, "Gimme those fucking keys."

He tossed me the keys and I put them in my shirt pocket.

There were about a dozen mailbags, and as I reached for one on top I looked up at the driver, who was half turned around in his seat, with his hands up in the air. He was shaking his head no. I kept grabbing bags until I got the up and down yes. I took the bag and placed it into the trunk of the Chevy. As I closed the trunk O'Neill said, "Let's go."

We got into the Chevy, turned around and before pulling away, I said, "We're not gonna tie them up or anything?"

"What for? Even if someone comes by and gives them a ride, it'll take them twenty minutes to get to a phone."

As we crossed the Bayonne Bridge, O'Neill threw the guard's gun out over the steel railing. I tossed the driver's keys.

"Jeez," I said. "I thought for a minute there'd be trouble and you'd have to slug the guy with your gun."

"No I'd never hit anyone with a gun. Bad press. People don't wanna read in the papers the words 'pistol whipped.' Thugs and niggers do that. We're neither."

There was morality mixed in there somewhere, which made Mitch O'Neill a complex character. He was easy to like, to dislike, to trust, not trust, fear and feel safe with, all at once.

I read in the papers days later that the haul was reported to be more that thirty thousand dollars. O'Neill explained to me how most of that had to go to "expenses." The truck driver was due a cut, as was O'Neill's uncle, who supplied O'Neill with all the dope on the job, the fact that there was a truck with dough on it in the first place, the route the truck was taking, and what kind of artillery would be onboard. I was paid a flat-rate two thousand dollars and was told it was clean money, not from the heist, and strongly advised not to spend it "fucking conspicuously." And that was it. That was my initiation into big-time robbery. It was just too easy not to be hooked.

For a week after the caper I showed up at O'Neill's joint every day, and every day O'Neill would tell me to get a "goddamn job."

"A convicted felon hangin' around town with no visible means of support is like a fuckin' bull's eye on your chest."

"A job? What the hell am I in the crime racket for?"

"Wise up. Ya think I wanna be a two-bit bartender the rest of my life? I got plans of retirement. *Early* retirement."

He leaned across the bar and got about two inches from my face, looked up and down the bar at the ten empty bar stools and said in the strictest of confidence, "I got a nice little nest egg gettin' fatter 'n fatter a little at a time. Someday I'll be takin' that egg to a nice little fishing village on the coast of Mexico. Live like a fuckin' king." He wiped his rag across the clean space of bar in front of me. "You should do the same. If you're smart."

The next day I asked for and got a job at Decker's Hardware, having what I thought was a smart plan of my own.

O'Neill was looking up and down the bar at the two fixtures at either end, leaned around the taps and said, "I got somethin' I want to talk to you about—" Just then Dave Sands walked into the bar. "Later," he said.

"Well, speak of the devil," I said.

Dave came over, gave me a handshake.

"Dave Sands, Mitch O'Neill," I said between the two men.

They shook hands across the bar.

Dave said, "A pleasure."

O'Neill said, "What'll ya have?"

Their hands still clasped, "Scotch rocks" came out of Dave like "Bless you" to a sneeze.

I got a refill, put a five on the bar before Dave could even reach into his pocket and walked us both over to one of the four booths on the wall opposite the bar. O'Neill went back to his Racing Form, and the two shot-drinkers at the ends of the bar continued breathing.

"So, a vet, uh?" I said.

"Yeah," he said. Behind his eyes he was sending out the hounds searching for a question to ask me.

"And you," he finally said, "what was Korea like?"

With the look on his face he was about as interested in an answer as if he wanted to know if I thought it would rain tomorrow. There was another question stalled inside him, but I could wait. In the meantime, how was I going to answer this one? Yeah, it was a real vacation, coming across trenches full of dead Korean men, women and children that the Chinese and North Koreans had executed as disloyal citizens. And how me and other Marines

47

answered these acts of the darker side of the human condition with our own form of evil.

"It was cold," I said.

The air between us got stale. I waited.

"Yeah," Dave said finally. "I was working for an animal hospital in Brooklyn right out of vet school, but, you know, Brooklyn's no place to raise kids."

I snapped my back up against the booth. "Kids?" I said, lifting my drink to my lips.

"Yeah, two boys. Jake and Tommy."

The liquor reached the back of my throat and stopped right there. I put down the glass, swallowed and cocked my head into a question. Dave took a long, long slug of his highball, while I took out my pack of Luckies, and before I could shake out a cigarette, Dave had his hand out. We lit up, and we both took in a king-sized drag and blew the smoke out in opposite directions. Dave sat back, held his cigarette over the ashtray with his left hand and with the fingertips of his right he had a grip on the rim of his glass, turning it slowly clockwise. When he had it wound sufficiently tight enough, he installed a forced smile and said, "You know, Tom, all these years I've felt bad about…"

I waved him off, the smoke in my hand arcing through the space between us. "Bad enough you had to name a kid after me?"

"Well, that was kind of a coincidence really. My wife's father's name is Thomas so—"

"And who is your wife?" I asked, not knowing why I wanted to know, except that he was my friend and in all these years I had never thought of him as anything less.

"Judy Stone."

"Judy Stone? The prom queen?"

"Yeah, that's her."

"Judy Stone?" I said, dubious. "You married Judy Stone, the prom queen?"

Dave showed some redness and a more sincere smile. "Yeah. But how did you know she was prom queen? You were in—"

"My mom would visit me every week, telling me everything that went on in the neighborhood."

Dave blew out some smoke, puffing out his sullen cheeks. He turned his head and looked through the wall. "I miss your mom. She was the best mom on the block. Everybody said that. Was hard to watch her change the way she did after your dad, you in—"

I knew all right. The rich Smiths took away my father's reason for getting up in the morning, making him feel worthless. After having the store swindled out from under him in '34, the same year they gunned down John Dillinger, my father struggled through the Depression like everyone else, but he never robbed anyone. Maybe he should have. For years he could barely provide the three of us with a roof or food. At the dinner table each night facing pancakes or beans for supper, my father would start off any conversation with, "Well, if we had the store—"

But we didn't have the store, and as he lost weight and his suits became too big for him, he appeared to be getting smaller and smaller with each day. Then the day before the landlord was about to throw us out in the street, I found the old man roped up to a beam in the basement. That was when I was thirteen years old and when I started to think maybe Dillinger had the right idea. If someone robs you, you rob him back. And from that day on I hated the moneyed in general and the Smiths in particular. And I swore that very day, as I walked back up the stairs of the basement, that I would make someone pay.

"Yeah," I said. "She tried going on the best she could, but I didn't help much with the way I was carrying on."

Carrying on so much that it landed me in juvie. For the two years I was in the detention center, my mother waitressed at night and washed clothes for the neighbors during the day just to hold on to our two-bedroom rowhouse in Flatbush. Each week when she would visit it seemed like she aged by ten years. When I got out she moved us out of Brooklyn to Syosset, where we lived in half of a rented two-family house. For the next few years I tried to stay in school and out of trouble, and my mother got a job as a cashier at Sears in Hicksville.

"Anyway," Dave said. "With a kid named Tommy, it was hard for me to ever forget what you did for me back then."

"I didn't do anything, Dave."

"Oh yes you did. The whole neighborhood knows what you did. The DA offered you a deal if you would put the finger on me. And you didn't." He sipped his drink and pulled on his smoke. "And because you didn't, they threw the book at you."

"Dave, youd've done the same."

Dave shook his head. "I don't know."

"Hey, it's nothing to be all guilt-ridden about."

"Really? You know it's not that easy, after all that guilt the nuns drilled into our heads for all those years. Everything was a sin. You couldn't take a piss without committing a sin for Christ sake."

We both drained our drinks at the same time. I reached for the glasses to get us refills. Dave jumped up and said, "No, I got this."

When he got back, I picked up my glass, held it aloft midtable and said, "To bygones being bygones."

Dave held his glass up reluctantly and said, "If you say so."

"I do."

After the clink of glasses something heavy left the booth. What filled its place was old neighborhood talk of kids we remembered, places where we played or got in trouble. We talked about how we had known each other since first grade and before, having lived only one door apart on our street. After two more rounds, Dave said he had to go and make like a dad and husband. We said we should get together again, and we both probably meant it. At the door Dave turned and said, "It was nice meeting you, Mitch."

O'Neill sent back a grunt toward the vicinity of the door, and I went over and sat at the bar.

"So what'd you want to talk about?" I said.

O'Neill threw his rag over his shoulder, reached behind him and grabbed a bottle of whisky from the bottom shelf. He walked up and down the bar and refilled the shot glasses of the two bookends. He gave me an upward nod and tossed his eyes toward the kitchen door. Inside the kitchen was a stainless steel sink and the smell of ammonia.

"I got somethin' cookin' should bring us a big score."

He opened the kitchen door about two inches and peered back into the bar. After he closed the door he ushered me to the rear of the room near the back door.

"There's this bakery over in Port Chester, Arnold's it's called. They gotta lotta people working there. Every two weeks they pay everybody, and get this" his eyes widened, and he measured out — "they pay in cash." A smile found its way briefly to the outer edges of his bright eyes. "Should be hundreds of thousands. Enough maybe for my retirement."

"Sounds like a big job." Maybe it was even big enough for my goal of buying back the hardware store. "How many guys you gonna need to pull it off?"

"That's the best part," he said, putting a hand on my shoulder. "My uncle's had the place cased for months. Says the room where they keep the dough is like in a corner of the building, with its own entrance that's always open during working hours, which is practically twenty-four hours, since they bake bread round the fuckin'

51

clock." He went back to the door to the bar, did his peering act again and then came back to me. "Inside there's a door you need to get buzzed in to. They got a glass wall with a hole in it so you can talk to the four bookkeepers inside. We come in there wearing masks, put a gun through the hole in the glass, and after the pencil necks stop shittin' their pants, we get let in. From there it's routine. You hold a gun on four of the guys; I take one to open the safe, bag up the loot, tie everybody up and we take off."

He asked me for a smoke. I shook two out of my pack and we lit up. O'Neill took two deep drags, blew some smoke just past my head and said, "So, you in?"

I really didn't think the question needed to be asked. I took a step back and furrowed my brow. "Of course. This sounds like some real John Dillinger stuff."

"Dillinger," O'Neill said, as if spitting out a pit from some piece of fruit. "Dillinger was a reckless killer. And he had a very short career."

He threw down his half-smoked cigarette on the kitchen floor, stepped on it, left it there and then walked toward the door back into the bar.

"Dillinger," he repeated. "Sure, he stole a lotta money, but in the end what did it get him? A higher spot on the most-wanted list, and a shitty last movie to watch."

He held the door open for me and as I went past him, he lowered his voice and said, "I want more than that."

Back at the bar, O'Neill refilled the shot glasses of the two ghosts and told me to come by the next night to go over a few things about our upcoming project.

"Tomorrow's no good, I got a date with someone special."

"More special than dough?"

"This babe is classy."

"Oh, I see. And where are you taking this classy broad?"

"I figured we'd go to Louie's over in Port Washington."

"No, no, no. A classy dame you take to Miller's Inn."

Of course everyone on Long Island knows that's where you go for a swank time, but the place is always booked.

"Yeah, I tried. I can't get a reservation there."

O'Neill reached for the phone behind the bar. He gave me a wink as he dialed a number.

"Terry," he said into the receiver, "Mitch. Listen I got a friend needs a table tomorrow night. For two. Eight o'clock. Name's Decker. Yeah, yeah, thanks, I'll give you the next tip that comes in from Belmont. Yeah, take care."

He hung up the phone, poured himself a short beer and said, "Make sure you tip the maître d' ten bucks on your way in."

"Is that Terry?"

"No. Terry's the head valet-parking guy."

Seeing the baffled look on my face he went on, "A while back it was suggested to management at that joint that it would be in their best interest if the valets joined the Teamsters union. It took two *visits* from some associates of my uncle, but they eventually, uh, complied. Terry was a guy I knew up in Ossining. He needed a job, so…"

"And a valet has that kind of pull with the maître d'?"

"No. But a Teamster does."

He threw down the rest of his beer, wiped his mouth with the back of his hand and said, "So who's the classy broad?"

"Her name is Irene McKenna."

O'Neill rubbed his chin. "McKenna?"

"Yeah."

"Oyster Bay?"

"Yeah. You know her?"

"I know of her husband, Enzo Fiori."

53

With the look on his face, I didn't know how he got the name out without puking.

"He's the don of one of the dago families in the city."

"She says he's out of the country."

He gave a short laugh. "Yeah, that's rich. He's out of commission maybe, but he's still in the country. He's doing twenty to life up in Attica."

"No kidding. She said they were divorced."

"Yeah, some kind of racketeering and murder rap they sent him up for. I heard she divorced him all right, but he keeps close tabs on her. She's probably sitting on all his dough, and he don't want her to stray, if you get my drift. I'd be careful if I was you."

"You're jiving me."

"What're you? A fuckin' beatnik? No I'm not *jivin'* you, the guy's bad news."

I told him thanks and started for the door.

"The next coupla days I'll be spending time over at that place," he said, "checking out the laya the land. We'll need to meet Wednesday to go over things. And keep Fridays open."

"Why Fridays?"

He put his thumbs under his armpits and flapped his elbows up and down. "That's when the eagle flies."

When I got home I spent an hour in the garage beating up the bags before going upstairs to boil up some spaghetti. I poured a jar of tomato sauce on it, opened a can of beer and called it dinner. Before going to bed I spent the rest of the evening watching *Maverick* on TV, studying the charm of James Garner.

FIVE

The next day at work I found nothing could shake my good mood. In the morning I was whistling and singing while stocking the shelves. Frank Smith heard me at some point and said, "How can you be such a happy worker in such a crappy job?"

I turned and took a step toward him, and he took a half step back. I pulled out the biggest grin in my quiver and said, "You know, Frank, let me ask you something. How much would you sell this place for so you can get out of *your* crappy job?"

For a minute there was a look of curious interest in his face, but it was quickly replaced with a dismissive sneer.

"Why, you just win the Irish Sweepstake?" he said with hands on hips and a condescending shake of the head. "Because you'll never get the kind of bargain my father got from your old man."

This was the kind of statement I would otherwise give someone a good pounding for, but Frank Smith's skinny Ivy League ass wasn't worth it.

"Well, the truth is, Frank, I've been pretty lucky at the track lately, and I just might make you an offer someday."

He made some kind of pff sound and said, "You'd have to hit every daily double for the next ten years to get up enough to buy this place, Decker."

But I could see dilemma building in his tightened jaw. He would've loved to unload the store; giving me the satisfaction of owning it was another matter. Inside that overeducated brain of his, he was looking for ways to justify or rationalize the deal. I let him have at it for a while and continued with the stock and my whistling, then slipped into singing Jimmie Rodgers's "Honeycomb," at which point Frank Smith turned on his heels and walked away.

At home after work I put in a quick twenty minutes on the bags and had a shower, and second shave of the day, then pulled my one suit out of the closet and put it on. I'd only worn the suit a handful of times over the last four years. I bought it right after my discharge from the Marine Corps thinking I was landing with both feet squarely into a neat corporate society where I'd get a job in some office with a sexy secretary and make the kind of money to buy a wife and house and live knee-deep in contentment. But those jobs were all taken by WWII vets who were hired the minute after they brushed off all the ticker tape from their parades. I quickly found that there just were not that many jobs available for high school–educated killers. So in need of a job — any job — to get my probation officer off my ass, I walked into the hardware store, where Frank Smith was more than willing to put me in a subservient position.

* * *

As I rolled the Ford into Irene McKenna's driveway I noticed two other cars parked around the circle; a silver Mercedes and a black Lincoln, which I parked right behind. As I got out of my car I saw a large, square man dislodging himself from the Lincoln. Like every mobster you see in the papers, either in handcuffs or dead on a floor, he looked about mid-forties, north of six foot, barrel chested, bellied and legged, and had a cigar stub clenched between his teeth. He was wrapped in yards of black cloth that resembled a suit, and a fat white head balanced on top. His pockmarked face had features that all blended into one another; where nose ended and lips began would be a guess at best. He walked straight toward me like someone who never had to *ask* for your lunch money; if you were smart you gave it up willingly and quickly. He tossed me an upward nod, took the stogie from his mouth and said, "Hey, a word." By the end of the sentence he was six inches from my face, his bad cigar-breath even closer.

"Sure," I said.

"Come with me."

I followed him over to the side of the garage, where a garbage can was on its side and the garbage ripped up and strewn on the ground. He replaced the trash into the can and stood it upright.

"Goddamn raccoons," he said then came toward where I was standing on the driveway.

"I unnerstand you're takin' out Mrs. McKenna tonight." He took a quick look toward the front door. "Make it your last date with her." To make his point more succinct he poked my chest with the two fingers that were holding his cigar.

With some jujitsu I had brought home from Parris Island, I grabbed his wrist, stepped to my left and pulled him forward, tripping him over my right foot, all in one move that took less than two seconds. He made quite a splash on the white gravel driveway. To his wide back below me I said, "You ought to be careful where you point that stogie, pal."

He lumbered his way to a standing position, brushed off what he could from the front of his suit, spat on the ground and took one angry, large step toward me. Just then Irene McKenna came out of the front door and made her way down the marble steps. The contrast between her and this lug in a dirty suit was stunning. She was wearing a waist-length leather jacket unbuttoned over a tight black dress an inch above the knee on the bottom and on top showing a modest amount of cleavage. Her black hair was parted to one side, falling just over the corner of her delicious right green eye.

"Oh, I see you've met Sally. Sal, this is Tom Decker, of Decker's Hardware."

For whose sake she left out any qualifiers as to my position at the store, I'm not sure.

"Tom, Sal Buetti."

I stuck out my hand. "Pleasure."

He grabbed my hand with soft, pudgy fingers. "Yeah," he said, with all the effort of a groom at a shotgun wedding saying, "I do."

Sal started walking back to the Lincoln. "I'll see you next week, Mrs. McKenna," he said, still brushing off the last of the white dust from his recent encounter with the driveway.

"Okay, Sal, have a nice weekend."

He looked at me with small eyes. "We'll talk again soon."

"Sure. Bring one of those cigars for me next time."

I went around to meet Irene at the passenger door of the Ford, and as I reached for the handle she looked over at the Mercedes and said, "Would you like to take my car?"

I knew somewhere in this world there would be some who would take offense, feel insulted or put down by the offer. But I carried not an ounce of that feeling on me, and I felt also that Irene intended no offense. And besides, a chance to drive a machine like that was not unappealing.

"Sure, want me to drive?"

"If you don't mind."

As we pulled out of the drive, she angled her body as much as she could to face me and said, "So, where are we going?"

"I thought Miller's Inn, if that's Okay."

"Oh my. I feel special."

I turned my head to look at her and gave her a respectful up-and-down study. I said, "You don't know that you *are*?"

A noticeable crisp blush developed, dissolved and then turned into a smile before I turned my attention back to

58

the road ahead of me. I could feel her staring at the side of my face when she said, "Maybe."

Turning to look out at the traffic absentmindedly, she commented, "I thought that place was always booked solid. How did you get a reservation on such short notice?"

I adjusted the rearview mirror and said, "I got some connections."

Again I felt the stare on my cheek. I turned the radio on low and we traveled the rest of the way with talk of things like siblings — none for either of us — and parents, the same. We got in the weather and the price of gas, and by that time we had arrived at the restaurant entrance.

As we pulled up, a man of thirty something wearing a short, dark blue jacket with gold-fringed epaulets sprinted toward the passenger door and opened it to let Irene out. I came around and handed the guy the keys. I noticed on his breast stitched in gold the name Terry. I reached in my pocket, came out with a five spot and handed it to him. I said, "I'm Mitch's friend. Thanks for the favor."

"Don't mention it, enjoy your dinner."

He walked around to the driver-side door, but before entering the car he showed a touch of courtesy by waiting until Irene had turned and started walking up the steps before checking out her backside.

Inside I handed the stiff maître d' a ten-dollar bill without even noticing the transaction myself and said, "Name's Decker. Something not near the kitchen."

He scanned the room, moving only his gray eyes, and then through some kind of telepathy he had a waiter standing in front of us in two seconds. "Take Mr. Decker to table three," he told him, and to me he repeated the house advice of, "Enjoy your dinner, sir."

We snaked our way behind the waiter to our table next to a window overlooking the duck pond. At the table were two busboys silently moving around china and cutlery, turning a table for four into a table for two. We sat and I ordered a bourbon and soda; the lady ordered the same. It was then I realized that, other than a hint of perfume, her alluring face was devoid of any trace of makeup and was simply a bare display of natural beauty. I felt myself staring and quickly fell into nervous first-date talk, which came to an end when I said, "So who's this Sally character?"

She smiled and used her right pinkie to pull the three strands of black hair off the lashes of her right eye. With a soft shake of the head, she said, a little guarded, "Oh, he's just an associate of my ex's."

"The ex who's out of the country?" I said.

Her narrowing eyes announced the arrival of a jig possibly being up. Before she could respond, the waiter showed up with our cocktails. He asked if we were ready to order; we said no. When he left she said, "Your connections tell you something?"

"Yeah. I hear things, but don't worry." I raised my glass. "Here's to dark secrets. We've all got them."

We sipped with eyes locked. After a moment she disengaged to stare out the window at nothing in particular. Perhaps to one of the ducks she said, "I moved to New York City about four years ago to pursue my dream of becoming a Rockette."

"You were a dancer?"

"I was a dreamer. I had no training, experience, or anything. Like any young person who can do the lindy hop all night long in the high school gym, I thought I could make a living at having fun."

She turned those green eyes back my way. "I was so naïve. But I did get a job dancing for money at some third-rate nightclub in the Village. That's where I met Enzo. He drew me in with his charm and his money. I didn't know anything about him, but the air of danger around him was beguiling. It wasn't until after we were married that I saw more and more of his evil."

The waiter came back for our dinner order. Irene ran her index finger down the menu and asked a few questions. The waiter, a middle-aged man with gray temples and an abundance of patience, answered all her questions and nodded with a slight bow with each answer he gave. She ordered an appetizer in a language I didn't understand and an entrée of roast duck. The waiter did not write anything down. I didn't really know much about swank protocol, but I did know food. I ordered the sirloin, medium rare, with baked potato, sour cream, *and* butter. The waiter disappeared.

"So anyway," I said. "Sally?"

"Yeah well, Sally," she said, sitting back a little in her chair, then forward again, leaning against the table. "You see, the *unwritten* portion of my divorce contract was that I stay living in the house until either Enzo gets paroled or until Sal says I can go." She gave a weak shrug of the shoulders. "I'm not sure why, but it's best for me to go along with it for, uh, health reasons. I was lucky he gave me a divorce at all, really. And Sal, well, his role is just odd. He comes and goes unannounced. At times it feels like he's the property caretaker, and other times like he's the warden. What's your interest in him anyway?"

"Oh, I just find him an interesting character. He seems to be very, uh, protective of you."

She did an eyebrow lift with slight head tilt.

"Back at the house before you came out he made it clear that maybe I shouldn't want to be dating you. But maybe it's just my imagination."

"I think it's not up to Sally who I go out with."

I wasn't sure how to take that. Was it the green light, or should I take a number?

"Well it's certainly not up to Sally to tell *me* what to do either."

"That's between the two of you, I guess."

That's for sure.

When the food arrived I tried to be as human as possible and not get lost in the attack. We talked idle through appetizer and entrée, covering politics — we both couldn't care less — and religion, the same. TV was fun but not important, as were movies. For music we both seemed to have the same casual passion. The old stuff from our teen years was defendable; she liked Vaughn Monroe, I Peggy Lee. The sisters Andrew and the brothers Dorsey were worth a listen now and again. As for today's rock and roll, we were both converts.

We finished our entrées and as darkness fell over the duck pond outside, we ordered coffee. When it was put on the table in front of us, we both sat back, waiting for it to cool, and stared at each other's face. My patience paid off and she revealed the first smile. It grew from the sides of her mouth, slowly migrating up and out to the corners of her eyes. I answered in kind.

"So why do I get the feeling, Tom Decker, that there is more to you than just paint and a handsome face? It's like there's a storm going on inside you and you've got the hatches battened down, riding it out."

"Well, it's something like that, actually. The storm will be over and sunny skies will come out when I have my hardware store back."

She lowered the coffee cup that was just up against her lips, placed it on the linen tablecloth and leaned forward.

"Oh, so you think that's it." Her right hand drifted across the table and touched my left hand. "You really think that's going to calm the seas, Tom?"

I don't know which made my heart pound more, the touch or the question. To help me think, I rotated my hand, palm up, and gently held the soft fingers that were resting on mine. I said, "Maybe I need a first mate."

She pulled her hand back gently and placed it in her lap. "Let's go," she said.

I paid the check and left what I thought was a substantial tip, picked up Irene's jacket from the hatcheck girl, left another tip and went outside, where I nodded to Terry, who dashed off into the dark parking lot to get the Mercedes. While we waited those few minutes my mind raced off into the future. I saw us on the marble steps of Irene McKenna's house. Irene made a silent follow-me motion and we stepped into the front hall. She stood motionless with her back to me, and I approached to help her take off her leather jacket. It got tossed onto the floor, and she stayed with her back to me, the zipper of her black dress commanding my attention. My hands were calm and followed the zipper down, revealing the white hollow of her lower back. I reached for her shoulders, barely touching them as she turned to face me, those eyes telling me everything. Her hands reached up behind my neck and pulled my head down gently. The kiss seemed to take up a hefty chunk of the space-time continuum before she took my hand and led me up the stairs to the bedroom. And that's where the full beauty of her body assaulted me and where we were both pulled into a vortex of desire and pleasure.

And that's exactly what happened.

In the morning I awoke to the alluring face of Irene looking down at me and the feel of her long hair brushing my cheeks.

"Want some breakfast?" she said.

I took in the real estate a few inches below her neck and said, "You mean from the kitchen?"

She laughed and threw a leg over mine and said, "Well if you want something in bed, that can be arranged."

After a few arrangements we got dressed and went down to the kitchen, where Irene filled the room with the smell of fresh coffee brewing and the sound of bacon and eggs frying. The sun was bright coming through the row of four double-hung, eight-paned windows over the sink. The kitchen was mostly white ceramic tile with dull stainless steel appliances here and there, making me think of old black-and-white movies of the thirties. As we were eating I noticed out the window that my friend Sal Buetti was wandering the backyard. I had the feeling he was not there to rake the leaves. I figured there was no sense putting off our unfinished business. I swallowed the last of my coffee, got up, put on my suit jacket and said, "I really should be going."

Irene came over to me and despite those long, shapely legs, she appeared small at that moment. She reached up with one hand and took possession of my jacket lapel. "I'd like to get to know you, Tom Decker."

"You mean more than just in the biblical sense?"

She positioned an inviting smile on her face that was lacking a I kiss. I filled in the blank.

"The feeling's mutual. I wouldn't mind finding out what makes Irene McKenna tick myself."

"So. An investigation is in order then?"

"No stone unturned."

I turned to make my way outside.

"See you."

"Bye."

Outside, standing by the side door of the four-car garage, was Sal in a cleaner suit than the last one I saw him in. He had his hand on the doorknob and said, "Hey, Decker, I got sumpin' I needa show you."

I knew this was going to be the slap-him-around threat; the one that follows the verbal threat. I knew the order hadn't gone out to bump me off or I'd be dead already. And I also knew that Sal had his own personal score to settle with me, so I needed to be ready to neutralize this situation quickly.

As I approached the garage, I noticed that both garbage cans were tipped over again with trash all around them on the ground. I entered the garage, which was empty except for what must have been a sports car under a tarp at the far end of the room and some gardening and mechanics tools about the floor and walls. Sal was just inside the door, standing in front of one of those flat, rotary lawn mowers. I stepped inside, closed the door and said, "What can I do for you, Sal?"

Sal took out a pack of cigarettes, lit one up and assumed the most gangster look he could summon from his apparently limited viewings of Edward G. Robinson movies. He said, "I got a message for you, tough guy."

He threw down his just-lit cigarette and made a move with his right hand toward the inside of his jacket. I knew the destination was going to be a shoulder holster and I instantly recognized that my assumption that I wasn't going to be bumped off could have been wrong. My next moves were generated by pure survival instincts, with a little help from a merciless drill instructor's teachings on getting out of any dangerous situation through the use of swift and unrestrained violence. I made a dive straight toward the big guy's chest, letting out a guttural scream as my left hand grabbed lapel, my right his right wrist, and pushed him backward right over the lawn mower. His two-hundred-plus pounds hit the floor with a good thump and my hundred sixty followed on top of him. His hand came out of his jacket with a pretty good grip on a shiny silver automatic. All he needed was an ounce more power than me and I was a goner. With the gun about two inches in front of his face, I made a quick forward jerk and smacked the rod right into his left eyebrow. It's a great place to hit someone if you want to get a lot of blood quickly. And to most people, even a cheap hood like Sal Buetti, blood brings panic. He surrendered his grip immediately, and the automatic came loose and landed on the floor about four feet away. I let go of his wrist, and he immediately went to his eye and started to clear blood out of it. I got up, kicked him in the groin and slowly walked over and picked up the gun.

As Sal got to a knee and was catching his breath, I found a rag next to a nearby Simonize can and threw it at him. He put the rag to his wound and said, "Goddamnit, I wasn't gonna shoot you."

"Sal, would you have taken the chance?"

The bruiser got out a reluctant, "No, I guess not."

I took the clip out of the gun, thumbed the bullets out, put them in my pocket and put the clip back in. I rotated my wrist, admiring both sides of the flashy chrome-plated weapon.

"Pretty," I said and handed it back to him. "So now tell me, Sal, what's this message you got for me?"

Sal slipped the gun back into its holster and tried straightening out his jacket with the one hand that was not applying pressure to a bleeding cut above the eye. He put a frown of annoyance on his mug and said, "You know what it is. The boss don't want you makin' time with the dame or hangin' round the premises." That last word came out of Sal's mouth sounding about as natural as a cat barking.

"You know you're going to need some stitches for that," I said, nodding up to his forehead.

Sal took the rag away from the gash over his eye to look at it and see how much blood he had lost. The blood that quickly dripped into his eye told him to put the cloth back, which he did.

"I'll tell you what I'm going to do for you, Sal. I'm going to let you go around telling the story about the door you walked into if you do something for me."

"I ain't makin' no deals with you," he said through the pain.

"Okay. If you want to continue this little dance party, I'm up for that. But Sal, I'm not some saloon keep late with a protection payment. I'm a crazy ex-Marine who has no problem snapping a neck now and then."

I let that sink into his thick skull for a minute, and then continued. "You know I have a few connections. I could let the facts of this whole incident here find their way up to people in your company's personnel department."

"Awright," he finally said. "Whaddya want?"

"All I want is a meeting with the don to plead my case. I want you to tell your boss that I'm respectfully requesting a sit-down."

That's how these mob types like to hear things. With so-called honor and respect as they put an ice pick through your eye.

"He's allaway up in Attica," he said.

I knew that of course, but I had a soft spot for this gorilla and let him think he told me something I didn't know.

"That's a long drive."

"Over four hours. I do it every Tuesday."

I wanted to get this meeting as soon as possible, but next week was going to be busy with O'Neill and the bakery.

"Okay, this Tuesday you're going to tell him — no, you're going to *ask* him — if I can come up to see him a week from this Wednesday."

"Not this week but next week," he clarified for his own sake.

"Right. Meanwhile I'll respect your boss's request and not see Mrs. McKenna. You tell him that, all right?"

"Awright."

"And get your ass to the emergency room."

SIX

The following Wednesday afternoon I spent my half day off at Mitch O'Neill's drinking at the bar and talking robbery in the kitchen.

"So what do I need to bring to this shindig?" I asked O'Neill.

"Just your piece. I've got everything else — masks, adhesive tape and aprons. And bring your own fucking gloves. You should own your own pair of gloves; you're a goddamn professional."

"Okay. Aprons?"

Some loud people came in the bar just then.

"I'll tell you later."

We left the kitchen and found Ned and Billy Connolly laughing at their own reflections in the mirror behind the bar. O'Neill went right to work serving the two regulars their automatic drinks, a bottle of Budweiser for Billy, and a shot of Four Roses and a beer chaser for Ned. I had another bourbon and soda appear in front of me as well. By the smell of toxic fumes starting to fill the room and the giddiness of the brothers, it was apparent that the boys had been working with either lacquer or some other brain-damaging product all day.

"Tommy me boy, how're you on this fine day?"

"I'm good, Billy, but don't you boys read the labels?"

Billy picked up his bottle of Budweiser, held it out at arm's length, then back closer to his face. He focused the best he could and read, "Choicest hops, rice—"

"No, the label on that can of lacquer you were using today."

From a stool over, Ned sharply corrected me. "Shellac," he said.

"Same thing. The fumes from that stuff's going to ruin what little's left of those pea brains of yours."

"Aaah," Ned said. "Been usin' that stuff for years with no problems." He swallowed the last gulp of his drink and slammed the glass on the bar, indicating a refill.

"Manners, Ned," O'Neill said calmly. The calmer O'Neill's requests were, the more seriously they had to be taken. He poured another shot and short beer slowly. It was clear O'Neill didn't like Ned; not many people did, really. If it weren't for his gregarious, easygoing big brother balancing off Ned's orneriness, the Connolly brothers would have been out of business years ago.

I tried to cut some of the tension. "He's Okay, Mitch, it's the shellac talking. Let me buy us all a round. You too, Mitch."

The brothers and I finished our drinks and O'Neill put new ones in front of us, then got his own shot of Bushmills 12 Year. I raised my glass and said, "To the paint industry. May it serve us all well."

"Slainte!" Billy said.

O'Neill threw his shot down silently.

Ned said, "Yeah."

After a minute, Billy was the first to break the silence. Pointing at the back page of O'Neill's *Daily News* behind the bar, he said, "I still can't believe the Yanks lost the series last week."

"Screw the Yankees!" I said. I still had a bad taste of baseball in my mouth from the whole Dodgers-leaving-Brooklyn fiasco. It all went silent again as the three entitled Yankees fans stared at me with looks of perplexed annoyance. They had no idea of what it is to be truly emotionally invested in your team. They were so used to having a championship bought each year that when they did lose, they were miserable. Whereas a victory like the Dodgers had two years before in '55, beating the goddamn Yankees, was to be cherished.

"Oh that's right," O'Neill said to Billy and Ned. "He's a Dodgers fan."

"*Was* a Dodgers fan," I said. "And if it weren't for the Dodgers being distracted by the fact that they were being sold out, *they* would've been in the series instead of the Braves."

"Well you can thank O'Malley for that," Ned said.

"I think it was the mayor," Mitch said. "He's the one who could've built the new stadium that O'Malley wanted in Brooklyn."

"No," I said. "It was neither of them. It was that fuck Robert Moses. Nothing gets built in or around the city without his approval."

"Who the hell's Robert Moses?" Billy said.

I wasn't about to go into a civil engineering lesson over spilt milk. I threw down the last of my highball, asked for another and sat quiet.

"Robert Moses is the puppet master," Mitch said. "He's the reason we can drive anywhere in the five boroughs or Westchester or Long Island. But hell, Tom, you really can't blame him for the Dodgers losing the pennant this year."

"And you guys can't be all broken up and miserable over the Yankees not winning the series once in a while."

"I'm not miserable, Tommy me boy," Billy said. "I haven't been miserable since, mm, let me see. Probably that day in Sicily when my commanding officer had his brains blown out in front of me by some Nazi bastard with a lucky shot and a fuckin' death wish." He leaned close to me and softly said, "I got the son of a bitch though." He then settled into his blarney pose and continued, "We were in this little shit village and we spotted the guy up in the church bell-tower. Nobody could get a shot at him from the street, so I decided, 'Screw it, I'm going up after him and ring *his* fuckin' bell.' It was personal. So I'm climbing the stairs and then a ladder, and

I can hear him get off four or five shots and then it goes quiet. I opened the trap door and there he was, reloading. I coulda just shot the fucker, but I was so mad, I wanted revenge. I got behind him, had him in a chokehold with my left arm, took out my bayonet and stuck it in his ribs. Course that was after he killed three more guys in the company. Now that's a miserable day. But" — I knew this was coming — "you must have had your share of misery in Korea, right, Tommy me boy?"

Maybe it was the three hours of drinking, or maybe it was the enigmatic fondness I felt for Billy Connolly, but I decided to finally give him something.

"Yeah. I had a moment of misery."

Billy's face went soft and he sat motionless. Even Ned put down his drink and spun on his stool to face me.

"It was a typical frozen-ass December. We took off for about a ten-mile march in the sub-zero weather. We all knew we'd be hiking in three foot of snow in boots that were made for the sands of Iwo. We didn't have winter linings for our field jackets either; all we could do was put on two or three extra skivvy shirts or a second utility shirt. We were going to take some godforsaken hill back from the Chinese, so we could get the hell out of that fuckin' reservoir."

"Jesus," Billy said. "That sounds pretty damn miserable."

I lit up a Lucky and shook my head. "Not really." I took a deep drag and a gulp of my drink. "We get to the base of the hill and got pinned down for three days without being able to move. Fuckin' Chinese attacked us day and night. But each time they did we killed scores of them. Each morning we had to check each other's foxholes to make sure nobody was frozen in. Eddie Martinez woke up one day with his legs frozen literally in a block of ice. We had to chop him the fuck out."

"Fuck," Ned said.

"We finally got some air support and claimed the hill in the name of democracy. Then three days after we took the hill we got orders to leave and continue with our, quote, 'fighting retreat.'"

"Christ, Tommy," O'Neill said. "For Marines, *retreat* had to be miserable."

"A little demoralizing maybe. But we finally get back to the safety of Hungnam. We lost thousands of guys, thousands more wounded just from frostbite and shit, and after a few days the captain calls me into headquarters."

"You're getting a medal," Billy said.

"No, I already had that by then. No, he calls me in and says, 'Decker, I got news from the States for you.' I say, 'Yes, sir.' He says, 'Your mother has died.'"

I put out my cigarette and finished my drink and didn't bother to look over at the three blank faces.

After a minute I looked up at Mitch and said, "But you know, Mitch, you're right. It wasn't Robert Moses, it was the fucking bullpen."

Four more drinks were poured and two cigarettes lighted up before Billy finally couldn't hold in his heritage any longer. "A man loves his sweetheart the most, his wife the best, and his mother the longest," he said.

We all drank to that.

***

The following morning I woke up with lead marbles in my head. I got dressed and when I bent over to tie my shoes, the marbles all rolled forward, banging up against the inside of my forehead. I made sure I got to work on time; I didn't need any crap from Frank. I went straight to the break room to get some coffee and ran into Dottie G. I hadn't seen Dottie since my date with Irene and I was really not in any mood to listen to any snippy comments so early in my hangover. I had to admit though that she looked a little cuter than usual. She was actually wearing another color besides black, a red silk blouse with small mother-of-pearl buttons, the top two undone. Her hair was a little different too; it was still short and black but with bangs added to draw your attention to the pale blue eyes set in her pleasing face. Throw in her usual tight black slacks and she made an adorable little package. When she saw me she came up close and studied my kisser.

"You look like hell, Tom. What did that broad do to you?"

"No," I said. "Bourbon did this to me, I just need some coffee is all."

"You need more than coffee. How 'bout I buy you lunch today?"

I think I surprised the both of us when I answered immediately. "That's a date."

The morning passed without my having to encounter Frank, and at noon I met Dottie at the diner. She was already there in a booth by a window. I slid in across the vinyl and said, "Hi."

She lowered the plastic billboard-size menu a few inches, peered over at me and said, "Hello, Tom."

I didn't need to waste time on the menu; I knew what I wanted — meatloaf, mashed spuds, peas, and gravy everywhere. I started to flip through the Select-O-Matic jukebox. I dropped a quarter in and Dottie looked up and said, "Play E twenty-four."

I pushed the buttons and then picked two songs of my own. In a few seconds Patti Page's voice came out of the ceiling somewhere singing "I'll Remember Today."

I said, "I figured you for something more bebop."

"Yeah. I like that too. I'm just feeling a little melancholy today."

"What is it? Boy trouble?"

A frown bracketed her mouth. "Please, boys are no trouble for me."

Angie came over and took our orders. Patti Page was done and Buddy Holly started singing "That'll Be the Day."

"Yeah, I guess you probably *have* a boyfriend."

"Not really. Are you volunteering?" She knew there was no answer coming back so she continued. "I try to keep my life uncluttered. I live a Zen kind of existence."

"Zen? Deep."

"Not really. I'm just following wherever the way takes me. What guides you, Tom?"

"Well, nothing exactly. I pretty much follow the way too, except I don't think about it all that much."

Angie came to the table with a Coke for me and tea for Dottie.

"So," Dottie said. "You don't wonder about the universe? Life? What it's all about? Do you think there's a God?"

"Well, it's not whether I think there is a God or not. I simply don't *care* if there is or isn't. It's all a big mystery to me, and anyone who tells you they have it all figured out is full of shit."

"Pretty bleak."

Angie delivered our lunch. I didn't waste any time; I scattered some salt and pepper on the dish and dove in. Dottie was watching with her mouth open in wonder.

"I don't think anyone's coming to steal your food, Tom. You can take a breath now and then. Is this how you ate at Miller's Inn with Miss Money Momma?"

I stopped to look up, my knife and fork in my fists pointing up to the ceiling.

"Actually we had a very pleasant evening. I was on my best behavior. I even used a napkin and not my sleeve."

This brought out that cute overbite smile.

"Do tell."

She was looking for the report I had promised I would give her.

"Well, she hasn't been a rich bit, er, person all her life. She married into money and then divorced out of it. She's actually very nice. I think you'd like her."

With that last statement Dottie opened her mouth, exposing her chewed tuna sandwich. She took a sip of tea, then held up an index finger, making a circular motion.

"She's got you wrapped right around."

I shook my head no and disappeared again into my lunch. After three quick forkfuls, I stopped and said, "You know, I think you got her all wrong, Dottie. Really, Irene is pretty down to earth. She lost her dad when she was little — "

"Yeah, I'm sure she's all sugar and spice. Just be careful. There's just something about her."

"Okay. Just for you."

"So, when are you seeing her again?"

"I don't know. There's a complication."

"Complication?"

I swallowed the last mouthful of diner grease and chased it down by draining my Coke. I gave a look of mild exasperation and said, "Oh, you know, schedules and whatnot."

"Yeah," her mouth said, but her eyes said, "bullshit."

We finished our meals, Dottie paid the bill and we went back to work, where I managed for the rest of the day to still stay clear of Frank Smith.

After work I went straight to O'Neill's for a briefing on the next day's bakery job. There were two extra barflies at the bar that Mitch was talking to, but when he saw me come through the door he immediately motioned me to the kitchen and left his patrons in midsentence. We went to the back door and he started right away.

"First," he said. "What are you doing about work tomorrow?"

"I'm calling in sick in the morning."

75

"That's good. I was going to tell you to do that. You don't want to ask for the day off ahead of time. It'd look like you had something planned. Your boss would have asked what're you doing, then you would've had to make up a story, put lie on top of lie. Sick is sick."

I took out my pack of Luckies, and Mitch put out his hand. We went silent for the time it took to light up, then he was right back with, "You got gloves, right?"

I said yes.

"Okay, gloves, your rod and a mean-ass attitude."

"Mean-ass."

"Okay. No booze tonight. Fill your tank with gas, go home and get a good sleep. I'll see you here five a.m. fucking sharp."

"Roger."

After stopping to fill up with Hi-test I stopped at the A&P on the way home, picked up a couple of Swanson's TV dinners and five little Drake's Coffee Cakes. At home I put on some sweats and went right to my little gym in the garage. I did upper-body weights, then the speed bag, and back to the weights for the legs and finally beat up the heavy bag. I was there for an hour and a half and worked up a pretty good sweat.

Upstairs after a shower I heated up the two TV dinners and ate them with a bottle of club soda, then enjoyed three of the Drake's cakes. After eating I went to the couch and found *Dragnet* on TV, with Jack Webb playing a cop about as realistic as the phony drill instructor he plays in the movie *The D.I.*, which I had just seen a few months ago. What a joke; Jack Webb, a loser who flunked out of Army Air Force flight training and then got a "hardship" discharge, and he's telling the American citizenry what a DI is like? Bullshit. The only excuse for the movie's phoniness is that it did take place at the San Diego Recruit Depot, which any Marine who came out of Parris Island knows is a fucking breeze.

Before turning in I cleaned my pistol, put it in a small brown paper lunch bag, along with a pair of thin leather gloves and a pair of sunglasses, rolled down the top of the bag, forming that perfect little handle, and placed it on the floor in front of the apartment door. Sleep came easy, with no dreams, not even one of my nightmares of frigid carnage that visit me most nights.

SEVEN

Bakers have the worst hours of any job I know. I had to get up at four fifteen in the morning to be able to get washed, shaved and dressed, get in the Ford, stop for a coffee, then drive the few miles to O'Neill's bar in time to meet him in the parking lot on time.

I found O'Neill at the back door smoking a cigarette and reading the early edition of the *Daily News* like he was waiting for a bus to take him to some boring job in a factory. He opened the passenger-side door, letting in the foul smell from the garbage cans up against the back wall of the bar, and sat down wordlessly. He placed two overnight carryall bags each the size of an Electrolux vacuum on the seat between us. I eased the Ford to the parking lot exit. Before entering the sparse traffic on the boulevard I asked, "You need coffee?"

"Had coffee an hour ago. You know how to get to Port Chester?" Without waiting for an answer he said, "Go."

We both put on sunglasses, and we drove for forty-five minutes in silence until we got to the crest of the Whitestone Bridge, when O'Neill looked east out the passenger-side window, hooked a thumb toward the distant water and said, "Your buddy, Robert Moses. Building another bridge right over there. If it were up now we'd be in Port Chester already."

"Moses," I said with disgust.

O'Neill again looked through the window and said to the glass, "Nice sunrise," and didn't care who heard him or if he got an answer back.

I glanced over to see the top tip of the sun and the bright orange-white sky, the color of a Good Humor

Creamsicle, glowing over the water of Long Island Sound.

"Yeah, fuckin' early's all I know."

"The early bird," O'Neill said rather cheerily.

"I guess. So, we gonna switch cars somewhere or what?"

"No. No need. You should use your own car whenever possible. It's *your* car. If you get pulled over, you got the papers, you feel comfortable. A hot car or hot plates is risky. You get pulled over, you're all nervous. Don't look good. Cop says to himself, 'Sumpin's wrong here.' Next thing ya know there's gunshots or a chase. At's no good. No, we're gonna park this car behind the diner that's right across the street from the plant. It's where all the workers go for their lunch and coffee breaks. And with these aprons" — he pointed at the overnight bags — "we'll just look like a coupla cooks breezin' along to our coffee break."

On the other side of the bridge we followed the sign for the northbound NY Thruway. Most of the road on this stretch was under construction, and by the fourth flagman I let out a long sigh.

O'Neill gave out a humorous grunt. "Your buddy again. But don't worry — we're goin' home a different way."

By the time we got to the town of Rye, on the southern border of Port Chester, it was coffee-break time for the construction workers, and most of the men were sitting on the guardrail drinking coffee out of steaming paper cups, and the heavy equipment — the dozers, the graders — was off to the side, allowing us to make some better time. I pulled into an Esso station to make my phone call to the store with my fake stomach virus.

"Decker's Hardware," the bright sunny voice of Dottie G. said. "Dottie speaking."

"Dottie, Tom."

79

"Hey there, daddy-o."

I've heard that expression tossed around by many people, always sounding untrue, like an engine not hitting on all eight. But Dottie paired the term nicely with her sweet voice and set a smile in my mind.

"Hey, scout," I said, not knowing where that came from.

"Scout. I like that. What's up, Tom?"

"Tell Frank I'm not making it in today. Stomach virus I guess."

"Oh, I'm sorry to hear that. Should I bring over some chicken soup at lunchtime? It's no bother, really."

"No, that's okay. I'm not sure about eating, plus I might be at the doctor's."

"Well, okay, I'll pass it on to Mr. Happiness. If you need anything though—" She paused, then said, "Of course I guess your *girl*friend will be nursing you back to health."

"No, I don't think so."

"Oh," she said, and I was taken aback by how many emotions could be attached to one word — she squeezed in surprise, thankfulness and hope, among others.

"Thanks, Dottie. I'll see you."

"Bye."

After a few miles we entered the industrial back lots of Port Chester, an area filled with gray concrete-block or red brick buildings one or two stories high at most. Some were connected with covered walkways or great silver pipes and ducts. All were connected to power lines that ran up and down both sides of the streets. Steam came hissing out from rooftops, from holes in the ground, from vents on the sides of buildings. From one block east came the deep metallic sounds of railroad boxcars squealing and rumbling into one another. Tractor-trailers roamed the streets grinding gears and backing up to loading docks with oblique stripes of yellow and black. The parking lots were slowly filling up with workers, who entered their buildings crisply through steel doors in uniforms of gray and green, logos embroidered over every breast pocket, names stitched in every color — Mark, Tony, Steve. The neighborhood smells ranged from the putrid stench overflowing garbage dumpsters to the eye-burning synthetic chemical concoctions to the choking, enigmatic amalgam of organic and inorganic bouquets. Finally, after a mile and a half of this manufacturing pastiche, the air slowly became sweeter with the scent of baking bread.

The redbrick bakery came up on the right, taking up a two-hundred-yard street block. It was bordered on three sides with a parking lot, partially filled. Most of the roof, where it was one-story, was crowded with smoke stacks, heating and air-conditioning units, and a bumper crop of those swirling silver vents that reminded me of Hershey's Kisses. One end of the building was three-storied and full of windows abuzz inside with secretaries and executives.

"That's our door right there," O'Neill said, pointing to a bronze-colored steel door on the right side of the building that was reached by four concrete steps with black pipe railing. "And here's the diner. Pull in, park in the back."

The diner — like every other diner in North America, a stainless-steel-and-glass tube with some neon — was just about directly across the street from the corner of the bakery where we would be entering and exiting. I pulled into an empty space behind the greasy spoon while O'Neill opened one of the grips between us and pulled out two white aprons.

"They don't have the Arnold's logo, but it shouldn't matter," he said. "White is white."

I turned off the engine and took the ignition key off the key ring and tossed the ring full of my other keys under the seat. We both slipped the aprons over our necks and tied each other's strings behind one another's backs.

"We'll put on the gloves just before goin' in," O'Neill said. "You *do* have your fucking gloves, right?"

"Yeah," I said like a child answering to whether he has washed his hands before dinner.

"Okay." He looked at the bag nearest me and said, "Grab that. Let's go."

O'Neill zipped his bag closed, picked it up and stepped outside. I picked up my bag, which felt empty and said, "What's in here?"

"Over a hundred grand in a few minutes."

I got out, squatted down and placed the ignition key on the pavement inside the left front tire. We crossed through the empty parking lot of the diner, got to the street curb and waited for the traffic stream to let us cross. On the other side of the street were two guys in aprons about to cross toward the diner. The shorter of the two was marbled with chocolate stains all up and down his apron. The taller guy's apron was as white as a nun's habit and starched stiff.

"Whadda we do here?" I said like a ventriloquist.

"We say hello."

The cars slowed down and we stepped onto the avenue, meeting the two cooks in the middle. Tall Mr. Starchy had slick black hair and mean eyes that bore a hole through my chest.

"Hey," O'Neill said.

Short, marble-chocolate guy said, "Hey."

Three or four steps out of earshot, O'Neill said, "Don't look back." As we stepped onto the sidewalk on the other side of the street he said, "Gimme a smoke."

I shook one out of the pack as he turned to face me for a light and to get a view over my shoulder at the diner entrance. "It's okay, they went right inside," he said, and we continued toward the side door of the bakery.

At the bottom of the concrete steps to the door, O'Neill flipped his cigarette off into the parking lot. At the top of the stairs by the door we both gave a quick look around; no one in sight. Gloves went on, and O'Neill pulled out a Wolf Man mask and handed me a Howdy Doody. I looked at him; he smiled. "Ready," he said. I nodded. "Soon as we go in you stick your piece through the hole in the glass, got it?" I nodded again. He pulled on the heavy door, which did not open easily, but when it did we both rushed in.

"Open the fuckin' door!" O'Neill said loudly yet calmly.

I stuck my automatic through the round hole in the glass and pointed it directly at an older guy with rimless glasses who was about a foot away from the glass. With his eyes fixed on my gun, he started blinking with fury as he reached over with a shaky, liver-spotted hand and pushed a small black rectangular buzzer. The buzz was loud and the vibration felt like an eight on the Richter. And even after O'Neill and I were inside the room and the door had closed behind us, the guy's hand was still on the switch.

I looked over at him, said, "Hey, how 'bout it?"

He increased the blink rate but took his finger off the buzzer. I looked at him little closer. The guy had to be mid-sixties, and in the space of the three seconds we were in the place, his color had gone from pink to white.

I told him, "Sit down on the floor, pop."

He sat. O'Neill gave me a look. I shrugged.

The three other accountants all appeared to be in their thirties. With their suits in various shades of gray, they practically disappeared into the bank of gray steel filing cabinets behind them. One of these jokers had on one of those green plastic eyeshades. At hip level O'Neill waved his gun and had them all move over to one side of the room near where the old man was sitting on the floor.

"Who's got the combination to the vault?" O'Neill said.

All three suits looked down at the old man.

O'Neill with a slight sigh said, "Over here, gramps. Open it up fast and don't make me have to start shooting you in the kneecaps."

The old man complied with shaky effort.

O'Neill addressed the three standing men. "You guys got a gun in here?"

The guy standing in the middle, a tall, well-built high school quarterback type — the guy who would give up his subway seat to the little old lady; the guy in the bar who got pummeled every night with phone numbers from every hot chick in the joint — raced his eyes over to a wall locker across the room and then raced them back and said, "No."

O'Neill gave a short nose laugh and then walked over to the locker. On the inside of the locker door he took pause to take in Marilyn's perfect porcelain-white body and nipples the color of cotton candy before removing the shotgun that wasn't there. He checked to make sure the gun wasn't loaded, then turned to the liar and said, "You, Pinocchio. Over here."

The guy stepped over.

"Stick your arms straight out, palms down."

The guy put his arms out and O'Neill laid the shotgun across the backs of his hands.

"If I hear that gun drop, I'll plug ya."

O'Neill tossed one of the bags onto the three-foot-wide steel table in front of me, which was bolted to the wall and had steel legs that were bolted to the floor.

"Everyone on the floor under the table there," he said. With his chin he pointed to the bag. "Wrap 'em all up to the legs of the table."

"What about Pinocchio?"

"Him too. But do him last."

I pulled out eight rolls of white adhesive tape, the kind that was on the handle of every sandlot baseball bat I ever struck out with, and had each person put their hands behind their back and around a leg of the table. I wrapped all their hands using up four of the six rolls of adhesive. They weren't going anywhere.

After I took the shotgun off Pinocchio's hands he groaned quietly and rubbed his forearms. "Take a seat," I said and then wrapped him up to a leg.

With the other empty grip O'Neill went to the vault, which was just a four-foot-wide steel door in the middle of one wall. The door had a combination dial and a wheel like on a tugboat. A few twists of the old man's wrist and a hard aport, and the door opened, revealing shelves floor to ceiling filled with stacks of currency. O'Neill looked over at me, and through the holes of his Wolf Man mask I could see his eyes sparkle. I nodded; Howdy was already smiling. He told the old man to get back on the floor and started filling his bag with money.

There was some movement on the floor and I heard someone say, "Martin, you okay?"

The old man didn't look good. His eyes were closed, his head tilted back and to the side, and his breathing was almost a snore. I took a step toward the wheezing man. O'Neill looked over and then right back to his work without slowing down the transferring of cash. "Gimme the other bag," he said.

I tossed him the bag. I looked at the other three guys on the floor. "He got a bad ticker or something?" They all shrugged in unison, like they didn't even know the man.

He was breathing through his nose, each exhale making a low plaintive rumble from down deep inside somewhere. In between his breaths I heard the clean, solid sound of two zips closing up two fully packed carryall bags. O'Neill kicked one of the bags, which, with its weight, only traveled a few inches toward me, and said, "Let's go."

I noticed the top shelf in the vault still had a few stacks of currency on them. I nodded in the direction of the shelves and said, "What about those — "

O'Neill cut me off. "I said, let's go."

After taping up the old man we stuck our guns in our waistbands under the aprons, picked up the two bags of dough and headed to the door. I took a last look at the old geezer on the floor. The last breaths I saw him take were shallow and slightly violent, jerking his body.

O'Neill stuck his head out the door to the parking lot and checked for traffic, pedestrian or otherwise. We dropped our masks on the floor and switched to sunglasses.

"Okay," he said. "C'mon."

Outside, the weather had turned November. Gray clouds blocked the sun and there was a faint, cold dampness in the air, settling a dreariness upon the world that should only be viewed from the inside of a saloon somewhere. In thirty seconds we were halfway across the boulevard. I couldn't help looking straight into the windows of the diner, where I saw Mr. Starchy staring at us. From the corner of my eye I could see his head turning toward us as we rounded the corner of the diner on our way to the rear parking lot.

When we reached the car I retrieved the key from behind the front wheel and opened the trunk, where we placed the two bags of loot and the aprons. Inside the Ford I turned the key and woke up the 125 horses. From his pants pocket O'Neill pulled out a folded piece of loose-leaf paper. I glanced at it to see that it had large numbers down the left column and a short sentence next to each number.

"Out of the lot turn left," he read off the paper. "Go for two lights, then another left on Mill Street."

I followed his instructions carefully, all the while monitoring the rearview mirror. After three or four more turns we were heading generally northeast, and soon the landscape turned from city gray to a country pale green. We were driving through tunnels of bare-branched maple and elm, passing stonewalls with gates and mailboxes, but no houses could be seen from the road. The damp day turned quickly to a light mist and then to a rain hard enough for me to have to turn on the wipers. The hypnotic sound of the wiper motor whirring and the blades streaking across the glass to slap at either end of the windshield had me sing-song counting out loud in rhythm with the blades — "One hundred *thousand,* two hundred *thousand,* three hundred *thousand*" — until O'Neill finally reached over and turned on the radio, filling the car with the carefully TV-packaged sugary pop sound of Ricky Nelson singing the teen hit "B-Bop Baby."

"Christ," I said, yet I tapped along with the beat on the steering wheel.

We passed a sign saying "Entering Connecticut," then a few miles down the same road another sign said "Entering New York."

"The fuck are we," I said after twenty minutes.

"We're heading north to a town called North Salem, New York, from there we'll make our way west to Route 9, which goes down along the Hudson."

"I know Route 9." I knew it from the Nelsonville bank job.

"Yeah, I'm sure. Just listen to my directions. And gimme those sunglasses."

He took my shades and his own and tossed them out the window into a wooded section of the road we were on.

"Hey, man. Those cost me ten bucks."

He looked at me with a false dim-witted expression on his face and said in his most mocking tone, "Hey, man, go buy yourself a fuckin' sunglasses factory."

And he started to laugh, slapping his leg, laughing deeper and deeper, slapping his leg harder and harder, until I caught it as well and started laughing with bouncing shoulders, pounding my hands on the steering wheel. I laughed until tears came and I had to wipe them away to see the road. It must have been five minutes before it all subsided. And then I said, "fucking factory," and it all started over again, both of us laughing like two patients in the dentist's office on gas.

"By the way," I said. "Why did you leave those last few stacks of dough in the vault?"

O'Neill turned toward me and leaned back against the passenger door. He said, "Singles are a waste of time, and the hundreds draw attention. There's plenty enough in what we got"

"Oh."

The rest of the journey to Syosset was spent mostly in silence, broken up only by O'Neill calling out directions or one of us saying, "fucking factory." On Route 9, about four miles south of the Bear Mountain Bridge, as I was looking less and less in the rearview mirror and thinking more and more about the look on Frank Smith's face when I made my offer to buy him out, I noticed a state trooper in his car on the side of the road watching the traffic for moving violations. I knew I was under the speed limit, but sometimes that's not enough. After I went past him I focused in on the mirror and watched him roll off the grass shoulder, onto the road and gain speed.

"Shit," I said.

O'Neill looked straight ahead and said, "What?"

"Trooper behind us."

The cop turned his lights on and came up close behind us. I waited to see if my guardian angel, whom I'd fired years ago, had decided to come back to bail me out. The copper let out the siren.

"Damn it." That angel never gave a shit about me.

"Listen," O'Neill said. "When he asks, we're looking for a place to do some fishing in the river."

"Where's your fishing gear, boys?" I impersonated.

"Oh, right here in the trunk, Officer."

O'Neill was not amused.

"Don't worry," I said, "I got something."

When pulling off a job, you want to have a story for why you are where you are. I figured I'd use the story I had ready for the Nelsonville job, since we were near that neighborhood.

I slowed down, coasted to a stop on the shoulder of the road, rolled down the window and waited. It seemed like an hour. The cop got out of his car and put on his trooper hat, which was very similar to a Parris Island DI's, and walked toward my window. He looked about my age, had a square face with sharp features as if cut like the crystal that's only put out on Easter. He was tall, well over six feet, and even with his trench coat on because of the rain I could tell he was fit and not one to be fooled with. But I knew a few things about cops. I knew, for example, that most were veterans, and that most of the veterans were out of the Marine Corps — and of those, most had seen combat. When he got to my door, he had to bend in half to get his head down to window level.

"Sir, may I see your license and registration, please," he asked with politeness right out of the academy.

I'd had it ready before he even got to the window, and handed it to him. This is usually when most people will say, "Is there a problem, Officer?" I don't do that; I wait for them to bring it up; I have absolutely no idea why I'm being stopped — I'm a totally law-abiding citizen.

He studied my license and said, "You live in Syosset, Mr. Decker?"

"Yes."

"What brings you around the Peekskill area today?"

"Well, we're just coming back from a visit across the river up there at West Point."

"Oh. You have friends there, do you?"

89

"Well no, not exactly. You see I was in the Marine Corps, spent some time in Korea. I just wanted to see where all those chicken-shit officers came from."

I thought I could detect a smile on his otherwise emotionless face.

"What was your unit in Korea?" he said.

"I was with 2/7."

"A grunt, huh?"

"Yeah. Were you there?"

"Yeah. I was with MAG-33."

MAG-33: Marine Aircraft Group 33. He was probably a pilot, meaning an officer.

"Oh, uh, sorry there, uh — "

"Captain," he said. "Would you mind stepping out of the vehicle, sir?"

He started walking toward the back of the car, and after I got out and followed him, I said, "You know, skipper, you guys really saved our asses on more than one occasion."

"Save it. Come back here."

My heart was pounding, making breathing difficult; my hearing was fuzzy, with pressure pushing against the inside of my skull. I watched the traffic on Route 9 going by like a swift river, but I heard nothing. I thought of O'Neill possibly turning psychotic and feared he might be coming out of the car blasting. To prevent that, I had to rein in my fear. I got to the rear of the car and saw the cop staring at the trunk. My hands were shaking; I put them in my pockets. The cop pointed at the trunk handle and said, "You better take care of that."

I was stunned with confusion for a moment. I caught O'Neill's profile through the rear window for a second; he was leaning forward reaching under the seat. I struggled with the cop's meaning. Did he want me to open the trunk? Then I looked more closely. The license plate is located right below the trunk handle, and the plate

90

was missing a bolt and hanging askew. O'Neill cracked his door open.

"Oh sure," I said with thick words. "I'll pull into the next gas station and take care of it."

"Do that," he said. Then he stuck out his hand. I looked at it for some time, slightly puzzled. Finally he said, "Semper Fi."

Suddenly it felt like Christmas morning and the last day of school all in one.

I shook his hand firmly like he was a long-lost friend. "Semper Fi."

I stopped at the next Esso station, fixed the license and then the rest of the drive back to Long Island went without incident. We pulled up to the back door of O'Neill's bar at just after noon. The rain had stopped by then and the sun was shining on the parking lot pavement, lifting up wisps of steam into the air. Outside the car I noticed the garbage cans had been emptied, and the air smelled as if it had been freshly cleaned with an odorless disinfectant.

We brought in the two bags and placed them on the stainless steel table in the middle of the kitchen, and we both stood there looking at them without speaking for several moments. Finally O'Neill said, "Go make sure the front door is locked and the 'Closed' sign is in the window."

On my way back to the kitchen, in the middle of the dark bar room, I heard that beautiful solid sound of one of the bag's zippers being opened. Back in the kitchen O'Neill was quiet and motionless, gazing at the inside of the bag like a young man who had just seen for the first time a real live woman's naked breast. A feeling of reverence filled the air, as if a celebrity had just entered the room. The green of the money against the tan leather of the bag seemed the most perfect combination of any two colors in the rainbow. I walked over slowly and bent over to stick my nose just inches from the cash. The rich clean-paper-and-ink fragrance was heady. The money was new and had not yet been tainted by the smell of any man's aftershave, or the perfume, lipstick or powdery smell from a woman's pocketbook.

I reached my hand halfway toward the top of the open bag, stopped and looked at O'Neill, requesting permission with my eyes. He gave a slight nod, and I picked up a pack of twenties and flipped them with my thumb like they were a deck of cards.

After a while O'Neill seemed unable to move an inch closer to the money, as if the vision before him was not real and would disappear if he were to move in any direction or disturb the air around it. He looked into my eyes, avoiding a glance at the two bags, and said, "Dump it all out."

I took the first bag, gripped both hands on opposite edges of the zippered opening, turned the grip upside down and watched the packs of fifties, twenties, tens and fives come pouring out like a fiscal retching. A few packs slid off the table's edge on to the floor, like junk mail I ignored them. I emptied the second bag and piled the money higher, adding to the mail on the floor. I tossed both bags off to the corner of the room and proceeded to stack the different denominations. O'Neill's part in the counting process was to hand me a pencil and paper and then stand back and watch. After an hour and a half of adding and re-adding, I stopped and wiped my brow with the back of my hand, took a deep breath, blew it out and said, "Three hundred twenty-one thousand four hundred sixty dollars."

After over an hour of silence, O'Neill finally made a sound.

"I think this calls for a drink," he said.

"No shit."

EIGHT

"One Dead, Half Million Stolen" read the headline in the paper the day after the robbery. Seemed the old man didn't make it. The inflated amount of money reported didn't bother O'Neill. "That's the press for you, or maybe some insurance fraud on the part of the bakery," he said. But reading that the old guy, Martin Thompson, "husband and father of three, grandfather of two," had suffered a heart attack "no doubt brought on by the traumatic stress of the hold up" — that was when a fistful of reality came up from behind me, spun me around and slugged me in the stomach. I hadn't felt such guilt since the first time I entered the confessional with masturbation on my soul. "Bless me, Father, for I'm worthless and weak."

At his bar the day after the stickup O'Neill, of course, had a different take on the situation.

"The cost of doing business," he said, blowing off a tragic death as if brushing so many peanut shells off his bar. "Course that could put pressure on the cops to step up the investigation. But if they had anything we'd be in cuffs already. No, we got away clean."

Clean, I thought, relative to what? Yeah, we didn't litter on our way back to my car maybe, but I didn't know about leaving a guy tied up and gasping for life as being all that clean.

O'Neill lit up a cigarette and blew half the smoke my way. I took out a smoke of my own and as I took a light off his cigarette, he said, "But what are you worried about anyway? You're not goin' all soft on me, are you? Your hero, Dillinger, killed people left and right. On purpose too."

"Yeah. But like you said, he didn't have a long career."

O'Neill watched me smoke two cigarettes to his one and felt moved to say, "You know what you need?"

"What?"

He turned up the brightness in his blue eyes and gathered up a flat smile. He looked up and down the barren bar and said, "A trip to Vegas."

"Vegas?"

"Yeah. Strictly business of course. We gotta clean up that dough."

He read my furrowed brow and said, "I'll explain on the drive out there."

I furrowed some more.

"Yes. You're gonna hafta ask that prick boss of yours for some vacation time."

"That's okay. I'm going to be *his* boss pretty soon."

Lines like commas appeared on the right side of his mouth. "Yeah. We'll talk about that. Meanwhile, get the week after next off."

It had been over a week since I spoke to Irene, what with the robbery and my deal with Sally. So on the Wednesday following the bakery caper, I figured it was time to give her a call. When everyone else in the store had finished their coffee and the break room was empty, I got to the phone and dialed her number.

"Long time," she said. "Thought you shipped off somewhere without me."

Hearing her full voice put a stir in my chest that a woman's voice hadn't done in a long time.

"No, no, I've been busy with a few things. Actually I was hoping we could get together toward the end of the week, Friday or Saturday."

"That would be fine. But I was hoping for something maybe a little sooner. Why don't you come over for a drink after work today?"

It was going to take a very creative excuse to turn down an offer so tempting. How could I explain that I was planning to spend the afternoon of my Wednesday — half work day — driving upstate to see her mobster ex-husband and negotiating with him, like she were chattel, and getting him to see his way to allow me to date her without rubbing me out? Any other ex-husband I wouldn't have had a problem with — I'd either ignore him or kick his ass — but criminals, especially so-called "organized" criminals, are usually to say the least, unstable. And they have an unwritten rule, like all their rules, about dealing with their women. Of course, all their rules can be broken, bent, sidestepped or just plain forgotten if the don says it is to be. Fortunately, lying and evasion come easy for me no matter how serious or superfluous the actual need to lie.

"After work. Damn, I'm visiting a Marine buddy of mine in a VA hospital upstate. But I'll be back probably around eight or nine, if that's not too late."

"That will be great. I'll have a little something fixed for us to eat then."

"Great, see you then."

On my way out of the store I ran into Frank Smith in the parking lot. The day was cold, gray, a bit windy, and I was wearing my old military field jacket, hunched shoulders and a turned-up collar. Frank was just stepping out of a brand-new out-of-the-showroom '58 Corvette. It still had the price sticker on the side window, but I didn't have to look at it to know they were selling for well over three grand. Despite the fact that Frank owned it, the sight of the car made my heart race. It was silver, with white coves and whitewall tires, and from any angle you looked at it, it screamed speed. I'd heard they were coming out with dual headlights but hadn't seen them until now. The way they stuck out from each fender, plus the oval grill, gave the vehicle a certain jet-age quality. I got up close to look inside and saw that it came with seat belts, which you were going to need, since I also saw that the speedometer now went up to a hundred sixty mph.

I didn't want to give Frank the satisfaction of letting him see my envy, but for a Corvette, exceptions have to be made. I looked over at him and said "Nice" with a strained sort of man-to-man frankness.

"It's more than that."

It was. But "nice" was all I was dispensing that day. He stood there with his aviator sunglasses, wearing a camel hair topcoat a darkish beige color that matched his hair. The coat was unbuttoned, and with his hands in his khaki trouser pockets, and a white silk scarf around his neck hanging down over the front of a powder-blue shirt, he was the very picture of success in a postwar America. Rockwell could not have painted it better. I waited for him to turn and take a few steps toward the store door.

"By the way," I said, making him stop and turn around, "I'm taking a few vacation days off next week. Monday through Wednesday, maybe Thursday."

I hadn't had a vacation in over a year, so I knew he would have to force himself to give me the days. With the last-minute request that was killing him, and the homely frown on his noble face, I knew I was going to be on the winning side of this encounter. He stood there for a full minute trying to think, I'm sure, of some way to make his decision not look like he was in any way acquiescing.

He turned his back to me again, and as he was striding toward the store entrance, he gave a slight turn of the head and appeared to be speaking to his shoulder when he said, "Make sure you line up someone to cover for you."

Game, set.

I would talk to Dottie G. about covering for me the next day, the thought of which made me curiously happy. I shook off the curious and got in the Ford, pulled out of the lot, stopped to gas her up and headed north for a trip through the poor farmlands of upstate New York to the Attica Correctional Facility. After four hours of passing barns with collapsed roofs, I rounded a mountainside and got my first view of the prison. As I got closer, the first feature that stood out to me — besides the repulsive, depressing atmosphere — was the great, gray wall with its antigrappling rounded top. The wall surrounded the entire complex and had to be over a mile long in total, and after parking the car, I found the visiting procedure was like trying to get over that wall.

I entered the door that said "Visitor Center" into a narrow rectangular room about fifteen by thirty, with old wooden chairs in rows as if set up for a union meeting in the Legion Hall. Three of the chairs were being used by three heavy black women of grandmother age. The walls were made of unpainted concrete, and at the far end of the room I met the first of the platoon of guards that it must take to put a two-person meeting together.

"Fill this out and bring it back," he said in his surliest, trying his best to make me feel like a common criminal. I took the small card without comment. He was a roundish, bowling pin–shaped guy standing behind chicken-wire glass in a small room made of steel walls put together with rivets the size of hubcaps, covered in twenty years of gray paint. I took the index card over to one of the sidewalls that had a shallow outcropping of concrete for a writing surface and took one of the short, stubby pencils provided to fill in my information. After breaking the points of two pencils I finally got the card filled out and returned it to the headpin behind the glass.

He looked at the card and raised an eyebrow. "You're here to see Fiori? What happened? Sally fuck somethin' up yesterday?" His tone was a shade more jocular now, but I maintained an attitude of detachment. He pointed to a door to the left with stenciled lettering that said, "Pull When Buzzed."

I stared at the door for almost a minute before I heard the buzz. On the other side was another guard and another world. I was in a hallway where the concrete block walls went up for twenty feet, and then there were iron bars for two feet where they met the ceiling. The air smelled vaguely of food cooking, but nothing that I could recognize. It wasn't bread baking, or meat roasting, or vegetables boiling; it was a hodgepodge of aromas that was barely carbon-based. The air was full of a constant commotion coming from all directions. Mostly it was the sound of steel, doors clanging shut, gates sliding open, or bars being rattled. Cutting through the metal jangle were men's voices, yelling mostly, some in anger, some in laughter.

In this dimly lit long hallway the guard at the door I had come through asked me to empty my pockets, remove any jewelry and place it all into a gray, galvanized pail, which he then took and put on a shelf next to a row of about twenty other pails. He let me keep my pack of Luckies but not my lighter. I was directed to stand on two red footprints painted on the floor and to lean forward placing my palms against the wall. Another guard came up behind me and put his hands all around and up and down me in the all-too-familiar pat-down. When he was sure I wasn't smuggling in a Tommy gun, he pointed to the far end of the hall, where another guard used a large brass key to open a door made of iron bars. On the other side was yet another hallway, with two more guards at either end next to their two doors. The first guard sent me down to a second guard, who took another, bigger brass key and opened his solid steel door for me.

Finally I was in the Visitor Center meeting room. It was about the size of a basketball court, with a ceiling again twenty feet high. At the top of all four walls near the ceiling were barred windows letting in plenty of daylight but no scenery. All that was visible was a cold, gray sky. The room was filled with gray steel tables for four, all bolted to the floor, and wooden chairs that were chained to the tables. Mostly couples, and one large Spanish family, occupied a few of the tables. There were four guards in the room, one by each of the two doors, and two in corners opposite each other. The guard at the door I had entered nodded toward somewhere near the center of the room and said, "Take a seat. Your inmate will be out soon." I found a table that was the farthest from everyone else in the room, including the guards, and sat down.

A male prisoner and his female visitor ended up their visit with an argument that had to be broken up by two guards, who then escorted them both to their respective exits. Two minutes later Enzo Fiori was brought into the room. I recognized him immediately from pictures in the papers. He was handcuffed in front and had a guard following close behind him. I stood up for him to see me, and he turned his head slightly toward the guard behind him, then pointed to me with his chin. They moved together in step with each other and made their way to my table, the whole time Fiori keeping his eyes in a cold stare right on me.

He stood at the chair across from mine as the guard removed his handcuffs, still staring at me with his deep brown eyes. He was taller than me by an inch or two but thinner by twenty pounds. His hair, although silver gray, was thick and healthy looking and swept back almost pompadour style. His nose was Roman, his lips thin, his face clean-shaven and smooth as granite, and his skin was not as pale as most jailbirds' tends to be but slightly tanned. He was mid to late forties, prime gangster age, and even in his drab prison uniform of navy-blue denim, he wore it like it was a three-hundred-dollar Italian suit.

He sat down, still reading me with the icy glare. I took out my pack of cigarettes and shook one out toward him. He took it, placed it between two fingers and then raised his hand as if in a classroom. One of the corner guards came over, produced a lighter and lit his smoke. He finally took his eyes off me, looked up at the guard and said, "Thanks, Marty."

Marty held the flame out for me and I fired up.

"Oh say, Marty, how's the boy. Did he get into Syracuse?"

The guard's face lit up about as bright as the flame from his lighter.

"Oh yeah, got a full football scholarship too."

"That's great. If I lose any money on the Orangemen now, I'll know where to come to complain."

He and Marty had a good laugh, then the guard moved back to his corner and Fiori came back to me. "So," he said.

"Well first," I said, "thank you for seeing me."

I thought I'd try the respect approach first; see how that went.

"Cut the crap. You're here because you want me to give you the go-ahead to start fucking my ex-wife."

Okay, screw respect, the gloves came off. "Well no, not exactly. I'm here because I want you to give me the go-ahead to *continue* fucking your ex-wife."

Then it was my turn to put on the icy stare. I took a long drag on my smoke and exhaled toward the table to our left, making sure Fiori saw that I was still showing at least a fair amount of respect. But at the same time I wasn't kissing this guy's ring. If he was going to kill me, he was going to kill me, but I wasn't going down without a pair of balls.

He sat on the edge of his chair, put his forearms on the table and clasped his hands together. His thin lips formed a flat smile, but the rest of his face didn't get the message.

He leaned in halfway across the table and gave me a nod to come closer. "Listen, tell me why I shouldn't just make a phone call tonight and have you out of my life?" He pulled back again into his chair, tilted his head and waited.

"Look, Enzo. May I call you Enzo?"

He blew out some cigarette smoke forcefully and opened his hands, fingers spread and palms up, which gave me the clear impression that he could care the fuck less what I called him.

"Look, I'm just a guy who works in a hardware store with a boy-meets-girl story. I met your ex, we seemed to hit it off, and maybe we can have a few good times together. That's it. But I also understand that she still lives in your house for some reason, and I don't care what the hell that reason is, really." I tried to make my tone emphasize that last statement. "I'm not interested in you, your business or anything else other than trying to show Irene a good time. And if you give me a minute I'll try to tell you who I am and — "

He leaned back onto the table with a sudden move and cut me off. "I know who you are."

I fumbled for words, but before any came out, he said, "I know about you, your store, about your father, your reform school, prison record. I know about your medals and your war-hero bullshit. You don't think I know who the fuck you are, Decker?"

I took a full drag on my cigarette, trying to think of an answer, and came up blank.

"And I know about your *special* skills too."

He put his cigarette out in the tin ashtray on the table and put his hand out for another smoke. When I shook one out of the pack, he grabbed the whole pack and put it in his shirt pocket.

"I was gonna give you the pack," I said, holding back the word "asshole."

"I'd rather *take* them. You know about taking things that don't belong to you, don't you, Decker?"

"If you mean Irene, I — "

He laughed. "Let me tell you a little story," he said, taking out my pack of Luckies and going through the whole lighting procedure, only this time all Marty got was a cold nod that silently said, *Thanks, beat it.*

"I got this sister, see, the baby in the family, the one my parents spoiled rotten. She meets Mr. Wonderful while she's at Columbia, right. Nice enough guy but he's a pinhead. My sister marries him but he ain't makin' enough dough to provide for her the way my old man thinks she should be provided for. The guy's got a third degree, or whatever, in marine biology. Marine biology, the fuck is that?

"Anyway the old man says to me, 'Give the guy something unimportant to do so's he can make a few extra clams 'n buy a house in the suburbs, grow fuckin' tomatoes in the backyard, I don't know. But mostly, of course, it's a grandkid the old man wants — you know? — before he croaks." He went quiet for a moment to savor his free tobacco, looked at the cigarette from several angles and then continued,

"So I have the guy running some numbers, delivering some packages cross town once in a while. Half the time he don't even know what he's carryin'. But I'm worried he'll do somethin' stupid one day and get pinched. Then I'm lookin' like the bad guy. So finally an opportunity comes up that's just perfect for the guy. I get him a job where all he has to do is show up and maybe piss off his boss once in a while and report to me every so often. So okay, he's happy, he's makin' some dough, my old man's off my back, everything's hunky-fuckin'-dory. The only problem is, every time he gives me a report, he's gotta tell me every tiny little fuckin' thing that has gone on at work since the last time we spoke. The guy's a detail nut, photographic memory, doesn't miss or forget a thing that crosses his path."

I put out my smoke and shifted in my chair.

"Don't worry. You're gonna love this." He gave a quick 360-degree check around the room. "So one day not long ago, he comes to me with a bit of information. The surprising thing about this information was not the info itself, but the fact that he brought it to me alone, without going to anyone else first. Turns out the guy's learning. He coulda gone to the cops or his boss, but no, the guy's got smarts all of a sudden 'n comes to me."

So I bit. "What's the info?"

"No, Decker. Not 'what's the info?' 'What's his *job?*' is the question."

His flat smile spread a little more, got the eyes involved. "In my business you find we have many irons in the fire. We do a little work with some of the local unions, you know. We play both sides of course. Sometimes we take a little from management to have the union look the other way. And we also get a little somethin' from the union coffers. It's like a double jackpot, you might say. Anyway, the job I got for my brother-in-law…" He paused and played this up like he was strutting the stage. I waited with full give-a-shit fixed on my mug. "I got him in the BCWI," he said.

I shook my head.

"Bakery and Confectionery Workers International."

At "Bakery" I started to feel hot. By "International" I knew my face was glowing red.

"That's right," he said. "He's the shop steward at Arnold's Bakery. I think you know where it is. You even passed him on the street. Him and his friend from the chocolate department. Right there in the middle of the street, plain as day."

Starchy? I must have looked to Fiori as quizzical on the outside as I felt inside.

"He spotted your phony aprons right away. And as you drove away he got your plate number. I got connections and tracked the car to you."

It felt as if the room temperature had just gone up ten degrees. I needed a drink of water; my mouth felt as dry as a ten-year-old catcher's mitt.

Fiori stretched his arms up high, brought his hands down behind his head and laced his fingers. "And leaving one dead behind." He tsked. "That's a homicide rap you're lookin' at."

I folded my arms across my chest with as much fake nonchalance as I could pull out of thin air.

"Yeah, you remember the old man you left for dead. People hate seeing innocent bystanders getting killed during the commission of a crime. Cops don't like it. *Girlfriends* don't like it."

He waited for a response that he knew wasn't coming. I could feel his gloating wash over me. I felt like I had just been given a body shot that put me on one knee holding on to the middle rope. I slowly climbed up to the top rope and got my wind back and tried to act as if he just landed a glancing blow.

"And what?" I said. "He says he saw us there, and we get five upstanding citizens who swear we were playing poker on the night in question."

"And the jury's gonna believe two convicted felons against two hard-working blue-collar family men."

He leaned into the space over the table between us. "Listen, relax," he said after a while. "We're gonna go into business together, you and me. First of all you're gonna hand over some of that half mil."

"Three hundred forty thousand," I said.

He brought his hands down from behind his head and waved me off. "Papers said half mil. We'll negotiate numbers at a later date. More important is the little job you and your mick friend are gonna do for me in a few weeks."

At which point all I could think of was Mitch O'Neill and how he was going to receive this news.

"I guess the question for you Decker, is, what is Irene worth to you? And do you want her to know you're just a common criminal, and a killer, just like me?"

Suddenly a guard from one of the corners called out, "Two minutes, Fiori."

Enzo Fiori got up from his chair, pulled on his shirt cuffs and said, "Listen, to show you I'm not a bad guy, go ahead have fun with the ex. But treat her right or I'll have Sally take care of you."

"Sally better take care of himself."

"What's that mean?"

"Ask Sally."

He turned and gave one of the guards the high sign. As he was being cuffed he said, "I'll be in touch."

Later that night I pulled into Irene's driveway and naturally I had to run into Sal Buetti. He was in his Lincoln, engine running and overhead light on. I parked behind him and got out of my car to find the temperature must have dropped to about thirty. As I walked over to his window, I could smell the cigar from ten feet away. I found him reading the *Long Island Star-Journal*, wearing a forest-green sharkskin suit and dark sunglasses.

"Sal," I said. "How's tricks?"

He pulled the shades down a quarter inch and peered at me over the rim with his slate-gray eyes, revealing a small Band-Aid along the top of his left eyebrow. He took the cigar from his mouth and said nothing.

I stared at the Band-Aid and said, "How many?"

"How many what?"

"Stitches."

He crumpled the paper into his lap. "Six, wise guy."

"Have you heard from your boss today?"

"Yeah," he said with a throat full of disgust. "I got the message. I'm just waiting here for an associate to come by with some kind of special assignment."

I held up my hands and turned my head in a defensive pose. "I don't want to know about it."

The two lights on either side of the house front door went on and we both turned to look.

"Is she expecting you?" Sal said.

"Oh yeah," I said and strolled up to the door and let myself in.

I found Irene in a kitchen full of the warm aroma of something roasting in the oven. She was at the sink with her back to me. I said, "Hey."

With both hands low in the sink, she turned her head and without seeing me said, "Hi."

Her hair was in a ponytail that hung down over a plaid flannel shirt. The shirt was tucked into a pair of jeans that still had the new dark blue color to them and were rolled up into a two-inch cuff at her bare ankles. Her shoes, a pair of brown penny loafers, completed the casual scene. I walked up behind her and put my hands on her hips, keeping at arm's length.

"Pennies or dimes?" I said.

"Huh?"

"In your shoes."

She stopped the circular motion of her hand on the piece of china in the sink. "Oh. Dimes, of course."

I was a little disappointed in the higher denomination, but I let it go for now. She put the dish in the drying rack and turned to face me. We both looked down to verify the coins in her footwear, and when we brought our heads back up we found our eyes meeting, leading to smiles and a kiss.

"Meatloaf okay with you?"

"Perfect."

Dinner was delicious, included wine and went on for hours with our talking and listening to each other on various popular subjects of the times. What the hell are they going to do with that Sputnik thing circling the earth? This Kerouac guy wrote a book on pep pills — big deal. Who knew the South was so backward down there in Little Rock? The conversation went on effortlessly and could get deep at times and then in a blink turn sharply silly. After dinner and in the glow of wine and lust, we drifted upstairs to the bedroom, where Irene lit candles, creating an atmosphere made for only one thing, and we tended to it.

In the morning I awoke first and propped my head up on one elbow to watch Irene sleep, like they do in cheap romance novels. I found myself to be under the influence of no particular emotion, feeling or need. The running commentary that usually goes on in my head nonstop and judges everything that comes in my path was at a standstill — or at least was paused. The teeth-grinding drive to settle scores, to squash memories of fierce battles waged on both foreign and domestic soils, had seemed to diminish overnight. My mind had either melted away these harsh compulsions or frozen them, holding them trapped in solid rock and time, hidden like fossils in an ancient dried seabed. Being at peace would not be how I would describe the feeling that morning, but a calmness ruled me and I would have done anything to hold on to it.

When Irene woke up we spoke few words. I went down to the kitchen before her and found a bright, sunny morning bursting through the windows. I made coffee and breakfast mindlessly with my eyes mostly outside in the cold backyard of late November. Irene came down and we ate with a silence that was broken only by the demure sounds of metallic tapping on china. Maybe it was the coffee, but soon the familiar sober restless feeling came upon me and I made a papery excuse for leaving, dropped my dishes in the sink, said, "Call you next week," and left.

I had heard of it and seen it on TV, but only right there in front of me did it become a nightmarish reality. In Irene's driveway, as I stepped outside, was the ugliest automobile I had ever seen in my life. I approached it pursing my lips in an oval, not unlike the grill on the hideous car in front of me, and let out an airy whistle. And sure enough, there on the side of the rear tailfin was the name. "Edsel." I wondered who would purchase such a thing, when a man quite a few years younger than me, putting him at around voting age, stepped out of the ill-formed tin crate and walked toward me. He was my height and build, with a head of wavy black hair that contained half a tube of Brylcreem. He was dressed mostly in gold watch, a timepiece big enough to be the first thing you noticed on him, second only to the meanness in his black eyes. The rest of his wardrobe was also black — topcoat, suit, tie and gloves. He was everything you would want in an up-and-coming gangster. In his face was a demanding need for respect that I presumed had been there ever since when he extorted the first drops of milk from his mother's tit.

"You Decker?" he said, not really wanting an answer. "I'm Tony."

"Of course you are," I said.

I put out my hand knowing he wouldn't get the joke, and he looked at it with a frown like it was a worthless penny on the ground. I put my hands on my hips, looked at the car and shook my head.

"That's some car there," I said.

Although he did seem pleased that someone admired his new set of wheels, he reacted — as I knew he would — by saying, "I'm not here to talk about my car," and gave a shrug of the shoulders that said, *The iron in my holster is heavy, man.*

These young ones you can have fun with. To fill their own perceived image of the hard-ass mobster, they play a role that never comes off as true. The look of a phony killer for me is always easy to spot. And for all his bravado and tough bluster, he really couldn't do a single thing that was not a direct order from the don, which made him a toy for me to play with.

"Well you know, Tony, I really *do* want to talk about your car."

I looked up through the bare trees to the sun-flooded sky and said, "I just want you to know, Tony, that it's such a beautiful morning and even your ugly-ass car is not going to ruin it for me."

He let loose with the shrug again and said, "You know you got a big mouth, Mister. Someday someone's gonna shut it for you."

I took a menacing step toward him, bringing me right up to his face. I said, "Is today that day?"

We gave each other matching cold stares and I really would've loved to have knocked some of his teeth out, but I broke off the stare-down when I lightly said, "So where's Sally anyway?" I stepped back, letting him think he'd won that one, because he would have stood face to face all fucking day.

"Sal's been reassigned."

I looked at him as if waiting for an explanation of the euphemism. I had an actual soft spot for Sal and hoped he hadn't been bumped off because of me.

"Reassigned?"

"He's been demoted's all. He's runnin' round collecting numbers for a while. It's whatcha get for bein' a pushover."

I gave him a slow up-and-down look-over. "And you're no pushover, are you, Tony?"

"Fuckin' right."

He looked like he had more to say but didn't quite know how to get it started. I gave him a minute to simply remember the message his higher-ups gave him to pass on to me, and then another minute to formulate some grand intimidating manner and tone in which he could verbalize the message through his limited vocal motor skills.

"Well, Tony, I'd love to stick around and sing your praises all morning but I've got a job to get to in the real world." I took a few steps toward my car.

"Hold on," he said. "I ain't through with you yet."

He made the mistake of grabbing for my forearm. He had his hand on my sleeve and hadn't even had the chance to squeeze his fingers before I had his wrist with my right hand and with my left hand I locked my thumb with his and gave a counterclockwise twist, bringing pain to every molecule in his arm. He was down to one knee before he could say "Ow."

I looked down at his young face crooked with pain. He reached for my hands with his free hand and I gave a minute amount of pressure to make him quickly change directions.

"Let's go over the rules, Tony. Actually there's only one rule. Don't fucking touch me." I gave him a few seconds to let that register through the smarting. "Do we understand the rule, Tony?"

He gave no verbal reaction, so I gave some more twist.

"Yes!"

"Good," I said and let him go. He got to his feet quickly, shaking his arm.

"I ain't gonna forget that, chum," he said, still trying to put on the James Cagney.

"See that you don't. Now, what else do you have to tell me?"

"I need a meeting with you and your mick buddy. And soon."

"Okay." I figured the sooner the better for me as well. "Tomorrow night, Friday, at O'Neill's Bar. You know where that is?"

"Yeah."

"Okay, around six."

"Awright."

NINE

"What!"

"He knows everything," I said.

"Christ almighty."

O'Neill was taking it about as I expected. Luckily there was no one in the bar to witness this little breakdown.

"Those two guys we passed in the street," I said. "One of them was Fiori's brother-in-law. He's the shop steward at the bakery."

"Fuck," he said. "You and that fuckin' broad."

"No, Mitch. It was you and those fucking aprons. Fiori said that's what tipped the guy off."

O'Neill glared. I'd never had the need to correct him when he was wrong. I don't know if he ever had been wrong. Certainly not since I'd known him. I didn't know exactly how this was going to play out.

"What's the little guinea bastard want?"

"Says he's got a little job for us. And that he wants part of the half-mil take from the bakery hit."

"You tell him there wasn't no half mil?"

"Yeah. He said that was negotiable."

"Wait a minute. What's the difference between a half mil and our three hundred forty thousand?"

"A hundred sixty thousand dollars."

"Right. That's probably just about what we left on those last shelves. And I bet I know who's got it."

"Who?"

"Well, think about it. Your shop stoolie. If he was sharp enough to spot those aprons, he was probably smart enough to watch us from the diner and see us go in and out of the money room. After we take off he goes in the room to investigate. Fuckin' guy's got just enough mob in him to smell how to make a buck on the situation. Son of a bitch."

"Think he's got all the dough?"

"Probably not. He'd have to talk the other guys into the scheme. But I don't think a four-way split of a hundred sixty grand would be a hard sell. Anyway, doesn't matter who has it; Enzo Fiori don't, didn't get his tribute. His brother-in-law is holding out on him."

O'Neill went silent for a few moments and then gave out a few short laughs, like he just remembered an old joke. He laughed a little harder and smiled as if very satisfied with himself. He poured himself a shot of Bushmills and built me a bourbon and soda, then held up his glass and with a wide grin said, "Let's drink to our new partnership with one of the five dago greaseball families of New York. This is gonna be fun."

"What's the plan?"

"The plan is this. You go home and pack for our trip to Vegas. We're leaving Saturday."

"Okay. But first we got to meet with this Tony guy tomorrow night."

"Who's he?"

"He's the new punk who's stationed over at Fiori's place in Oyster Bay. My guess is he's got the dope on whatever this job is they want us to do."

When Tony showed up at six fifteen Friday night, O'Neill's Bar was busy.

"You're fucking late, greaseball" was O'Neill's greeting as he looked up and down at the adolescent goon, who was still in black and wristwatch. "You'd think that phony gold watch would keep you on time."

"It's twenty-four karat."

"Maybe it's your car then. You got a car that can do over twenty miles an hour?"

"Oh, he's got a car all right," I said.

Tony took his time looking at us one at a time. "Traffic," he said flatly.

O'Neill got one of his regulars, Eddie Duggan, to work the bar while the three of us made our way to the kitchen. Before closing the kitchen door behind us, O'Neill looked back to Eddie, who was pulling a beer for himself, and said, "And don't fuck me, Duggan."

"Okay, junior, what is it?" O'Neill said to Tony once we were inside the kitchen.

Tony took his time settling in, broke out a pack of Salem cigarettes and through impoliteness or just knowing better, didn't bother to offer one to O'Neill or myself. We took two from my pack of Luckies and lit up. After we all took in a good collective drag of smoke and exhaled in three different directions, Tony spoke up.

"It's a bank," he said and looked at O'Neill and me like that bit of information was meant to dazzle us into criminal ecstasy. He took a step back and leaned his backside on the sink, flicking ashes onto a pile of dishes. I eyed O'Neill and saw the muscles in his jaw working viciously.

"A bank," O'Neill said with impatience. "Well, now we know that money's involved. Can you give us any real information on the job, kid?"

"All I can give you is what I know. I know it's upstate somewhere and that there's some kind of factory nearby that pays all the workers every two weeks, and then the workers come to the bank during lunch hour to cash their checks. On those paydays the bank keeps extra cash in the vault, maybe over a million. And the boss wants us to hit it two weeks from now."

"That's not enough time for me to case the joint," O'Neill said, almost raising his voice. His dislike and mistrust of Tony was coming dangerously close to the surface. I was ready to head off Tony should he go

114

somewhere that would jeopardize an already dicey situation. A provoked Mitch O'Neill would not do any of us any good.

"You ain't gotta worry about that," Tony said. "My people are taking care of all that. Alls we gotta do is wait for instructions" — he flicked an ash — "and follow them."

O'Neill looked at me with irritation hidden in his eyes and needing a place to unload it. He slowly redirected his gaze to settle on Tony's small black eyes. Tony put on a fair display of baleful airs himself, but he was no match for O'Neill's years of finely tuned callous character. And I thought, by O'Neill's silence, he was showing a merciful degree of restraint by not tearing the punk apart. But restraint for O'Neill was a hard position to hold indefinitely.

"So," I said. "When can we expect to receive these, uh, instructions?"

"Right before the job," Tony said. "The boss wants to do it as close to Christmas as possible."

"What's the deal there?"

Tony wrinkled his mouth to one side. "Fuck if I know."

"Christmas bonuses, you dumb wop," O'Neill said with a half laugh and a grin on his face. "Your boss has smarts, I'll give him that. By the way, who's givin' the orders on this job, what with the big boss up in Attica'n all?"

"The guy over me is my father."

"And he is?"

"Enzo's brother."

O'Neill glanced my way with a knowing look that said, *I knew this wise-ass had to be related to someone.* I nodded.

"Well," O'Neill said, "there's a lot I'm not crazy about, but — "

"But you'll do it," Tony said. "Or you're lookin' at armed robbery and homicide for that bush-league job you guys pulled at that — what was it? — a pastry shop?"

O'Neill's face and neck turned red; his eyes from under a palpable scowl were fixed on Tony's presence. He dropped his cigarette butt on the floor with false calmness and stepped on it, pivoting his foot like a dance step. I took a step toward the space between him and the kid. I put my hand on Tony's shoulder and walked him toward the door.

"Well thanks for coming by, Tony," I said. "We will await further instructions."

I closed the door and looked back at O'Neill, to see he hadn't moved or changed expression in the slightest. But somehow critical mass had not been reached and no blood was shed.

"When this is over," O'Neill said, "me and that punk are gonna have a little parlay."

"Only seems right. But they do seem to have our asses over the proverbial barrel."

"Maybe not," he said with a nod and a wink.

***

The following week was the trip to Vegas, which was not uneventful. O'Neill got a bland car from Hertz to drive and loaded the trunk with our ill-gotten gains. Taking turns driving, we headed straight nonstop for Nevada. We decided not to drive our New York plates through the Yankee-hating states of the South, so we mapped out a route that took us through maybe not the most interesting but what we thought should have been some of the safer states, like Iowa, Nebraska and Colorado.

About a hundred miles outside Lincoln, Nebraska, the cold grayness of December greeted us, along with news flashes on the radio about two teenagers who were crisscrossing this barren, cold state on a killing spree, and at the first roadblock we came upon, the reality of it all was heart pounding. There had to be a dozen patrol cars from as many forces and branches of forces. O'Neill and I knew we would pass for adults and not teens, but the sheer aggregate of law enforcement was disheartening. We passed through this first barricade easily though, with a state trooper's permissive wave. Later down the road we heard that the teen killers were a boyfriend-girlfriend duo that had the whole region in a panic. At the second roadblock, added to the state and local black-and-whites was the unmistakable olive drab of the military. The National Guard had been called in and by then the number killed by these two — updated on the radio every hour, on the hour— was up to seven. By Colorado the roadblocks and the radio eased up, and the weather started to warm up.

We got to Vegas on Monday morning and after checking in to a cheap motel, we went right to work. The plan was simple and went smoothly from start to finish. In the morning we each would go to separate casinos with five to seven thousand dollars, buy some chips and gamble for two or three hours, losing a few hundred dollars and never winning. Then we cashed the chips in for clean money and met back at the motel, went out for a meal, came back and hung around the pool for an hour or so, and then went back out at night to different casinos and repeated the process. We did this for three days and nights, until we had a total of three hundred twenty-three thousand dollars of clean, spendable cash.

"Now," O'Neill said, "in case you're wondering, I kept ten grand of the actual robbery dough for a special purpose. I'll explain later."

After a full night's sleep, we left Vegas early Thursday morning. It was somewhere around Denver we heard on the radio that those two teen killers were apprehended after a total kill count of eleven, including the girl's parents and her two-year-old sister. At a Route 6 gas station I picked up a newspaper and got a look at a picture of the two murderous creatures. The girl was plain, with a round face and short curly black hair and looked like she could have just stepped off the dance floor of *American Bandstand*. The boy had a face that should have been on a postage stamp representing American juvenile delinquency. He had blondish hair combed back in classic teen-idol pompadour style that I'm sure ended behind his head in a DA. With menacing eyes set deep in his face, a square jaw and from his lips a dangling cigarette, which seemed to be there for decorative purposes only. He looked like he was trying for a James Dean kind of image, although with his general look of unawareness, I doubt he would know James Dean if he tripped over him and then kicked his ass for being in his way.

Something about this kid's picture, his two-dimensional demeanor, made me think of Tony Fiori. The same type of depraved lawlessness, of crime with no purpose, of killing for killing's sake, was the impression I got from my cursory knowledge of both these miscreants. Empty souls who were destined to live short lives with unfulfilled dreams of payback to a society that owed them. I was sure in a few days the early life of this plains killer would be inked all over the country, with tales of abuse at the hands of all those around him, form his parents, relatives, friends and his school, to the odd gas station attendant down the road. The same would be said of Tony, I was certain, in the not too distant future. And that made me wonder. What would be people's impression of me, should I have the misfortune of having my mug show up in the papers? Would a grainy black-and-white photo of me show that I was actually driven with a sense of pride in my work or that I was out to right a wrong? I hoped the image would say, *Sure, I robbed, but only from banks and such, never from Joe Blow on the street.* And really, who didn't like to see some guy get away with the big score, to see the greedy one-sided institutions of finance getting their pockets picked? Yeah, the gun was an issue, but I hadn't had to use it yet. I'd burn that bridge when I came to it.

We pulled up to the bar in Syosset late Saturday afternoon. We took the two bags of dough and brought them into the bar and then O'Neill immediately opened up for business.

"Come around tomorrow afternoon," he said. "We'll go over the split and some other stuff."

"Like that ten grand of dirty money?"

"Oh yeah, that too," he said and laughed. "You're gonna love what I got in mind for that. See you tomorrow."

I drove straight home, got into some sweats and went down to the garage for a two-hour session of weights and punching. After a shower and two beers, a nap was in order. On the couch in front of the TV it was somewhere in the middle of *Victory at Sea*, with its glorious stories of World War II battles on the high seas — battleship guns assaulting the night sky with fiery blasts, sending carnage airborne to destinations unknown — when time caught up and drowned me in a dreamless ocean of sleep as black as the waves on the oval screen in front of me.

TEN

At O'Neill's on Sunday there was a lot of activity on both sides of the bar. O'Neill was serving drinks to more patrons than I'd ever seen in the joint, every bar stool was taken, and two of the three booths were occupied. The attention of everyone in the place was on the two guys behind the bar up on two stepladders. They were wearing gray work shirts with "Fulbright Electronics" stitched on the back and were struggling putting up on a shelf in the corner of the room the product of our new space-age technology — a new color TV. The talk rumbling up and down the bar was all football. The Giants needed a win to stay in the race for the conference championship, and if the two TV installers didn't get a picture going in the next few minutes, there was going to be an ugly scene.

I leaned into the bar between the Connollys and tried to get O'Neill's attention. Billy Connolly's red face became aware of me and he put his thirty-pound arm around my head in a friendly headlock.

"Tommy me boy, what're ya drinkin', then?"

The brogue was about three or four drinks thick and his query was not so much a question as it was an order.

"I could use a bourbon and soda, Billy."

"Mitch," he hollered, and I expected every Mitch within thirty miles to show up soon at the door. "The lad here needs a bourbon and soda."

O'Neill nodded and rigged one up and brought it over. He opened his eyes wide to me and looked up and down the bar. "You believe this shit," he said. "Word got out fast I was replacing the black and white with color." He lowered his voice. "We'll talk at half time."

One of the TV installers came off his ladder, folded it up and carried it outside. The other guy was still up fiddling around with the two antennas that formed a V on top of the set. The screen was a jagged rainbow of alternating vertical, horizontal and diagonal florid streaks.

As O'Neill was about to answer a call for beer at the end of the bar, Ned Connolly grunted, looked up at the clock behind the bar and said, "Mitch, see if you can get that guy to move his ass and get that thing tuned in. We're gonna miss the fucking kickoff."

O'Neill threw his towel over his shoulder and said, "Ned, you can always go home and watch the fucking game with your wife."

Ned mumbled something about needing the Giants to win, but it was lost in the babel of all the juiced-up sports fans around us. He had the look of a man with something more than just team pride on the line with this game. It was more than likely that he had some money, money the wife didn't know about, riding on the outcome of the upcoming contest. And he would no doubt lose, as gamblers do, which is why a yoke of grumpy unpleasantness was always hanging around him. Ned was the guy on the side of the road muttering under the hood of a car. The guy who comes into the emergency room needing stitches in a place that makes nurses blush. Ned was a hammered thumb, a bounced check. He had a need for more and always ended up with less.

Finally a corner of the room burst into living color and, as they say, a hush came over the crowd. Only one person could gather his thoughts amidst such a warm glow of chromatic bliss. While everyone else in the bar was lost in the dazzling spectrum of the green grass and white lines of the gridiron, it was Ned who declared, "Thank Christ."

The Giants had already beaten the Steelers 35 to 0 earlier in the season, so a win here was pretty much a foregone conclusion. But the Steelers kept the game close, and near the end of the half two things became apparent. The Giants might blow it, and Ned Connolly was losing his shirt. At the two-minute warning, through his clenched teeth Ned let out a "God damn it!," and when the half ended a fully articulated "Fuck!"

On the screen in glorious color was the score: Steelers 14, Giants 7.

In the kitchen during half time, O'Neill laid out his plan for what was to be done with the ten grand of the bakery money. "We're gonna set up those fucking guineas," he said. "We'll plant the dirty loot on that union stooge, what's his name."

He held out his hand for a cigarette and said, "What *is* his name anyway?"

"I don't know. The big boss just called him Mr. Wonderful."

He laughed, said, "Yeah, that fits."

We smoked, not speaking for a moment, listening to the din of the full bar on the other side of the door.

"This Wednesday night is good for you, right?" he said.

I nodded.

"Okay, we're gonna take a little trip. Meet me here just after midnight."

"Got it."

Then O'Neill unlocked the door to the pantry and went inside. He came back out with a brown leather briefcase, the kind that has two straps with small brass buckles holding it closed. He put it on the table, opened it and motioned me to look inside.

"This is yours. A hundred grand. Don't spend it all in one place."

Inside were packs of different denominations — fifties, twenties and tens — each pack with a rubber band wrapped around it. I looked back up at O'Neill and when my eyes landed on his face, a broad grin quickly went flat, as if he were trying to hide a part of his nature that had been locked away from everyone including himself for possibly a lifetime. I didn't make anything of it. I had too much respect for my oddly affable friend and mentor. "Cool, man," I said. "I think I'm about to make the name of that hardware store legitimate."

O'Neill ran the water in the sink to put out his cigarette and tossed it in the trashcan. With his back to me he said, "Why don't you hold off on making any offer for a while? You know, until you can show some way that you're buying the place with money that you got on the up 'n up." He turned to face me, wanting a response.

"Yeah, I can do that."

"And anyway, are you sure that's what you want to do?"

"Well," I said, dazed for a moment that there could be other options, "it's been my plan ever since getting back from Korea. Before that actually."

O'Neill gave a slight shrug. He tossed his chin toward the brown leather on the table. "Hundred grand. A lotta dough."

I tried to think of other choices besides the hardware store, but ever since I walked up the basement stairs of our Brooklyn home, dry-eyed with rage, the Smiths had been in my cross hairs, as if they themselves kicked the stool out from under my old man. Someone owed me something, and I wanted to collect. But even if I did get the store back, would I consider that payment in full? I had no answer for that.

"Yeah," I said, picking up the briefcase. "A lotta dough."

I walked out the back door.

I went from the bar straight to Irene's and was there in twenty minutes with a drink in my hand, Irene by my side, and the Giants letting the game slip away. The house had a whole room dedicated to TV watching. The walls of the room were panels of natural-colored yellow pine with a clear high-gloss finish of varnish. The window and doorframes, as well as the baseboard trim, were painted an off-white muted sandy color in an oil-based soft gloss. We were sitting on the couch close to each other holding hands with our feet up on a mission oak coffee table. In the middle of a lackluster third quarter I yawned and Irene said, "They don't deserve to win this game. They have no rushing game, and they have the worst fumbling record in the division."

How does a man react to a woman saying something like that? I placed my index finger under her chin and guided her gently, introducing her lips to mine. The kiss was soft and brief and afterward she pulled back a few inches, taking me in with a smile. "Hungry?" she said.

We drifted into the kitchen, where Irene ducked into the fridge and came out handing me a bottle of beer, and then went back in for a platter of sliced meats and cheeses, a head of lettuce and a tomato.

"Sandwich okay with you?" she said.

"Only if you have rye bread."

"What do you take me for?" she said, and then produced a loaf of rye from a rolltop breadbox. I reached out for the bread she had placed on the table and suddenly felt my cheeks go hot, and my hand stopped in midreach. Printed on the cellophane bag was the familiar red-and-white lettering of Arnold's Bakery. A strange feeling of hand-in-the-cookie-jar came over me.

"What's the matter?" she said. "You said rye, right?"

"Yeah, yeah. I just thought of something I've been meaning to talk to you about."

She was spreading mayonnaise on a slice of white bread and without stopping said, "What's that?"

"Well, I'll be coming into some money soon, and I was planning on making an offer to buy the hardware store."

"Really."

I thought I could detect a note of skepticism in her tone, but I couldn't be sure.

"Yeah, an uncle I've seen once in my life — my mother's brother out in Iowa somewhere. Never married, no kids. I guess he made it big in the farming equipment business. Had some major holdings that he left to my mother, so it gets passed down to me. Coupla hundred thousand, how about that?"

She finished making her sandwich, cut it in half and took a bite. She nodded slowly as she chewed. I took a bite of mine and waited for a verbal response. I watched her swallow then take a long slug of beer from the bottle. I could watch her for hours, but I had a lie to push through Congress and I've always found that the more elaborate you can make the lie, the more plausible it becomes. The sheer effort it takes for your mark to comprehend the convoluted fabrication finally wears them down, and they believe you by default.

"Apparently ole Uncle Floyd invented some kind of attachment for a tractor and sold it to John Deer, who paid him in stock that went through the roof after the war."

She had another swallow of beer and let out an unrestrained belch. "Is that all you want to do, buy an old hardware store?"

"Well, yeah. I thought, you know, get the store back to its rightful owner. Put Frank Smith in his place."

"Put Frank Smith in his place, by giving him more money that he doesn't need? I don't know, seems to me Frank and that store have been part of a war that's been going on with you for a long time. Maybe it's time to move on to a different campaign."

I chewed that over with my sandwich and found of the two, the sandwich was going down a lot easier. I looked at her deeply, trying to get more out of her than just what was before my eyes, but she wasn't giving out any hidden information.

"And where would you suggest that be?"

She showed an expression on her face of mild exasperation, as if the question was as relevant as being asked to name the Seven Dwarfs.

"Tom, I like you. And I like being with you for who you are, not what you do. As long as you're not a liar, murderer or a thief, you're who I want to *continue* to be with."

At that point I would've liked to know a few more names than just Dopey and Grumpy. But instead, there I was, trying to build a relationship upon lies. However, it was a situation I was familiar with, and I only needed to break out my rather formative rationalizing skills. I mean first, who doesn't lie? To me it's a part of self-preservation, an essential part of our will to live, and a behavior in our blood that's been passed down from caveman days. I picture an ancient troglodyte who just killed a wildebeest in some neighboring tribe's territory. When caught with the carcass by the tribe chief and asked if he's responsible, is he going to admit to the transgression and risk being clubbed to death? I'm sure *my* ancestor would have answered, "Hell no, it was dead when I got here!" We lie to keep ourselves safe, to save face, to make ourselves look good to others, sometimes to spare others our true opinions of them. "The truth will set you free," they say. Yeah, or it can get you killed. And for women to demand or even expect the truth from their men at all times seems a bit naïve. I mean, do they really want to know how that dress looks?

Later, I enjoyed the fruits of my lying and spent the night in Irene's bed. In the morning I got up early to leave for work. Irene rolled over from her stomach to her back and said groggily through the hair covering her face, "See you tonight?"

"Sure."

Outside in Irene's driveway December was starting to feel like that holiday cold I remembered from Brooklyn days. It was see-your-breath cold and the sun was fighting a losing battle trying to punch through a sky that was as gray and dull as the backside of a mirror. When I thought the day couldn't get any grayer, I saw that malformed mistake of a car, Tony Fiori's Edsel, entering the driveway.

He parked the heap, got out and walked toward me. He was all in black again, which now included a cap, the kind you see on old men in sports cars, except that this one was made of black leather and looked more like just a greased-up hairdo. He got a few steps from me, lobbed a glance toward the house and said, "Enjoying yourself?"

I took a moment, then said, "Oh, you mean Auntie Irene," trying to match his meanness. "Yeah, she really knows how to, uh, entertain."

The fingers on his right hand went into action clenching and unclenching, forming a fist every three seconds. I didn't have the time to watch adolescent hormones developing, so I made a move toward my car.

"Wait a minute, pal," he said. "I got a message for you and your mick friend."

Brushing off the derogatory tag like a mosquito at my ear, I said, "What?"

"My old man needs a meeting about that thing," he said as if the FBI was tapping the air around him.

"First, what's your old man's name?"

"Vito."

For some reason I immediately pictured in my mind a butcher with fat arms and bloody white apron.

"Sure, where and when?"

"At the old man's office in Queens next week."

"We'll meet in Queens. But it will be in the White Castle parking lot on Northern Boulevard."

There was no possibility that Fiori was getting us on his turf, and I'm sure he knew that. This was probably a test to see how dumb we were. And the kid didn't put up an argument.

"White Castle. Where's it at?"

"Just get on Northern Boulevard and follow your guinea nose."

ELEVEN

Wednesday night I met O'Neill at the bar some time after midnight, following his only instructions, "Wear black."

In a few hours he got rid of the four half-drunk patrons, whose eyes were all silently fixed on the TV up in the corner as if they were children gazing upon Mary's apparition, when really all that was going on was Steve Allen's annoying replacement, Jack Paar, droning on about has-been Walter Winchell like anybody but himself cared. O'Neill flicked the lights, both of them, and broke the spell, and all four patrons shuffled out the front door. He went into the kitchen and came back out with a small lunch-sized brown paper bag. On the way to the back door he opened the bag and showed me a three-inch pack of money wrapped in some kind of clear plastic.

"Saran Wrap," he said. "The greatest invention in all of mankind."

I must have looked unimpressed, so he said with a great grin, "Stuff 'll keep this dough dry for centuries."

He still wasn't getting the response he wanted and rolled up the top of the bag, said, "Let's go."

It was December cold as we got into O'Neill's car. Inside the car he opened the bag again, peering in with a grin and asked, "Got your piece?"

"Yeah, why?"

He looked over at me with disappointed eyes that said, *don't you know anything?*

"You know a guinea you can trust?"

I could have given him a dozen or two off the top of my head, but I didn't want to disturb his Saran Wrap buzz.

"So where we heading?" I said.

"Great Neck. A section called Great Neck Gardens. Your friend Starchy the shop steward lives there. It's amazing how easy it is to get a hold of union records."

We smoked two cigarettes each on the way to Starchy's — Mr. Wonderful's — neighborhood, which consisted of a square mile of brand-new houses, as if unrolled from a giant bolt of instant community. We turned off the main road onto one of the quiet lanes lined with tall, bare trees and dim streetlights. The neighborhood was a grid of crisscrossing streets, each block had eight houses on a side, and each house's backyard met the backyard of the house on the next block over. O'Neill was following directions he had written down on an envelope, quickly finding the right street and then the number on a mailbox that also had the name Gaudiello on it.

"That's it," he said. "Right there."

The house was a modest Tudor with an addition added over the attached garage. The addition didn't match the style of the original part of the house and looked foolish. In the dark I could just make out that the house timbers were painted a dark brown and the stucco a common beige. We drove by without slowing down and reached the next corner, turning right and then right again. We went one more block and parked in the dark middle of the block equidistant from the two streetlights on either corner. O'Neill put the paper bag inside his coat. We both pulled our collars up and stepped out of the car.

We walked single file in the narrow patch of grass between the sidewalk and the curb so as not to make any loud footstep sounds on the concrete. We walked briskly under the lights on the corners and crossed over almost tiptoe in silence. The third house down was the house that backed up to Starchy's. Like every house on the block, it was dark. We crept up the driveway and along the side of the garage to the backyard. With the temperature in the teens, I was hoping that the locals were humane enough to not have left any dogs out in their doghouses. With the new moon there was nothing in the sky but blackness and the mysterious distant stars. The darkness worked in our favor for a while, until O'Neill made a dash from the corner of the house to the fence that separated the two backyards and ran right into a swing set, rattling the chains of the swings. I came up right behind him and grabbed the two seats of the swings to hold them steady and stop the noise. We both stopped moving and breathing. After what seemed like an hour's wait, nothing had stirred in the house and we approached the fence. It was a picket-type barrier, low enough that we could straddle it without getting our balls ripped off.

Two feet from the other side of the fence and still some thirty feet from Starchy's house was a toolshed in the form of a tiny barn. The door in front of the shed faced the back of Starchy's house. We edged our way around to the front and O'Neill pulled the door open wide. He took a quick look inside, trying to penetrate the darkness, and then took his hand off the door to reach for the bag of money inside his jacket when the door, which must have had a spring hinge, whipped back, closing itself with a slam that sounded like a thunderclap. We both froze and stopped breathing for the second time. A light came on inside a window on the second floor and we both dodged around to the back of the little barn, each of us going to opposite corners and peering around to get a glimpse of the back of Starchy's house. Then another light went on in the house behind us, grabbing our attention, and we both dropped to the ground between the shed and the little fence. I looked between the pickets of the fence, which fortunately were only about an inch apart, giving us some cover from Starchy's rear neighbor, and saw a pair of garbage cans behind the neighbor's garage. Like a hurdler I dashed over the fence, got to the cans, silently tipped one over, pulled out some of the trash, tossed the lid in front of the guy's back door and made it back over the fence and prone on the ground in three seconds flat.

Both back doors opened at the same time letting out a dull yellow light that cut through the cold night and flooded the two backyards. I was pressed up to O'Neill and felt him moving around like a man in a straightjacket. I looked over to see he had his Colt in his hand. I'd seen O'Neill in various situations of stress and he usually handled them with aplomb, but I had never seen him cornered, and in the years I'd known him I'd lost track of how many times I'd heard him take the ex-con vow, "I ain't goin' back to the joint." I could make out his thumb on the hammer and felt my heart pounding against the cold hard ground under me. Gunplay would not make this night turn out well for anyone. I wanted to put my hand on O'Neill's piece and gently lower it to the earth, but I didn't want to tip a desperate predicament over to a calamitous one.

The neighbor stepped out his door and landed his bare foot right on the garbage-can lid. "Shit!" he said and then, looking over at the garbage cans, added, "Goddamn it!"

Starchy, who was outside also by this time, called out, "Phil?"

O'Neill pulled back the hammer, making a clicking sound that to me sounded like gears grinding on a Mack truck.

"Hey, Vic," the neighbor said. "Goddamn raccoons."

"Better you than me, neighbor," Vic Starchy said.

Neighbor Phil started picking up his garbage, and Vic retreated into his house. We waited for Phil to go back inside his house and for all the lights in both houses to go out and then waited for everyone to fall back asleep. Finally O'Neill got up, went around to the front of the little barn and studied the small window on the shed, which had a small pair of shutters on either side, nailed to the wall. He felt around one shutter, then took out the bag of money and stuffed it up behind it, wedging it between the shutter and the wall.

"Let's get the hell out of here," he said.

On the way home I asked O'Neill, "What do we do now, call the cops?"

"No. We gotta wait for the right time."

***

A year before my father made his exit through the basement of our Brooklyn home, I had my confirmation on an altar deep in the heart of St. Mark parish, confirming that I had been sufficiently brainwashed into the Eucharistic adoration society that was the Catholic Church, and I guess that's when I got my con game working, because the priest, the nuns, my parents — I had them all thinking I had fallen for it. As a reward for this fraudulent perpetration, my parents offered to take me out to dinner at a restaurant of my choice. I had no problem choosing the eatery I wanted. It was White Castle. This was a burger joint where the burgers were the size and shape of a Scrabble tile, loaded with onions and four-day-old grease, topped with a pickle slice, and squeezed between small white buns, with tops perfectly toasted to the color of forty-weight oil. This was a delicacy made for a twelve-year-old, to be enjoyed eaten comfortably in the backseat of a Chevy.

It was in the parking lot of that very same celebratory hashery where O'Neill and I were waiting for Vito Fiori. White Castles were small buildings complete with parapets festooned with fake turrets. They were indeed painted white with blue lettering, but where we parked in the rear of the "restaurant," all the white paint in Pittsburgh couldn't cover the stain around the exhaust fan, which had turned the wall around it the darkest shade of gray possible without being black. Minutes after we parked and got out of our car, Fiori made his entrance on time in a Fleetwood Caddy as black as a hangman's hood and driven by Tony Fiori. He beckoned us over to his car, which was not going to happen. O'Neill had somehow acquired for the occasion a brand-new Buick Special as black as Fiori's but with a stripe of chrome streaking across the side panels like a suave bolt of lightning. We beckoned back.

From the driver's door of the Caddy emerged young Tony, who went and opened the back door, out of which stepped Vito Fiori, who was taller than his jailed brother at around six foot but shorter than his son by two or three inches. Both he and Tony were in traditional gangster garb — long black overcoats, black gloves and shoes; the only difference between the two was that senior's swagger carried a lot more cachet. As they both approached us I noticed the final touch on Vito that said "mobster," a tiny ruby set in a thick band of gold on the pinkie of his right hand. The two stopped in front of us, hands were not extended.

I opened the back door, both hoods slid into the car, and O'Neill and I got in the front. I turned to face Vito, who removed his light gray Homburg, revealing black hair that wanted to be curly but was slicked back and flat on his head. He had the same brown eyes as his brother, and he was clean shaven as if from two minutes ago and had a look on his face that suggested he had way too many items on his busy schedule, *So let's get this over with.*

By way of the rearview mirror, O'Neill spoke first. "I don't like goin' into a bank with only three guys," he said flatly. "And I know nothing about the place, since I ain't been able to case the joint."

"I told you—" Tony snapped with much hand gesturing, until his father put his hand on Tony's arms, lowering them and shutting the kid up without taking his eyes off O'Neill in the mirror.

"First, O'Neill, there will be four of you on the project." He looked over at me. "I believe you know Mr. Buetti?"

O'Neill glanced at me, shook his head, and I nodded to Fiori.

"Listen," Fiori continued, "it has to be that way. The fewer people who know the details, the less chance information can get out and find its way into the wrong hands. I'm sure you agree."

I'm sure O'Neill did agree but he certainly wasn't going to say so.

"Of course," Fiori went on, "we could have a certain shop steward go blabbin' to the cops."

O'Neill's eyes went off the mirror for a second, and I saw the corner of his mouth twitch upward as if tweaked by a tiny electrical jolt.

"Here's how it's going to work," Fiori said, waiting for everyone's attention, and when satisfied he'd had it, he continued. "Next Thursday, the day before the job, one of my guys will drive all four of you up to a place where we've arranged for you to stay overnight. It's about an eight-minute drive from the bank. My guy will explain the whole plan of the job on the way up and you can rehearse it in the house where you'll be staying." He stopped to pull on his ear.

"Got it so far?"

No one spoke.

"Good," he said, looking out the window at absolutely nothing. "Now, we've been working on this job for months and if everyone does what he's supposed to, we should all be either rich." he leaned forward two inches toward the front seat. "Or as in your cases, free to go about your daily rat race." As he sat back and put his hat on he asked, "Any questions?"

O'Neill finally turned around and squarely met Fiori's fixed stare halfway between them.

"First," he tilted his head toward me, then back to Fiori. "why you need the two of us? You got plenty of goons who can pull this off, why us?"

"You're right, I do have qualified men who could probably do the job but," Fiori looked over at his sullen son briefly, "there are risk factors."

"If it's so risky," O'Neill said, "what about Buetti and this—" he stalled for a moment, looking over at Tony. "your kid here?"

"You'll see when you get upstate. Their part is relatively risk-free."

Fiori reached for the door handle.

"One more thing," O'Neill said. "I want it clear that when the operation starts rolling," his eyes went straight to the center of Tony Fiori's pupils. "I'm the guy calling the shots."

"Pff," was Tony's impulsive reaction.

"Well, as a matter of fact, O'Neill," Vito Fiori opened his door and put one foot onto the parking lot asphalt. "that's exactly how it *has* to be."

The two men walked to their car and drove away. O'Neill sighed heavily.

"Jesus Christ," he said.

Before leaving to go back to Syosset we grabbed a half-dozen burgers each and sat in the car eating. I can't say it didn't bring back pleasant dining memories. We finished eating and tossed the trash into an overflowing receptacle in the corner of the lot as we drove out, and it was three stoplights before one of us spoke.

"What do you think?" I said.

"I think it needs some work. The main thing I don't like is Tony Fiori. And this Buetti, what's he like?"

"Sal Buetti is a dedicated soldier who's loyal to the don, but I don't know his feelings for these two guys. Could be he'd do anything for them; could be he'd double-cross them. I think he's an honest guy though, for what that's worth. But you're right about Tony. He's a fucking problem. Unpredictable in a predictable sort of way."

"Yeah, well, we've got three days to come up with an angle. We're not going into this thing without an insurance policy protecting our asses. And I ain't doin' it for free either."

His voice was thick with resolve, like phlegm from a bad winter cold. His eyes were looking straight ahead through the windshield six days up the road planning, revising the plan, calculating odds, recalculating. He was like that for the thirty-minute drive back to Syosset and only spoke when we reached the bar and I was getting into my car to go home.

"We'll talk tomorrow," he said.

TWELVE

Two days later Irene called me at work in the morning and said she was free for lunch and would pick me up at the store at noon. When I came out into the parking lot to meet her, the sun was bright and warm on my face. It took me a minute to focus through the glare, and when I did I found her and another figure standing between two shiny Corvettes. Up close my dread was personified. Frank Smith was chatting it up all cozy and charming like he knew how to do so well.

"Didn't know your girl had a Vette," he said to me.

"I didn't either," I said as I got up close to Irene for a small kiss.

"It's under a tarp in the garage most of the year. Since I don't see it I never remember to take it out. Something about the sun being so bright today, I just said, 'Hey, why not?'"

"It's always a good day for a Corvette," Frank said. Then the two of them went into car talk. Fuel injection — he had it, she didn't; RPMs; rear axle ratios; zero to sixty; blah, blah, blah. I was hungry and I said so.

"I only have forty-five minutes," I said, cutting them off in the middle of positraction. "Or the boss'll dock me."

"Oh, you wouldn't do that, Frank, would you?" Irene said.

Frank easily untwisted the dilemma with an answer that netted out to his favor. "No, of course not. As long as you bring him back safe and sound."

Irene reached to open the driver door but Frank got to it first and opened it for her. I was rounding the front of the car and looked over to see Frank reach for her elbow to guide her into her seat. When he saw my eyes on him he snapped his hand back to a safe distance. We pulled out of the lot onto Main Street, and after Irene shifted into second she said, "He doesn't seem like such a bad sort."

"He's a prick."

She laughed and almost missed getting the car into third gear. "My, someone gets a little grumpy when he's hungry."

I let it go. "Where are we going for lunch?"

"A little out-of-the-way place I know of."

Five minutes later we pulled into her driveway. An hour later she dropped me off back at the store.

"See you later," she said.

"Yeah."

As I walked across the parking lot back toward the store entrance, Dottie G. was coming out to take her lunch break. She looked toward Irene's car leaving the lot and said, "Haven't gotten wise to her yet, Tom?"

"*She* hasn't gotten wise to *me* yet."

She looked up at me with deliberate eyes. "Yeah, I guess it would take a special woman to really get to know you—" She placed an engaging smile on her face. "And you know you wouldn't have to look very far to find such a woman." Then she skipped off to cross the street to the diner. Somehow I think she knew my eyes followed her all the way across the street and into the diner entrance.

The rest of the day at work was uneventful; only one run-in with Frank, but it was a trying one. He was quite taken with Irene of course, and asked, "Where did you meet her? And what the hell does she see in you?"

"Right here at the store."

He furrowed his brow. "Don't we have a rule about dating customers?"

I gave a shrug.

"I think I might just put one in place so I can move in," he said, arrogance coming off him like steam off a hard-worked racehorse.

"I don't think she's your type."

"Please," he said with weighted condescension. "When she dumps you I'll be more than ready to take over."

After that conversation I had an almost pleasant conversation with the prince of grump, Ned Connolly, who came in without his brother Billy just before closing needing some mineral spirits to clean out the day's brushes. Our talk was brief and I kept it free of the subject of gambling.

From work I went home for a workout, shower and change of clothes and then went over to Irene's after dark. I saw the ugly Edsel parked in front of the garage with Tony not in it. There was a light on inside the garage and an intuitive curiosity moved me to peer into the window of one of the three garage doors. I could see Tony Fiori alone, carrying a hard briefcase, ascending the pull-down staircase that led to the attic space above the garage bays. I figured that this was something I should investigate to gain some intelligence on him and his bunch.

The thought of intelligence skipped through my mind and reminded me that it was something lacking in great quantities back in Korea. Some decent information on enemy troop strength and locations might have saved thousands of Marines' lives around that bloody reservoir. There was a day back then that I'm constantly trying to block out of my consciousness, but somehow it still creeps through the barbed wire on cold nights like this and suddenly I'm back there and it's as real as the IRS and I can feel the bitter foreign cold and hear the wind and bullets snapping through the air all around me and I can see the blown-up parts of Marines I had known for only a few months yet it seemed like I had known all my life, and I can taste the black-red blood in my mouth and my feet turn cold as if trudging up that bullshit hill that we would kill and die for, just to take it and give it back in a matter of days. Many men were killed that day.

But not me.

When I saw Tony coming back down the stairs I got back in my car, started the engine and turned on the lights. When he came out the garage side door and saw me, I turned off the lights, cut the engine and stepped out of the car as if I had just gotten there.

Tony said, "Hey," and took two steps toward me, which meant I should drop everything and rush to his needs. "Hey, instead of screwin' round here, shouldn't you be gettin' ready for our trip upstate on Thursday?"

"I'll be ready. What time are we leaving?"

"I don't know yet. I'll let you know," he paused for effect, "when you need to know."

He got in his car and drove away.

I found Irene in the kitchen getting ready to put something in the oven.

"Wait," I said, "let's go out to eat. And there's someone I want you to meet."

"Oh, who's that?"

I told her about Mitch O'Neill, talking him up to make him out to be something between the older brother I never had and sage mentor, which he was in a felonious sort of way.

We went to a little pizza joint around the corner from the bar. The china in the joint was as thick as the spaghetti sauce, and the tablecloths were fake plastic red gingham. After dinner we walked to O'Neill's arm in arm, leaning into the cold wind.

It was a Tuesday night, seven shopping days until Christmas, and O'Neill's was getting festive. The Christmas lights that hang on the walls year round were turned on and the place had a handful of non-regulars, folks just out of the office Christmas party who were determined not to go home sober. I introduced Irene, and O'Neill put on a large, cardboard smile, and said, "Pleasure. What can I get you two kids?

We told him what we wanted and he went to the middle of the bar to get the ingredients.

When he came back with my bourbon and Irene's rusty nail, he leaned both hands on the bar, making his shoulders hunch up close to his ears. His blue and Irene's green eyes met in a locked stare. O'Neill looked up and down the bar and back to Irene and found her fixed stare right where he'd left it. He turned around and poured himself a shot of Bushmills, turned back around and said, "Tommy tells me you're Enzo Fiori's ex."

Irene held up her glass, said, "Long may he rot."

O'Neill smiled with his eyes, clinked his glass with hers and they both threw down the liquor and landed their glasses on the bar at the same time. O'Neill looked over at me and winked. But I wasn't sure what kind of wink it was; it could have been either approval or warning. The bar was too busy for him to stay to chat very much, so we had one more drink and left the holiday spirit of O'Neill's Bar & Grill and drove back to Irene's.

The next morning I was up early to leave for work and Irene had planned a day of shopping in Manhattan, so we both walked out of the house together. Of course right there in the driveway close to the garage in the bright cold morning sun was Tony Fiori leaning on his ugly car, collar up, rubbing his gloved hands together, more I think to break the boredom than to keep warm. From the garage, which was about thirty yards away, Tony called over to me, "Hey, noon on Thursday at O'Neill's. Don't be late."

Like a reflex I shot a glance at Irene, who had narrowed eyes on me, a look of suspicious disappointment embossed on her face. I was struck dumb for a moment and couldn't think of anything to say to either of them, so I just shook my head with a smirk as if to say, *what a kidder,* and got in my car. But Irene wasn't buying it and from my rearview mirror I could see her taking a few steps toward Tony while watching me drive away. It was going to take some Fred Astaire steps to dance around this one. But I'm always up for a lying challenge, and on the upside, I owed Tony Fiori a sock in the jaw.

The first thing I did after getting to work was to get someone to switch days off with me, since I needed the next day, Thursday, off for the drive up to Fiori's job. Andy Ellis in Plumbing was happy to do it. Then I figured I'd just call in sick again on Friday. So all that was out of the way. But the rest of the morning I felt a little absentminded. I couldn't get the picture out of my head of Tony and Irene standing in the driveway as I left her house. At coffee-break time I tried to get to the break room before anyone else to use the phone in private and call her. I had a few lies to possibly go with but I had to see if she had spoken with Tony and if so what he had said, before I decided which concocted road to go down. The problem was, how did I explain that I was associating with the mob because they were blackmailing me with information they had concerning a robbery and homicide I was involved with? This was going to take skill all right. I dialed her number just as Dottie and Frank entered the room, which now added discretion to my lying task.

"Hey, Irene," I said when she picked up the phone.

"Before you say a thing, hear this. We're through."

"Wait a minute, what did that mug tell you?"

"It doesn't matter, good-bye."

"But," I said, then the line went dead. I said "Bye" to the dial tone and felt a flush come over my face. I turned to get a cup of coffee as if nothing had happened, and when I finally took my eyes off my coffee cup I took in

Dottie's face, which had one of those smiles made by drawing in her lips. She said nothing, just poured herself a coffee and put enough sugar in it to sweeten a deal with the devil.

"You guys hear that Elvis Presley just got drafted?" I said.

Frank gave a short laugh through his nose. He said, "Trouble in paradise, lover boy?"

I sat down wearily next to Dottie, who was rolling her eyes.

"Buzz off, Frank," I said without looking at him, having no need to see the satisfaction in his face.

"Yeah," he said. "I got a phone call to make anyway." He walked out of the room and I heard him whistling his way down the hall to his office.

"Jerk," Dottie said. "How about lunch on me today, Tom? Whaddya say?"

I looked at her with no in my lips but yes rumbled up from somewhere deeper.

"Sure."

She got up, put a hand on my shoulder and said, "Good."

I watched her little frame walk out the door and a glimmer of solace pierced my gloom like a narrow shaft of sunlight cutting through the air of a dusty room.

Sometime later I looked for Frank to tell him I needed a little time to leave the store to take care of some personal matter. I thought I would make one more desperate effort to go see Irene and fabricate a story that Doubting Thomas himself would believe. Frank was nowhere to be found, so I got Donny Borg from Gardening to cover the paint department while I drove over to Irene's place with a deceitful stratagem that just might work. But as soon as I entered the driveway I saw that I would not even get a chance to use it.

Parked right up near the front door were two very familiar shiny Corvettes.

I don't know which emotion came first, betrayal or amazement over the swiftness in the changing of events. Whichever, I felt my heart break like a wicked curveball low and away. And Frank Smith on the mound made it all the worse. I pulled out of the driveway, and a pyramid of emotions was being built in my head — anger and jealousy among them — and on the very top was revenge. But I had to push that all aside. There were other events going on in my life at that moment that had to do with my very freedom, and worrying about a simple love affair would not do me any good. Revenge could be put off, because that would take planning, anyway. Jealousy was a luxury I didn't need, and I tossed it off like a cigarette butt. The anger was a tough one though. I needed to get to some familiar surroundings, and all I could think of was going back to mixing paints back at the store, get my mind on the mundane. And when my head cleared somewhat, I found that was exactly where I was.

When I got to the paint department I saw that Donny had a line of five people waiting impatiently for paint. I told him to go back to his peat moss and in a few minutes I had everything under control. I kept busy during the rest of the morning. When I wasn't helping paint customers I was running to the storeroom for stock to replenish empty shelves or roaming the store for any department that was particularly busy and needed help. It was this fervid push of activity that made lunchtime arrive quickly, and soon Dottie and I were skipping over to the diner.

After we sat down in a window booth and gave our order to Angie I noticed two guys enter the joint. They were both kind of bulky looking wearing work clothes, the kind you would see on a loading dock — khaki trousers, plaid flannel shirts under parka jackets. One was hatless, with salt-and-pepper hair, the other wore a hat

145

like a paperboy on the street corner hollering "Extra, extra!" They surveyed the place for seats, noticeably not looking in my direction, found two stools at the counter, sat down awkwardly and ordered coffee. I saw a hand waving in front of my face and I heard my name being called. It was Dottie.

"What?" I said.

"I said, do you have plans for the holidays?"

I hadn't had plans for the holidays since getting back from Korea with no parents and no desire to celebrate any part of the human condition.

"No," I said. "Why?"

"Well," she said, but was interrupted by Angie arriving with our food.

"Anything else, kids?"

"I'm good, Ange, thanks," I said. Dottie shook her head no.

I had the day's special in front of me, which was honey-glazed ham steak, oven-roasted potatoes and peas. Dottie had a sandwich I wasn't interested in. I started in on my dish.

"Anyway," Dottie said, "there's this party a friend of mine in the city is having on New Year's, and I was wondering if you'd like to go to it."

With that the atmosphere in the booth changed. I had never been asked out on a date by a chick before and the feeling of being put on the spot was odd. I swallowed a mouthful of ham and took a deep look at Dottie, who seemed to have just turned into a different person than the one I worked with. Other than the darling overbite, everything about her looked different to me. Her eyes were a deeper, more inviting blue, she looked taller even though she was sitting down, and her bangs were looking less schoolgirlish and more vamp-like.

"You mean, like, uh…"

146

"A *date*, yes. You can say the word, Tom, it won't kill you." She sounded like she could care less if I accepted or not.

I thought about my schedule over the next few days, and just thought I couldn't count on how, what, or where I would be that far into the future.

"Well, let me think about it."

"Sure, that's cool. By the way, could you give me a ride home after work today? My car's battery went dead this morning."

I told her that wouldn't be a problem.

After we finished eating we got up and walked to the cash register to pay the bill and on the way we passed by the two lugs at the counter, who remained silent and with eyes straight ahead. We dashed across the street, cutting through traffic and the icy air, and got to the entrance of the hardware store, where I stopped and told Dottie I was going to stay outside for a minute to have a smoke. She went inside, and I lit up a cigarette and paced up and down, flapping my arms for warmth, all the while keeping an eye on the diner door across the street, waiting for the two heavies to come out, which they did about halfway into my smoke. I watched them get into a '55 Pontiac two-tone, white and turquoise. They drove away quickly, using up a fraction of the excessive power of Pontiac's new V-8 engine.

I don't know why but they bothered me.

THIRTEEN

A few minutes before closing Dottie came into the paint department ready to leave. She had on a black beret pulled down over her ears and a Navy pea coat with its big collar turned up and a red-and-white scarf that must have been six-feet long wrapped around the outside of the collar and covering the lower half of her face.

"You ready for the Yukon?" I said.

"Have you looked outside lately?"

With no window in the paint department I had to say, "No."

I put on my coat, my old field jacket with its winter liner, and we walked toward the front door. I looked out the glass door at the white parking lot and snow-covered cars. As we stepped outside, the first sense to be assaulted by a snowstorm is the sense of hearing, which hears nothing. All sound is swallowed up by the whiteness. Walking through the parking lot to my car, I felt big flakes the size of pancakes landing on my bare head. About halfway to the car Dottie slipped and grabbed for my arm and held on for the rest of the way, until I opened the door of the Ford for her to get in. Up in the glare of the streetlights, where a snowstorm is always measured more accurately than by any weatherman, the snow was streaking sideways through the light's ball of illumination. Looked like the start of a good-sized storm.

I started the engine, turned on the heat, lights and wipers, and pulled out into the street, which was slightly slick with fresh snow. I drove slowly, and Dottie gave me directions to her apartment in Woodbury, about a ten-minute drive from the store. We went by way of the Jericho Turnpike, which hadn't been plowed yet, with only two or three inches of snow accumulating so far. At a four-corner intersection in the center of Woodbury, Dottie told me to make a right.

"About halfway down the block is my place."

After we passed a deli, travel agency, stationery store and a bank, Dottie said, "At the bar is my building."

By building she meant the two-story brick arrangement that had a doorway between the bar and a fish store, and apartment windows up above. I parked in front of the bar.

"Listen," she said, "are you hungry?"

I had turned on the left blinker to pull off the curb and into traffic but stopped and looked past her to the bar, which had a neon palm tree in the window and a sign that said "Duke's Paradise."

"They got some great burgers in there," she said.

"Yeah, I could eat." *And I could use a stiff drink.*

The bar was the usual setup; entrance into the middle of the room, bar to the left, booths against the wall to the right, a few tables in the middle, and kitchen door and a hall leading to the restroom doors off the back wall. A tall, thin, blonde waitress of middle age was at one of the occupied tables. She looked up at us and said, "Hey, Dottie," then tilted her head left and right and said, "Anywhere." We took a booth.

I sat facing the front door, as I always do, and surveyed the joint. The walls were plaster, with molding configured to form large rectangles around the room. In each rectangle were murals of tropical scenes, beaches, waterfalls — a lot of blue. And of course there was a palm tree in each mural. The booth itself was of relatively new construction, done with cheap pine but stained and varnished nicely for the mahogany illusion. After a while the waitress came over. She looked at me and winked.

"Snowin' hard out there yet, sweetie?" she said to Dottie.

"It's starting to, yeah. Aunt Marion, this is Tommy Decker, from the hardware store. We work together. Tom gave me a ride home tonight."

"Nice to meet you, Marion," I said and extended my hand. Marion put a bony hand in mine and gave a firm handshake.

"Nice to meet you too."

Dottie looked over at the bar and said, "Where's Uncle Duke?"

"Your uncle's workin' the kitchen tonight. Joey didn't show up, so Roy Maine is at the bar workin' off his tab. What can I get you two to drink?"

"A bottle of Bud for me," Dottie said.

"Bourbon and soda," I said.

As Marion was writing the drinks down on her pad, Dottie looked at me and added, "I think we're having burgers too."

I nodded yes.

Dottie said, "I'll have mine with cheese and — "

"A slice of Bermuda onion, medium rare," Marion said.

Dottie nodded and looked at me sheepishly.

"Cheese for me," I said. "Medium rare."

Marion pointed at me with the eraser end of her pencil and said, "Fries?"

I nodded. She didn't bother to ask Dottie.

"Got it," she said and walked off to the kitchen.

I looked up at the black-and-white TV in the corner over the crowded bar and saw Chet Huntley, whose head was at a forty-five-degree slant on the screen, and he was going on about something, but I couldn't make out what he was saying. There was film of the Berlin Wall, with people trying to look through rolls of barbed wire and crying in what looked like anguish.

"So," I said. "Your aunt and uncle run this place?"

"Yeah, they bought the whole building actually. They gave me a good deal on renting an apartment upstairs."

"Not over the fish store I hope."

"No. I'm right upstairs over the bar." She looked around at the noise. "It usually quiets down after midnight."

Marion came over and placed our two drinks down on the table, looked at Dottie and said, "Your uncle says hey. Burgers'll be out in a jiff."

Dottie's bottle of beer came without a glass and as Marion turned I said "Wait," and was just about to ask her to bring one when I saw Dottie wipe the top of the bottle with her palm and then take a good enough swallow to bring tears to her eyes.

"Yeah, hon?" Marion said to me.

"Uh, I'll have a beer with my burger please."

"Sure thing."

After she left I must have been staring at Dottie, because she looked up at me and said, "What?"

I shook my head and held my glass up, said, "Cheers."

She dished out a little snarl and a belch.

I glanced up at the TV again, it was showing a picture of Elvis Presley reading a letter next to a Christmas tree, and then David Brinkley's face came on, and then Chet's again, and then the news was over and a string of commercials ran, trying to get us interested in real life, where you needed cigarettes and dish soap and bathtub cleanser and automobiles and corned beef hash and Betty Crocker and Maxwell House coffee and Motorola TVs and toothpaste and frosted flakes and beer and razor blades and aftershave and other TV shows and aspirin to take away the pain of it all.

The food and my beer seemed to show up in no time. Marion, looking down at us said, "All set?"

Dottie had her burger loaded with ketchup and halfway in her mouth before I could answer, "Yeah thanks, Marion."

With the burger in both hands I felt really hungry. I took a large bite and before I could even begin to chew, some kind of reflex had me emitting a slightly audible "Mmmm."

Dottie looked up at me and said, "Right."

"Mmm," I said again, this time meaning yes.

With our mouths full we conducted a full conversation for the next few moments on the superiority of US prime by uttering only grunts and nods.

After my first beer washdown, I took a short break to ask, "So, your aunt and uncle live upstairs too?"

Dottie wiped the ketchup smile from her face, took a sip of beer. "No, they live in Huntington, still in the house where I grew up."

"You and them and your parents all in the same house?"

"No. My parents were killed in a car accident."

"Oh, I'm sorry."

The booth went cold for a few seconds.

"I was just a baby. Aunt Marion and Uncle Duke raised me. They've really been my mom and dad all my life. They have two kids of their own, my cousins Tim and Alice, but really we're like siblings. What makes the situation really special, though, is that my real mom was Marion's sister and my real dad was Duke's brother. So it was real easy to think of Duke and Marion as my mother and father."

"That's pretty cool. I think you're lucky."

She nodded and we both went back to work on our dinner. Marion came back when we were finished and we ordered two more drinks and settled into a comfortable talk.

"So," Dottie said after we got our daily workday minutia out of the way, "I don't want to pry but, uh—"

I cut off her pause, which was gently but clearly saying, *I told you so.*

"Yeah, it looks like it's over and, uh…" My pause said, *Yeah, you were right.* "I don't know. I thought we had something."

"You know what I think, Tom," she said, leaning into the table.

I took out a pack of smokes, offered her one; she shook her head no, and I lit up and sat back.

"I mean first of all, who marries a gangster, you know?"

"How did you know she was married to a gangster?"

She looked at me with the facial expression of someone who didn't live under a rock.

"And I think you didn't know her well, and she didn't know you at all. How could she, of course? You hide so much about yourself. But you can only hide *some* of yourself, some of the things you *do*, maybe. But you can't hide who you are to people who…"

She trailed off for a moment and I waited. I wanted to hear this. She looked to the label on her beer bottle, began that thumbnail-picking thing that beer-bottle label pickers do.

"It's like you try to hide parts of yourself under a coat of paint or something. But it would take more than a few coats of paint to keep me from knowing who you are inside. Believe it or not, Tom, you're just not that mysterious."

"Really?"

Her eyes came off the beer label and penetrated through me like X-rays.

"Yeah, really."

I felt myself trying to block thoughts of things I didn't want her to know about me, and of course then all I could think about were bank robberies past, present and future, and how much I found myself being attracted to her at that very moment. I smiled and said, "So, what do you think is under the paint?"

She swallowed the last of her beer, wiped her mouth with the back of her hand and leaned back against the back of the booth. She took a deep breath and exhaled more than she had taken in, as in exasperation, shrinking her into a concave position. But just as quickly she got bolt upright with a look of insight and determination. She put her palms on the edge of the table and leaned forward to where her small breasts were pressed on the table, her head more than halfway across, and with a crafty smile all around her mouth and eyes she said, "Some day maybe I'll *show* you what I think is going on with you."

Her smile lingered a while and then faded quickly, like a blown out candle on a birthday cake. She sat back as if she had just moved her rook and was waiting to see if I took it as calculated strategy or a bluff.

I put my cigarette out in the ashtray and said I should be going. We got Marion to bring over the check, which Dottie said she would put on her tab, and I didn't argue. We started for the door when Dottie said, "Just a minute," and walked to the kitchen door and stuck her head inside. I couldn't hear anything except the sound of china rattling and the hiss of beef frying on a grill. When she came back we said goodnight to Marion, put on our coats and stepped outside.

It was colder than it was an hour before and the wind was blowing the snow in all directions. The street was still not plowed and there had to be six inches down already. The hubcaps on the Ford were buried and the car was coated with windblown snow, giving it a sleek look, like an artist's rendering of the automobile of the future. I thought about how I'd been so preoccupied lately that I hadn't gotten my snow tires on or even put the chains in the trunk.

"Well, this doesn't look good, does it?" Dottie said.

I had no answer fast enough for her.

"You know I've got a couch upstairs. Why don't you stay over?"

I looked up and down the empty street, luminous balls of snow around each streetlight.

"You have real coffee? Not that phony instant crap."

"Yes."

"Lead the way."

We took two steps and were at the door to the apartments upstairs. Inside was a narrow foyer with a bank of mailboxes on one wall and a staircase that went straight up to a landing on the second floor at the back of the building. At the top to the left were two doors for the apartments over the fish store, and to the right the apartments over the bar. Dottie's was the apartment in the front of the building. Her door opened into the kitchen, with the living room to the right and to the left a hall to the bedroom. Dottie turned on the light switch, and the fluorescent light on the ceiling flickered and then lit up the room in a dull bluish glow. The old plaster walls and woodwork were coated in a stark white semigloss; the cabinets were metal with chrome hardware and painted an off-white hi-gloss.

"Come on in," Dottie said leading the way into the living room. The room was rectangular, with only two windows in the front-end wall that overlooked the street. One side wall was exposed brick, the other plaster painted a deep burgundy, and there was a half wall at the kitchen, with two tall stools at a counter. The general feel of the room was dark but comfortable. Dottie reached for a Tiffany-type lamp that had multicolored leaded stained glass and looked like a kaleidoscope melted over a small umbrella. When she pulled the short brass chain turning the light on, it actually seemed to make the room darker. The furniture all appeared to be second-hand; the only thing that stood out as new was the hi-fi in the middle of the brick wall. Lined along the wall on the floor to the left and right of the hi-fi were milk crates full of record albums.

"Have a seat," she said. "Something to drink, maybe?"

I sat on the couch next to the lamp, said no to the drink and took out my smokes offering her one. She said no so I put the pack down next to the lamp.

"Where did you get this?" I said, pointing to the lamp. "Is it real?"

It's from my grandmother. What do you mean, is it real?"

"Is it a real Tiffany?"

"A real Tiffany what?"

"You know. Is it—.

I looked closely at the base of the lamp, and sure enough it was signed. "Wow," I said.

"What?"

"It's signed. It's worth a lot of money."

"Yeah, well, it's pretty," she said and went over to her records. She walked her fingers along the tops of the album covers and picked one out and put it on the player. A saxophone came out of the hi-fi like smoke and filled the room with a soothing feeling. She stood in the middle of the room for a moment with her eyes closed, swaying slowly with the music. It was the type of jazz you couldn't get on the radio; the kind of music you didn't listen to — you felt it. Or you didn't. Dottie was feeling it and was not faking it like some do. I didn't listen to a lot of jazz, but I had listened to enough to recognize this horn player, who took over the listening space of any room where he was let in. You had to pay attention; his sound demanded it.

"Coltrane," I said.

Dottie opened her eyes and smiled. She came over to sit next to me on the couch.

We sat together quietly for the rest of the tune. The next cut was a little more uptempo but still not bebop speed. Dottie sat back with a look of serenity that could not have been broken with a sledgehammer. When I looked in her eyes, her repose froze me. I looked deeper and when I leaned in only a fraction of an inch she reached both her hands behind my neck and pulled me in the rest of the way. Immediately from the touch of her soft lips I felt a wanton, almost selfish eagerness on her part. There seemed to be a race that went with the music to see who would please who first, each of us catching up to, or waiting for the other, until we finally reached a pace that was tender yet passion-driven. The music and the action both stopped at the same time.

"I'll take that cigarette now," she said as she got up.

I lit a smoke and handed it to her, and then she walked over to the hi-fi without a stitch and turned the record over. She was a woman in complete harmony with her nakedness. I watched her every move, and she was comfortable with that, too. She came back to the couch, sat close to me, and I put my arm around her. It was then that I realized I too was comfortable. I didn't feel the usual anxiety I get after sex, the need to make up some excuse to split. I didn't want to get up for a beer, or get up to leave, or get up at all. I wanted to stay right where I was, listening to jazz, watching the snow come down outside the windows and smelling the hair of this lovely girl in my arms. I felt somehow that this was something I'd been wanting for a long time, and it was not anticlimactic now that I had it.

"So where's this New Year's party?" I said.

"In Greenwich Village. A girlfriend of mine from high school lives there."

We fell silent for a while and then she looked up at me and said, "Do you have all your Christmas shopping done?"

I gave a shallow laugh. "I think I just remembered one more person to put on my list."

The record ended and the hi-fi turned itself off, so I went over to the records to find something else to put on. The collection was varied, and when I found a Hank Williams album I was not surprised, and put it on. Dottie smiled.

"You have a lot of different kinds of records here," I said.

"I like a lot of different kinds of music. I have this fantasy of having a radio show where I just play all kinds of music."

I got back to the couch and she grabbed my arm, drawing me close to her, and put her cheek on my shoulder.

"Do you think people would listen to a show like that?" she said.

"I would. Why don't you make a move in that direction? Some training or school or something."

"Well, there are some schools in the city, but I don't have the time or the money."

Silence again held us, like a favorite aunt's hug.

"Dottie, I…"

"Shh." She pointed toward the window. "Isn't the snow beautiful?"

"Yeah."

We fell asleep later in Dottie's bed with me on my back and Dottie's arm across my chest. I try not to fall asleep on my back, because that's when most of my nightmares come, and that night was no different. With Dottie's arm weighing heavy on my chest, the same terrifying sequence of events begins — I'm pinned down, immobilized. I know I'm sleeping and someone or something is coming for me, a murderous presence is close by, ambush ready. I'm not armed and I'm in a bottomless pit of fear. Breathing stops. I wrestle with my muscles to wake myself up to stop the advance of a force that is inhuman yet primal. It has breached the walls. It is creeping forward in the shadows. It is single hearted in its objective to bring cowardice to me, like a knife of iced dread stabbing through my heart.

Tossing, shaking my head, willing myself with desperate effort to wake up, I finally rolled over to my side and real consciousness slowly came back into focus. Dottie was shaking me.

"Tom, Tom!"

I blinked my eyes open finally and recognized my whereabouts more or less. I scanned the room quickly. When I'm at home I usually calm myself by reaching for my gun, get up and reconnoiter the apartment to verify my safety.

"Who was sinning?" Dottie said.

"What?" I said, acting as if the question made no sense.

"You were talking in your sleep. You kept saying, 'Sin, sin!'"

"I don't know."

But I did know. In Korea, after stabbing that commie soldier in the throat with such righteousness, to get my own guys to stop shooting at me, I was going through his pockets to find a white rag or something to wave over the sandbags of the machine-gun nest. In one of his pockets was a photo of a girl of about twenty or so, and at the bottom of the picture was the name Xin. I found out later it's pronounced *Sin*. She comes to me in my dreams, sometimes to kill me, sometimes to make love to me.

"Maybe it was the nuns," I lied.

"Yeah, they must've really done a number on you."

159

Afterward, sleep did not come back quickly, my eyes kept trying to penetrate the darkness. I would see whatever I wanted to see in the shadows, either movement or stillness. When it was movement, my heart would race; when it was stillness, I had a chance to close my eyes and maybe fall back to sleep. After an hour of vigilance, I finally dozed off.

In the morning I awoke early to the smell of coffee. I walked past the kitchen, said "Hey" and continued to the front windows to assess the aftermath of the storm. It was still dark and the streetlights were on but there was no snow falling through their light. The street had been plowed, and a few cars and trucks were passing by. Some of the vehicles had chains on and I could hear them whirring over the bare pavement sounding like a steady stream of coins being poured into a sack.

Dottie came up behind me and handed me a cup of coffee. "Black," she said, not asking, just announcing.

There was no talk of "That was great last night." I think we were both hoping it was just the first of many nights together.

I asked her if she needed a ride to work, but she said her uncle told her last night when we were leaving the bar that he had put a new battery in her car, so she would be fine. I told her I was taking off to get to my apartment first for a change of clothes and I would see her later at work.

She said "Okay, see you later" as nonchalantly as if we had just finished a game of Monopoly. I laughed to myself and walked out her door.

When I got home, I washed up, changed clothes and then called in to the store and told the older Dottie in the office I was not coming in, feeling a little under the weather. I needed the day to get the Ford ready for the trip upstate with Fiori and company, and with the weather being dicey I wanted to get my snow tires on and make sure the engine was in finely tuned condition. Also I had to call O'Neill and see if he wanted to get together for a strategy meeting.

He did.

"Be at the bar at eleven," he said. "Bring extra ammo."

FOURTEEN

I met O'Neill at his joint later that Friday morning. The strategy, O'Neill explained, was to watch each other's backs so "these ginzoes don't try any kind of double cross." We waited about twenty minutes, and finally Sal and Tony and some new guy arrived. The trio walked in through the back door of the kitchen and after closing the door, Tony looked at O'Neill, cocked his head toward the new guy and said, "This is Allen."

Allen was definitely not out of the gangster mold, looking more like a public school math teacher with a nervous condition. He wore a light brown tweed fedora, which was pulled so far down that it rested on the tops of his ears, bending them over like wilted flowers. He was skinny but not tall. Over a brown plaid suit he wore a dark blue car coat with thick fur on the lapels, creating the look of a horse collar. His eyes were rimmed by thick black-framed glasses similar to Buddy Holly's but a little less goofy. He stepped toward O'Neill and actually stuck out his hand, which O'Neill ignored by saying, "Let's go."

Out in back of O'Neill's the parking lot was small enough for me to notice right away that there was an extra car besides Sal's Lincoln, the ugly Edsel, and mine. Parked off to the end of the lot was the Pontiac from the diner yesterday. And standing right next to the rear door was Tony's father, Vito Fiori.

"My old man wants to talk to you," Tony said to me, a Cheshire sneer on his face.

I walked over to the Pontiac, O'Neill following a few paces behind me.

"Mr. Decker," Vito said. "Do you have insurance with your car?"

"Insurance?"

"Yes, insurance. It's very important these days, what with accidents happening all the time."

He opened the back door of the Pontiac and said, "I took out some insurance on this car just today." He gestured for me to look inside, and when I did a wave of nausea rushed from my stomach to my head and then back again. In the backseat sitting next to one of the goons from the diner, who had his arm draped over her shoulder, was Dottie, a gag wrapped and tied tight around her mouth. She was shrugging, trying hopelessly to get the goon's arm off her. Her watery eyes were filled with more annoyance than fright, and when she turned them on me I felt a rage that had to be calmed. I turned and stepped up to Vito Fiori.

"Look," he said, "this is just to prevent any *accidents* from happening. Tomorrow's little enterprise goes along without a hitch, you'll see your girlfriend as soon as everyone gets back."

I leaned toward Fiori's ear so he wouldn't miss a word. "Do you know what a motivated Marine can do with a rifle from five hundred yards, Fiori? You won't even see it coming. The only *accident*, should she be so much as looked at crosswise, will be if I miss your head and put a bullet in your fucking heart."

He closed the car door and looked over my shoulder toward the Lincoln. He said, "They're waiting for you."

I gave one last look into the Pontiac's window and saw Dottie still trying to shrug off the ape's arm.

"Let's go," I said to O'Neill.

Back at Sal's Lincoln, Tony held the back door open expecting O'Neill and myself to get in.

"We'll follow you in Tom's Ford," O'Neill said.

"That's not the plan," Tony said.

There was stillness in the air for a moment, until Tony and Sal looked over at Allen, who said nothing but gave a short nod and slid into the backseat of the Lincoln, closing the door behind him.

"Try to keep up," Tony said to me and got in the front passenger seat, while Sal looked at me with a short frown as he removed thirty yards of thick black overcoat, folded it in half over his arm and placed it on the seat between himself and Tony before he got behind the wheel.

After we got into my car O'Neill said, "Don't worry, we're gonna fix these fuckers."

Before I started up the Ford I watched the Pontiac pull out of the lot and slip out of sight. "Fix" did not have enough fury in it, I thought. If I had the iron balls of that twenty-year-old Marine with the government-issued license to kill and was not held down by life's petty consequences, I would have gone after the Pontiac, killed every ego-inflated mobster scumbag in the car and rescued the girl of my dreams, and in doing so relieved the guilt for having been responsible for getting her into the situation in the first place plus satisfied a certain amount of rage I was feeling for the whole predicament I found myself in.

"Goddamnit!" I said.

We followed the Lincoln off Long Island, across the George Washington bridge, traveled a length of Route 17 and on up the New York State Thruway for almost three hours, bringing us deep into cow country, and exited into the battered town of Ravena, NY. It was a sad little burgh that looked even bereft of its one horse.

We made a turn onto Main Street, crossing over some forgotten weed-overgrown railroad tracks that hadn't seen a train in decades, and made our way slowly through the town. Not even the golden glow of a late-afternoon winter sun could bring any color to this drab little town. The wooden buildings had all the paint windblown off their walls long ago, making the overall appearance of the place as gray and rough as elephant hide. In the middle of the block the Lincoln's left turn signal started blinking. To the left was a three-storied cube of a building made of solid granite. It had an empty lot on either side and a parking lot in back that gave it a look like the rest of the buildings in town had abandoned it and it was making some sort of last stand. At the top of the front wall in relief lettering was the name "Carlisle Trust Bank." The front of the bank was mostly taken up by a double door of about twelve feet in height, and each door had to be four feet wide and appeared to be made of solid bronze, with its bas-relief of ancient money lenders tarnished a chalky white. There was a small window on either side of the door about the size of an entrance to a birdhouse, with each window fronted by thick iron bars that must have blocked any chance of daylight entering the building.

"Jesus," O'Neill said. "These jokers better have something up their sleeves for this."

As the town thinned out and turned back into rural farmland, Sal continued down the paved road for another mile or so until we came upon a factory complex that was on both sides of the road. It must have been time for the shift change because just as many cars were entering the gates as leaving. There seemed like hundreds of parking spaces in the lot and about half were filled. A sign on the top of one of the four buildings on each side of the road said "Atlantic Gypsum." Another half mile past the plant the Lincoln made a U-turn and we went back toward the town. About a quarter mile before entering the town Sal turned off the main road onto some kind of access road with a broken chain that had been stretched across the road between two small wooden posts. The chain was lying on the ground and had a rusted metal sign attached that said "No Trespassing." There were no tire tracks in the snow that covered the lane, and as we got about two hundred yards off the main road we entered forest and disappeared from sight of the highway. After a few twists we finally arrived at an abandoned four-storied wooden building with a sign on the roof that, if all the letters were there, would have spelled out "Ravena Fuel Depot." In what was once a parking lot, Sal spun the Lincoln around and soon we were back out on the county road and again heading into town.

After passing through the town we were on a stretch of the road where no houses were to be seen, only farmland, and that was hard to see because there was a berm of snow on either side of the road made by the state plow trucks. Sal slowed to turn at a blue mailbox with the name "Stanley" hand-painted on it and drove down a dirt driveway lined with poles carrying electric and possibly phone lines. After about a hundred yards the drive entered into a stand of pine trees, under which a fine, thin layer of snow like sifted flour lay on the forest floor. The driveway made a few bends before we finally came upon a farmhouse, which looked well maintained compared with what we'd seen nearby. There were no parking spaces per se; we just stopped our cars and got out. The trees were so close to the house that it appeared the house had just grown there between the trees.

O'Neill and I leaned against the right front fender of my car and lit up a couple of cigarettes. I nudged him and pointed toward the side of the house.

"What the fuck?" he said.

Parked next to the house was an orange-and-white two-tone '55 Chevy Bel Air that made it look like the snow was on fire. Allen came over smiling at us and said, "You like our getaway car?"

These were the first words we'd heard Allen speak. His voice was clear and accent-free, although his speech was almost refined, like Cary Grant's.

"You gotta be kidding," I said.

"C'mon inside, gentlemen."

I heard the trunk of the Lincoln slam shut and looked over to see Sal and Tony carrying two duffle bags over their shoulders. We walked up the stairs to the standard two-story clapboard farmhouse with wraparound porch, two gables on the front roof and everything painted white. Allen unlocked the door, and as each of us passed him to enter he handed out pairs of white gloves.

"You'll wear these the whole time we're here."

We all entered into the cold house and huddled in the foyer. Tony looked left and right at the bareness of the house and said, "Where'd we get this place from?"

"Doesn't matter," Allen said. "It'll never be traced to any of us. Go down and get the coal furnace going."

"The whaa?"

"I'll get it," Sal said, dropping his duffle bag practically on Tony's foot.

"Take a room upstairs," Allen said to no one in particular. "And settle in. We're eating in ten minutes."

O'Neill and I went upstairs and took one of the front bedrooms looking out over the cars. There were two small beds, and when I dropped my overnight bag on one of them it bounced up and down on the thin mattress and squeaky springs for the length of time it took O'Neill to say, "Jesus H. Christ."

I looked around the room, which was basically empty except for the two beds, a table between them with a small radio on it, and a few frameless black-and-white photos of ballplayers hanging on the walls. A couple of brothers probably grew up here with misguided team loyalties, since the photos were all of Yankees from eight or nine seasons ago. Only one photo was autographed — that of Snuffy Stirnweiss.

After a few minutes the house warmed up a bit and there was a faint smell of coal burning I recognized from winter days in our Brooklyn home, which also had a coal furnace. Downstairs in the kitchen O'Neill and I found

Allen and Sal about to prepare some dinner. Allen was putting a box of spaghetti into a pot of boiling water on the gas stove.

"Sal," Allen said, "Cook up some sauce. There's some stuff in the cabinet."

Sal opened all the top cabinets, moving jars and cans around, and said, "There's nothing here."

"Right there," Allen said, pointing to a can of Hunt's Tomato Sauce on one of the shelves.

Sal picked up the can and looked at it as if he had never seen canned goods before. He passed a quick look to O'Neill and me looking for help.

"I can't make anything out of this," he said.

Allen looked up from stirring his pot of spaghetti.

Sal opened the refrigerator, pulled a few drawers open. "Where's the garlic, onions—"

"Sal, you open that can, put it in a pot, heat it up, and voilà."

I went to the cabinets and in a few seconds came out with three small cans of spices.

"Here, Sal," I said and handed him some garlic powder, dried oregano and basil. "This might help."

Sal looked at the tins as if I were handing him a waste of time. By now O'Neill, who was sitting at the small kitchen table, was having a private, small laugh at Sal's bemusement. Sal looked over at O'Neill and said, "What are you laughing at? You're gonna go hungry. I don't see no fuckin' potatoes here."

All five of us eventually found ourselves at the table in a square dining room of plastered walls with peeling pale teal paint. Over a dried-up yellow oak table was a chandelier with two of the eight light bulbs working on it and many empty, rusted metal hooks where once fake crystal hung. Allen was at the head of the table, with Sal and Tony sitting on one side opposite O'Neill and me on the other, and a plate of spaghetti in front of each of us.

Sal got up before lifting a fork and went back into the kitchen and then quickly returned, standing at the swinging door between the two rooms. He looked at Allen with his sad, puffy eyes.

"Where's the wine?" he said.

Allen was tucking a dishcloth into the collar of his shirt, letting it hang down the front of his breast like a dinghy-white, very wide tie. "There's some bottles of beer in the fridge," he said. "Bring me one." He looked around the table, pointing his fork at the rest of us. "Anyone else?"

The table needed four beers, and Sal backed his way into the kitchen, shaking his head at the gathering of Philistines around the table. He came back with five brown bottles, and we all took a long drink of beer, put our bottles down on the table and settled into silent dining — that is except for Sal, who was battling to swallow his first forkful of food, nodding up and down like a horse trying to escape its bridle.

"Jesus Christ, that's awful," he said.

Allen wiped his mouth, putting some color into his tie. He looked at Sal like a mother who had to get a child to eat his spinach.

"Sal, you're gonna have to get used to this cuisine. You're gonna be here a while."

Sal shook his head again in resignation and, using his fork and a spoon, spun a lump of spaghetti the size of a baseball and made it vanish into his round face.

"How long's a while?" O'Neill said with a mouthful of food and adding to it.

"Till the heat blows over," Tony said as if he knew something no one else did. Everyone looked over at Tony and then to O'Neill, who was looking at nothing outside the perimeter of his plate.

"Something like that," Allen said. "We'll go over everything after we finish eating."

O'Neill finished first, brought his plate into the kitchen and washed it and then came back to the table with a fresh beer, sat down and waited patiently. After everyone else was done and the table cleared, Allen went upstairs and quickly returned with a small briefcase that he set on the floor next to his chair and pulled out of it a piece of paper with the floor plan to the Carlisle Trust Bank roughly sketched in pencil. Tony reached over and grabbed a corner of the paper to spin it around so he could read the words and follow the arrows.

"Where do we go in?" he said.

"First of all," Allen said as he turned the paper back around to face him, "*you* don't go in. Second, there's a lot that gets done before anyone steps into the bank."

He reached back down into the case on the floor and came up with four envelopes and passed one to each of us. Mine had the letter D on it, and I looked over at O'Neill's, which had an O on it. I took out the single piece of loose-leaf from the envelope and saw on it a column of times, and a brief sentence next to each time: "0600 — Leave house in Chevy with O," and so on.

"As you can see, gentlemen," Allen said, "every step of this operation is all mapped out for you. If everyone follows each direction at the precise time, you should be in and out of the bank and back to this place in less than two hours."

He removed his thick glasses and wiped them clean with the same dishrag he had been using for a napkin. Again Tony tried to move the paper to look at the bank's floor plan. Allen pulled the paper back calmly and turned it over to a blank side.

"Tony," Allen said, "what's the first step on your list?"

Tony took out the paper from his envelope and read the first line.

"Oh six oh oh—"

"Oh six hundred, moron," O'Neill said.

Tony put on a frown that was more a reaction to the meaning of O'Neill's statement than to the insult.

Sal elbowed the young thug. "Six in the morning," he said.

"Okay, oh six a.m. leave house with S, proceed to one-one-eight Curtis Drive."

Allen at that point took out two maps from his bag and handed one to Sal and one to me.

"Your to and from routes are highlighted," he said. "Don't forget to take them with you in the morning."

He then went over the whole heist in general and specific language. He had us move furniture around in the living room and dining room to simulate the bank's floor plan and went over each step of everyone's moves. When his eyes weren't on us they were on his watch. His comments were mostly either "Move faster" or "Take your time." After three hours of this he finally thought we had it right.

Good," he said. "Any questions?"

"Yeah," O'Neill said, strangely calm for someone being forced into a dangerous position. "Where are the nearest state troopers? What about the diversion? And what's with that fuckin' getaway car?"

"Good questions, sir," Allen said. "I was waiting to see who was going to ask them." He looked over at Sal and Tony with not just a little disappointment in his eyes. "As you have obviously surmised, there is no police force in this town, and with the state thruway nearby, the town is in the state trooper jurisdiction. I'll be leaving here in the morning just ahead of you four; in a vehicle I have out back. I'll be heading to that old fuel depot that's just waiting to be fire-bombed. That should keep the troopers busy while you are conducting the bank withdrawal.

"At the bank itself, there's a guard but he's not armed and shouldn't pose a problem, unless, of course, he has a heart attack or something." He paused for the benefit of

O'Neill and myself, I'm sure. "Should any of the bank personnel escape from the vault that you will have locked them in, or if someone on the street calls in suspicious goings-on, you guys should still get back here before the cops can get anywhere near close."

Everyone, including O'Neill, nodded.

"That Chevy outside," he continued, "that looks like it escaped from the circus was boosted two nights ago at Idlewild Airport's long-term parking from some guy vacationing in Europe who won't report it missing until he gets back a week from now. That hideous car is what every cop in the state will be looking for in the next few days. And there should be more than a few witnesses who see three guys in it going like a bat out of hell out of town heading for the thruway to make their escape. So when we pull out of town a day later in a plain black or maroon sedan, no one's going to look twice."

"Okay," O'Neill said. "One last thing."

He waited for Allen's and the whole room's full attention. When he had it he said, "I ain't goin' in no bank without any artillery."

Allen smiled at O'Neill and turned to Sal. "Sal, the duffle bags."

Sal went to get the bags, which were on the floor near the front door, where he and Tony had first dropped them. He brought them over to the dining room, one in each hand, and lifted them with a small amount of strain, placing them on the table. Allen opened the first one and pulled out four pairs of khaki trousers, four shirts, four Navy pea coats and four pairs of black shoes.

"Your uniforms, gentlemen," he said. "The sizes should all work, more or less." He then reached down to the bottom of the bag and came up with four nylon stockings. "And your masks."

He tossed the empty bag onto the floor up against the wall below the bay windows, opened the second bag and reached inside it. The first item out was a sawed-off double-barreled twelve gauge shotgun, which he handed to O'Neill, who immediately broke it open, inspecting the empty chambers, and then looked down the barrels with a look of approval on his face. Allen stuck his hand in the bag again and came out with what looked like a Colt .38 Special revolver and gave it to Tony.

"That's called a Colt Official Police handgun," Allen said. "And with the six-inch barrel it should make any civilian stop and take notice."

Tony smiled at the gun, opened the swing-out cylinder, spun it with the palm of his gloved hand and then snapped it back in place with a flick of his wrist. He looked very pleased with himself.

Reaching into the bag again with both hands, Allen looked at me and said, "And what every good bank robber needs is something that takes the starch out of any hero types in a bank heist." His two hands came out of the duffel bag cradling a weapon I had only seen in old black-and-white movies in the hands of the likes of Paul Muni or George Raft. There in front of me was the real McCoy, the darling of the ghosts of gangsters past, the aristocrat of criminal weaponry. The black steel was worn to the color of the buffalo on a nickel. The hardwood stock and pistol grip were smooth from handling. I took it in my arms and held it like a newborn, taking in every feature, including the drum magazine that could hold up to a hundred rounds. On the side of the receiver just below the rear sight I read the words.

"Thompson Submachine Gun."

I looked over at O'Neill, who was shaking his head and rolling his eyes.

"It looks good on you, killer," Allen said and turned the bag upside down, dumping out the remainder of its contents, ammo for all the weapons. He took the two empty bags and handed them to O'Neill. "Fill these with money tomorrow." Then he looked at each of the four faces in the room and picked up the floor plan from the table and placed it in his briefcase.

"We all have this memorized, right," he said looking straight at Tony. No one moved. He looked at his watch. "Okay, ten o'clock. Everyone to sleep, back down here at five thirty."

Sal, O'Neill and I headed for the stairs, and Tony went toward the kitchen.

"Anyone want a beer? How 'bout a game a cards?" he said.

"Tony," Allen said, motioning with his head for Tony to come to him. He was not loud, no exasperation or authority in his voice; he said Tony's name as if calling him over to give him a tip in the fifth at Saratoga.

Tony came up to Allen with shoulders slouched.

"What?"

"Bed."

Tony mumbled something in adolescent, went to the kitchen, pulled a beer from the refrigerator and followed O'Neill and me up the stairs to the bedrooms. Tony was in the room next to ours; the walls were so thin we could hear him curse when he knocked over his bottle of beer.

O'Neill aimed his eyes toward the wall and said, "That idiot is gonna be a big problem at some point." He sat on the edge of his bed, took one shoe off and held it by the heel, pointing the toe toward the sound of Tony's footsteps. "Bang," he said softly as the shoe recoiled.

We both lay down to sleep, which for me did not come easily when the first thoughts drifting in and out of my inner vision were pictures of Dottie in the hands of a couple of goons. I was not going over the plans of the next day's heist but instead how to rescue the embodiment of sweetness — Dottie G. I turned on the radio and pulled in one station from Albany that was still playing prewar big band music. It helped some, and I dozed off.

FIFTEEN

In the morning I got to the kitchen at five fifteen and found Allen at the table with a cup of coffee. He was fully dressed, with hat and coat. There were four beer bottles in front of him. Each bottle had a rag sticking out of it. I couldn't see through the brown glass, but I could tell there was a liquid inside the bottles. I poured myself some coffee and sat down across from him. In a minute everyone else was in the room.

"Everyone have a coffee," Allen said. "You can eat something when you all get back." He looked at Tony. With what looked like hope in his eyes, Allen kept his stare on Tony for a moment, then stood up and put two of the beer bottles in his coat pockets, and the remaining two one in each hand. He faced O'Neill and me.

"You two, when you're inside the bank, if Sal sees the cops, he's takin' off and you're on your own. Either shoot your way out or give up, I don't care." He looked over his shoulder at Sal and Tony at the table. "Our job is to get through this safely. If we come back to the don with money, that'll be a plus, but mainly we're here for behind-the-scenes support, with you two doing all the heavy lifting." He lifted his shoulders apologetically. "You got yourself into this, get yourself out."

He turned to face the back door with his hands full and waited.

"Tony," Sal said, looking at the door.

Tony, as if waking, got up and opened the door for Allen, who stepped outside. Tony closed the door. We sipped coffee as the sound of a car trunk closing was followed by car door closing and then engine starting.

Through the kitchen window we could see Allen slowly going by in a gray Plymouth.

At five forty-five O'Neill and I were in the orange Chevy following behind Sal and Tony in Sal's Lincoln as we crept over an inch of new snow on the driveway leaving the farmhouse hideaway. The sun was not due to rise for another hour and a half and my headlights were picking up a few lingering flakes of snow from last night's fall dropping from the pine trees. At the end of the drive Sal turned right heading toward town and I followed about seven or eight car-lengths behind. I kept a pace at some three miles per hour above the speed limit — not too fast, not too slow. After eight miles we turned left onto a paved county road, and three miles later we turned left onto Curtis Drive. There was a house right there on the corner and then not another for a half mile until we reached number 117 in a cul-de-sac at the end of the road. There was not another house in sight. Sal backed the Lincoln right into the short driveway behind a late-model Chrysler. I turned the Chevy around and parked on the street. There were no lights on in the front of the house.

Tony and Sal got out of their car silently with their stocking masks on, and Tony quickly went around to the rear of the house to cover the back door. O'Neill and I got our masks on and met up with Sal at the front door. The house was a two-story colonial, all white except for the door, which was a high-glossed black. We all positioned ourselves so we could not be seen from any of the windows. Sal nodded for me to knock on the door. I found the doorbell button first and pushed it in, and when the Westminster chime was only halfway through I rapped my knuckles on the door rapidly like someone who needed help. In a few seconds I heard footsteps coming down the stairs, the click of the deadbolt and then saw the doorknob turning. As soon as the door budged inward a fraction of an inch, I pushed it in the rest of the way, with Sal and O'Neill following me inside the house.

Staring at the sight of three scary men with guns was the half-covered-in-shaving-cream face of Lindsey Dearborn, Carlisle Trust Bank manager. He was wearing an undershirt and a pair of pinstripe suit trousers with the suspenders hanging down by his legs. He looked stunned but somehow not surprised. A woman's voice came from upstairs.

"Who is it, dear?" she said.

We ushered the manager into the living room out of sight of the stairway.

"Tell her to get down here," O'Neill said in a low tone and with a pistol at Dearborn's ribs.

"It's, uh, you better get down here, Laura," he said.

The woman arrived downstairs in a rose-colored chenille robe with roses embroidered on the lapels, and slippers of terry cloth the same color as the robe. She put the back of her hand to her open mouth upon comprehending the scene in her living room. With gray hair that was too long for her age, she looked a lot older than her husband, who could have been in his mid fifties.

"What do you want?" she blurted, sounding more indignant than frightened.

"They want money I'm sure," Dearborn said calmly.

"We don't want trouble," O'Neill said. "This is where I say, 'Everyone do as you're told and no one gets hurt.'"

By then Tony had come through the front door and closed it behind him, and Sal went to one of the front windows, keeping lookout.

"Go upstairs," O'Neill said to Tony. "Find the kid. Tell her to get dressed for school like normal."

Tony ran up the stairs and down the hall. We could hear a door open and close and then quickly open and close again. Tony appeared at the top of the stairs.

178

"She says there's no school today," he said. "Christmas vacation."

"Just tell her to get dressed," O'Neill said. He then turned to the husband and wife. He looked at Lindsey Dearborn hard, motioned with his pistol toward the stairs. "Upstairs finish shaving." To the wife he said, "You too. Upstairs get dressed. We're all leaving here in three minutes."

The old lady started up the stairs, with the husband following, then O'Neill and then me. Halfway up she stopped and turned, looking past her husband to O'Neill.

"Where are we going?" she said.

O'Neill shook his head. "Jesus Christ, lady. Why? You wanna call to cancel your beauty parlor appointment? Get moving."

"Laura, please," Dearborn said as calmly as if telling her they were going to be late for a movie.

O'Neill followed the old man to the bathroom; I went with the old lady to her bedroom, let her go in and closed the door behind her. Where was she going to go? If she jumped out the window, Sal would see her land in the rhododendron outside. Tony was standing outside the girl's room with its door ajar and Tony craning, trying to get a look inside. I walked down the hall and closed the door in front of him.

"Hey, I was enjoying the scenery."

I ignored him and went back to Laura Dearborn's door. In about a minute O'Neill came from the bathroom with the husband and walked him to the bedroom. O'Neill followed him inside the room a few steps. The wife was in a dressing alcove off to the side.

"Stop," O'Neill said.

Dearborn stopped.

"Where's your gun?"

"My what?"

O'Neill tilted his head. Dearborn was not dumb. He pointed to a nightstand next to the bed. O'Neill went over, opened a drawer and reached in for a small nickel-plated automatic and slipped it into his pocket.

"Two minutes," he said and came back out to the hall.

The three of us stood in silence for another minute, with O'Neill staring at his watch. Finally he knocked on the master bedroom door with his piece. "Let's go," he said. He then went to the daughter's door and knocked. "C'mon, sister, get out here."

The kid came out first. She was about sixteen years old, with short blond hair and eyes the color of Windex. She was wearing a red gingham blouse and black slacks that tapered down to her ankles, and a pair of black penny loafers and an air of teenage blasé. She walked past the three masked men as if she does it everyday.

As she took her first step down the stairs, Tony called out. "Hey, girlie. Where do you think you're goin'?"

She turned and looked at Tony with a crooked pout on her small mouth. She reminded me of Dottie, and suddenly a wave of anger passed through me leaving me feeling cold.

"Just wait right there," Tony said, "till I tell you where to go."

Laura Dearborn then came into the hall and looked over at her daughter's open bedroom door. "Gwen?" she said.

"What?" Gwen said, sounding as if it were the hundredth time that morning she had to answer the call.

Laura followed her daughter's voice, met her at the top of the stairs and clutched her hand. Lindsey Dearborn finally emerged from the bedroom in his three-piece suit and tie and ruby cuff links, clean shaven and smelling of Old Spice.

"Everyone down in the living room," O'Neill said.

Once they were gathered downstairs, O'Neill sat the bank manager down in a chair facing away from the front windows. Tony took out two black cloth bags from his coat pocket and put them over the heads of the mother and daughter. Tony looked at Sal, Sal at O'Neill. O'Neill nodded.

"Let's go, sweetheart," Tony said to the teen, grabbing her hand and leading her to the door. He stepped outside the front door and then Sal took Laura Dearborn's arm. "Just stay with me. Watch your step."

I went to the front window and watched Tony and Sal load the two hostages into the backseat of the Lincoln. Sal made his way back to the house while Tony got in the driver's seat, turned around and said something to the two passengers, and they both ducked down out of sight. He then took his mask off, started up the Lincoln, pulled slowly out of the driveway and drove off.

When Sal walked back into the house I couldn't help but ask, "You trust that clown with your Lincoln?"

"That's not *my* Lincoln. It's a stolen Lincoln. I don't drive anything else. Mine is back at Irene's, er, Enzo's place in Oyster Bay."

O'Neill went to where Dearborn was sitting and faced him squarely. "Okay, I think you get the picture and pretty much know what's going on and what has to happen now."

Dearborn nodded quickly, not so much with resignation as eagerness.

"My associates" — O'Neill glanced toward Sal and me — "and I don't want no trouble. We don't want anyone to get hurt." He pointed to the front door, to where Dearborn last saw his family walk away with one sterling criminal. "If you behave and we all get what we want this morning, everyone goes home a winner. Right?" He paused, bent at the waist toward Dearborn's face. "Right?"

"Right, right," Dearborn said.

"Okay. Right now you're going get in your car, like you do every morning, and drive to work. We're going to follow behind you — and believe me, as you may have guessed, we know a lot about you, your bank and your driving habits. If I see you going off course in any way, there will be a price to pay, get me? You're going to let the two of us into the bank through the back door, and then we wait for the rest of your employees to arrive. You will tell each one of them what's going on. I'm sure I don't have to tell you how important it is to get their complete cooperation. When the vault timer goes off, you open the vault; we take the money and leave." O'Neill paused, looked at me, checked his watch. "Questions?"

"What about my wife and daughter?"

"When all of us are at a safe place counting our money, they will be let go unharmed."

O'Neill shifted his gun from one hand to the other and grabbed Dearborn by the elbow. "Okay, let's go."

We all went outside. Dearborn got in his Chrysler, waited for us to get in the Chevy and then pulled out of his driveway. When we got to the main road O'Neill, Sal and I took off our masks and followed behind Dearborn a few hundred yards. On a stretch of road that had nothing but empty snow-covered cornfields on either side of the road, O'Neill tossed Dearborn's automatic out the window. We got to the parking lot in the back of the bank at eight thirty, fifteen minutes before the manager's regular time. The lot was empty, and while the bank manager got out of his car, the three of us put our masks back on and waited for Dearborn to open the door to the bank.

"Think this guy'll play it smart?" I asked O'Neill.

He shrugged. "I don't know what it's like to have a family. But I had a dog once." He looked over at me, and through the nylon mask I could not get any kind of facial expression. "Anybody try to fuck with that dog..." He trailed off, leaving the issue as vague as the features on his face.

When Dearborn had the door open we got out of the car, went to the trunk and got out the Thompson, the shotgun and the empty duffle bags. Sal closed the trunk and said, "Good luck."

O'Neill and I entered the bank with Dearborn while Sal pulled the Chevy closer to the lot exit. Inside, we walked down a short, narrow hallway lined with cardboard boxes against the walls on either side that gave the area the smell of musty paper. The walls needed fresh paint. There were three doors off the hall, a ladies' room, men's room and a door marked "Manager," and at the end of the hall was a door with a frosted-glass window. On the glass was the backwards word "Private."

Dearborn opened the door and we stepped into the main great room of the bank. The room was dark due to the small and few windows in the place. He then went to a bank of light switches on the wall and flicked them all on, lighting up the room from three ornate chandeliers made of a dull metal and glass, which hung down from the thirty-foot-high ceiling. The space was grand, with marble flooring and marble columns at each corner of the room. On one of the walls was a mural of some ambitious steam locomotive pulling a train of boxcars through the once-energetic pastoral lands surrounding the town of Ravena. The bank must have at one time held the fortunes of the railroad barons who summered up here in the country before the great crash of '29. In the center of the room was a table made of a thick slab of marble held up by four wooden legs the size of tree trunks. On the table the usual deposit slips, pens and a calendar.

At one end of the big room was an iron fence from floor to ceiling with a gate in the middle of it. Behind the gate, set back in an alcove, was the great round door of the vault standing silent and bold in the glow of its own shining silver. I took my place near the front entrance with Dearborn who took out his keys to open up the door for each employee as they approached the door. O'Neill waited out of sight of the door near the gate to the vault. The first to arrive for work was the guard, a tall white-haired gentleman in his late forties with pink cheeks and alcohol on his breath. His dim eyes, like magnets, went straight to my machine gun, and he seemed to gasp.

"We're being robbed, Phil," Dearborn said.

"Stand over there by the table," I said, pointing to the center of the room, the one place that was the farthest away from any alarm buttons.

He walked over to the table and quickly placed his hands on the marble as if holding on to a rocking boat. The next to arrive were three tellers at the same time, two middle-aged women not terribly attractive, and a young man in his twenties. He entered behind the ladies and took off his overcoat before he even noticed me. He wore a suit with lapels three styles behind the times and a bow tie. When he saw me he gave me an up-and-down glance that made me dislike him immediately. When I told the trio to move to the table, he had an air of being inconvenienced and not happy about it. The two women raced over next to the guard, but Bow Tie sauntered. I took a step toward him and poked him in the back with the Thompson.

"Move it."

He stopped in his tracks, turned and glared at me.

"Ronald, please," Dearborn said. "Just do as you're told."

After Ronald joined the others I pulled Dearborn aside. "Whose nephew is he?"

Dearborn shook his head. "The board chairman's son-in-law."

"You better put him wise, quick."

Dearborn nodded.

The last employees to arrive were the three male officers. They joined the group at the table without incident. I stayed at the door to escort any customers that might come in and told Dearborn to give his employees the scoop. He did so with a good deal of passion that I was surprised he had in him. The two women seemed to take the situation with much concern, probably being mothers themselves, and reacted with worry on their faces, touching the bank manager's arm as he spoke.

At exactly nine o'clock O'Neill called over to the bank manager, "Okay, Dearborn, who else do you need to open the vault?"

Dearborn nodded to the man standing right next to him. "Alex, here."

"Okay, the two a ya, over here."

The two men went over to O'Neill. Dearborn took out some keys and opened the iron gate, and the three went to the vault door. Everyone's eyes at the marble table were on the vault. Mine were on everyone at the marble table, but from the corner of my eye I could see O'Neill with his shotgun at the backs of Dearborn and Alex, who were loading money into the two canvas bags. Back at the table I noticed Ronald whisper something to one of the male officers, who nodded his head up and down.

"Hey!" I called over, loud enough to turn all the heads at the table toward me. I raised the barrel of the Thompson in Ronald's direction. "Shut up."

Ronald swallowed hard, making his bow tie do a little jig. Something about this guy was drawing anger out of me like a leach sucking blood. Was it the assumed privilege I thought he had? The fact that he was of draft age and instead of being in the army was at some soft job that was given to him? It was all that, plus the general smart-ass smugness that just came off him like cheap cologne. But there was something else I couldn't quite put my finger on. And then it came to me. He reminded me of

Tony Fiori. These two young men were going through life without a clue as to the larger, messier picture around them.

While this Ronald may not have had the evil criminal streak in him like Tony, he did have the look of someone who had not a thought in his head for his fellows. He would probably own this bank one day and would never know or care about the homeowners or farmers whose lives and livelihoods he'd be ruining whenever the bank faced the inevitable decision to foreclose on some of them. Both of these heirs apparent would never know the feeling of a situation being forced upon them. Like this bank robbery was for me. A quagmire for these two would be solved by Ronald throwing money at it, or Tony shooting his way out of it. And then the more I thought about Tony, the more I thought about Dottie and the place she could be in right then. The dark, burning rage in me was closing in physically on my vision. I was in a tunnel of anguish, with only the face of Ronald at the end of it, smirking in a confidence that under the circumstances made no sense.

I blinked and shook my head and noticed that he was looking over my shoulder at the door — the door that I was not paying attention to. I turned around in time to grab a customer who had come in and was about to run back out.

I had him by the back of the collar. "Where you going?" I said, as if on top of everything.

He was a short, round, very heavy fellow whose momentum had me hopping behind him before I got him to stop.

"Over there with the others," I told him, with a little shove toward Marble Island.

By then O'Neill was coming through the iron gate with Dearborn and Alex in front of him, each struggling to carry the two duffle bags. He had them place the bags near the door to the back hall.

The noise of loud sirens started leaking through under the sill of the front door. They got louder and louder until Ronald spoke up over the wailing.

"Looks like the jig is up, boys."

In seconds three fire engines ran past the front of the building, sirens, bells and horns blaring. It looked like the fire department and every state trooper were on their way to a blaze somewhere. O'Neill and I looked at each other with grins we could hardly hide.

"Now," O'Neill said to the group of bank people. Everyone please step behind the gate over there."

He walked behind them and ushered them all into the vault and closed the great door behind them, and then we made our way to the back door. Outside, the rising morning sun was bright and lit up a clear blue sky. The air was cold. Laden with cash we lumbered over to the Chevy, opened the trunk tossed in the guns and the money and then got in the car. Sal put the Chevy in gear and pulled out onto the side street and then onto Main Street, which was only just coming alive with a handful of pedestrians and five or six other moving vehicles.

O'Neill took out his envelope from Allen and read off the directions.

"Left on Main for two point six-tenths and then a left on Maple Hill."

On Main, Sal gunned it and raced through town as if heading for the NY Thruway. The left on Maple Hill was well short of the Thruway, and after four or five minutes we found ourselves driving south along the Hudson River, with railroad tracks between the river and us. We were passing industrial loading docks with barges waiting for materials to be loaded. At one of the docks was a corrugated tin shack with the name "Atlantic Gypsum" on it, the company whose money we now carried in the trunk of our car. Right next to the tin shack was a seedy-looking bar called "Dockside."

"They'll be drinking for a different reason tonight I guess," O'Neill said.

The excitement of having a very large quantity of money behind me suddenly diminished when I thought of the bigger picture, and Dottie. This was all for her if I ever got out of it. But that was as far as I could go; I couldn't advance the hypothetical, so I focused on the very present, of getting safely away from a bank heist.

After a half-dozen more turns on back roads we found ourselves on the road to the hideout. Before making the turn into the driveway we checked ahead and behind us to make sure no cars were in sight. We were clear, and Sal turned into the driveway. We parked between Sal's hot Lincoln and Allen's gray Plymouth, got out of the car and walked up to the house. It was only ten in the morning but I felt like I had just put in a long, hard day.

SIXTEEN

Waiting right inside the door was Allen, with nothing in his face except patience.

"Everything go to plan?" Allen said.

"Fine," O'Neill said. "I'm hungry."

"I'll fry some eggs," Sal said.

As the three of us were on our way to the kitchen, Tony came banging down the stairs. He got to the entrance and looked around the empty space.

"Where's the dough?" he said, out of breath.

Sal threw the keys to the Chevy right at his head, but Tony ducked in time and they went up against the wall and on to the floor.

"In the trunk," Sal said.

He gathered the keys and went out the front door. He made three trips to retrieve the money and the guns. As Sal, O'Neill and I were eating bacon and eggs in the kitchen we could hear Tony out in the hall saying "Holy shit!" several times.

As I stood in the kitchen and stretched I eyed the padlock on the door to the basement, where Mrs. Dearborn and the teen were being kept. I nodded toward the door and asked, "Everyone behaving themselves down there?"

Sal gave a quick look over to Allen, who without looking up said, "They're fine."

After eating, I said I was going upstairs to rest. The restless sleep from the night before plus the stress of the morning had caught up to me.

"You're on lookout in two hours," Allen said.

"Sure."

In the bedroom I took off my shoulder holster and gun and hung it with my pea coat on the back of a chair. I turned on the radio and the announcer was in the middle of reporting the bank robbery. I smiled when I heard "last seen in an orange Chevy heading for the New York State Thruway." I lay down on the bed on my back, and in a minute I was in that between time of sleep and consciousness, where something was keeping me from drifting off. Images and thoughts of Dottie had my nap tied up like a calf in a rodeo. I couldn't fall asleep and I couldn't wake up. Faint sounds were seeping into my transient state; it was like a whimpering. Was it Dottie calling for me in my dreams? I felt and heard myself snore and used it to wake myself up. Slowly gaining the acquaintance of the present reality, I sat up in bed, swinging my feet to the floor. I listened. The sound was coming from the other side of the wall, in Tony's room. I put my ear to the wall and heard what sounded like someone trying to catch their breath. I went out in the hall and down to Tony's door, opened it a crack and listened again. It was crying.

I pushed the door open enough to get a look inside and saw Gwen Dearborn sitting on the bed up against the headboard. She had her knees pulled to her chin and her two hands were full of covers tightly gripped and drawn up to her face. Her eyes were closed and she didn't seem to notice me. I closed the door and went back to my room to get the stocking from my coat pocket.

With the mask on I stuck my head in Tony's door.

"Are you okay, miss?" I said.

The girl was startled, pulling the covers up tighter to her face. I guess we all looked the same to her.

"No, no, I'm not."

I struggled for the words. "I just got here. What happened?"

She shook her head, saying nothing, and just rocked back and forth on the bed.

"Did...did he hurt you?"

"What do you care!" she said, not quite screaming but with a force and aim that hit its target.

"What did he do?" I said, not realizing how indelicate I sounded.

"Don't make me say it," she said and closed her eyes, shaking her head and shoulders violently as if trying to shake off the horror of it all.

I felt a similar helplessness as when I last saw Dottie in the back of that Pontiac. But this time there seemed to be a few more options open for me. They were not coming into my mind in exactly the clearest forms, but they were immediate and made me move quickly. I followed my footsteps down the hall to the stairs.

Downstairs I found O'Neill, Allen and Tony in the dining room. O'Neill was sitting at the table, his shotgun lying on the floor beside his chair. Allen was sitting at the small bench in the bay window that overlooked the driveway, and Tony was standing at the swinging door to the kitchen. Sal was not visible; he was probably on lookout somewhere. I put on the brakes with my anger for a moment and directed my talk to Allen.

"Allen," I said with much false calmness, "who had the envelope with the instructions to rape one of the hostages?"

My eyes stayed on Allen, whose eyes dashed over to Tony for a moment. Without turning my gaze from Allen I could see Tony slowly unbuttoning the pea coat. O'Neill's eyes were everywhere at once, but the rest of his body was silent and as still as a pallbearer. Still directing my words to Allen, I said, "You had to hear what was going on upstairs. You couldn't do something?"

Allen gave a slight eye roll. "He's the boss's kid, for Chrissake. And anyway, what's it to you?"

"Yeah," Tony said. "What's your beef? You had your part in this deal, and I had mine."

I took a step toward Tony. "And your part was to be a piece of shit?"

"My part was to keep the girl happy," he said, and a snarl crawled slowly across his mouth. "Just like my friends in the Pontiac back in Syosset are keeping your girlfriend happy."

I took another step toward the creep, at which point Tony reached into his coat and came out with the Colt revolver. I stopped moving but had trouble stopping the furious beast that was trying to get out of me and put a choke hold on Tony's slimy neck. A maneuver came to me; grab for the gun, disarming him, and then beat the punk's face into chaos. I moved an inch, and the entire room went into movement all around me.

I felt the pain before I even heard the bang or saw the flash from Tony's gun. The bullet hit my shoulder, spun me around and had me hanging on to the dull green paint on the wall behind me. I turned around to see O'Neill bending over for his gun as Tony took a shot at him and missed. From under the table O'Neill got a shot off and hit Tony in the legs, allowing gravity to bring him to his knees in an instant. O'Neill then got up and leveled the shotgun at Tony who had managed to get halfway standing up. When O'Neill pulled the trigger Tony's back was slammed up against the swinging door, pushing it in toward the kitchen as he slid down to the floor, leaving a blood smear on the door. Before Tony gurgled out his last breath, Allen got a gun out from somewhere and aimed it at O'Neill, who was of course by now defenseless, having used up both shells in his double barrel. I could only be a witness then, since my rod was upstairs hanging useless on the back of a chair.

"Mitch!" I screamed knowing it was too late.

Allen put a very well-aimed bullet in O'Neill's heart.

I went to O'Neill's still body on the floor. Looking down at my friend I was immediately filled with the feeling of permanence.

"Mitch," I said, not expecting an answer.

The room was now very quiet, with a layer of smoke hanging at just about eye level. The smell reminded me of the rifle range at Parris Island. Allen turned to me with his pistol aimed at the middle of my chest.

"Well," he said, "this is turning out even better than planned. Sorry, but you two guys" — he pointed his gun to O'Neill and back to me — "were never meant to return from this job. We were just going to leave you here for the cops." He looked over at Tony. "But that. Now that's a bonus. Never liked that jerk. No one did. But I'll be looking good to the boss for avenging his son's murder by taking out his kid's two killers."

He raised the gun higher and closed one eye. I felt nothing inside. I had only one thought. Dottie. A sudden noise to my left made me look in that direction but then just as quick I turned back to see Allen firing his gun while holding his stomach. Then yet another shot from my left hit Allen in the head. A sudden puff of pink mist and then physics, working in collusion with death, had Allen collapsing upon himself and landing on the floor in a lifeless pile of cloth-covered flesh and bones.

The room went silent again. I looked to the doorway on my left and saw Sal leaning against the wall holding his midsection, blood spreading down along his pant leg. My mind was trying to make sense of the last few seconds. I blocked out the pain for a moment but still couldn't figure out why Sal just shot one of his own. It couldn't have been to save my ass. I looked at the flashy automatic in Sal's hand and made my best guess.

"Oh I get it," I said. "You're going to kill me and have all the money for yourself. Is that it?"

Sal struggled to focus in on me, and when he did it was with a look of annoyance, like I had just asked him for a ride to the airport.

"Kill you? Hell, Decker, you and me go way back. I wouldn't ice you. I just never liked this Allen a whole lot. He's been known for leaving a lot of soldiers behind after an operation. Man's got no honor. And the money..." He looked down at the blood starting to collect on the floor below him. "I don't think money is gonna do me any good at this point."

I stood silent, taking in Sal's place in the universe. He was literally a dying breed, the last of the stand-up mobsters, a sometimes brutal gangster who was still in it to protect the neighborhood, even if that meant protecting it from itself.

I went to the kitchen, stepping over Tony's body, returned with some dish towels and when I approached Sal, he said, "Forget about me. I've seen this kind of wound before. Just get your ass out of here. Besides" — he nodded toward Tony — "I was supposed to watch out for that dope. So I'm done for either way."

I ignored him, told him to sit down on the floor, and put a dish cloth under his shirt and applied pressure.

"Hold that there," I ordered him. He complied reluctantly.

I got the other towel on my shoulder, sat down at the table and tried to put together a plan of action, which became quite clear in only a few seconds. We had to get our asses out of there. I looked over at Sal and smiled inside.

"How long you think the roadblocks will stay up?"

"Probably right after nightfall they'll give up"

I agreed. They'd keep up heavy patrols around the area, but by night the wind would be out of their sails and they'd pull in the roadblocks. Allen's original plan was to stay here in the house for forty-eight hours, but plans

194

change. We had to get somewhere for help with our wounds before it was too late for me to drive anymore.

"We've got to hang in here until dark then," I said.

Sal nodded.

"Sit tight," I said getting up slowly.

"The fuck am I gonna go?"

I walked upstairs to get the girl. I put on my mask and led her downstairs and to the basement door in the kitchen, all the while stepping over bodies.

"Don't mind the mess," I said, trying to lighten the horrid scene.

I unlocked the padlock and opened the door to the basement. Gwen Dearborn couldn't get down the stairs fast enough. I called down and told Mrs. Dearborn that we would call the police and tell them of their whereabouts in a few hours. As I closed the door I could hear the soft cries of mother and daughter gratefully finding each other in one piece. I closed the door and locked them in.

I spent the next twenty minutes getting back into my own clothes and helping Sal into his. I brought down the radio from upstairs and put it in the living room to listen to while I gathered the money-filled duffle bags, and then loaded both bags into the trunk of my Ford. The latest on the radio about the robbery was the local troop commander saying, "We are pursuing leads and will have an arrest within twenty-four hours," which is cop talk for we are chasing our collective tails. Then I stood over O'Neill's body for several minutes, thinking.

"What?" Sal said.

"I don't like leaving him here. The cops could link him to me."

"Listen, if ya need an alibi, I can get ya one no problem if we can get back close to the city. We always keep a stock of solid citizens who're ready to swear on a stack-a-Bibles you were with them for every hour of the day in question. And carryin' a dead body around is never a good idea. Whattaya gonna tell the cops ya get pulled over? An' whattaya gonna do with him once ya get back home anyway?"

He made sense.

"All right," I said.

When nightfall finally came Sal needed more help in getting to the car than I did, but we managed. His bleeding was not really slowing down that I could tell, so I figured I'd make him comfortable and hope for the best. I went back into the house and got a blanket to set him up in the backseat with. I got in the driver seat, started up the Ford, put it in gear, rolled a few feet up the driveway and stopped. I looked back at Sal.

"Just a minute," I said.

I ran back into the house and went to the dining room, looking around at the carnage. The smell was now a sickly mixed scent of blood and dust. My eyes swept the room until I spotted my target behind Allen's body. I had to kick him over a foot away from the wall so I could reach down behind him to pick up the Thompson submachine gun. As an afterthought I also picked up the automatic that Allen had used to kill my friend Mitch O'Neill.

It was nighttime dark when we finally pulled out of the driveway and onto the main road out of Ravena. We passed no roadblocks and only one state cop car, which was going in the opposite direction. From the map that Allen had provided I went by back roads for about an hour before finally getting to an entrance to the Thruway. Once on the Thruway I felt safe enough to turn to Sal and ask how he was doing.

"I'm cold," he said, sounding like someone had added turpentine to thin out the thug in his voice.

"Just hold on. I got an idea where we can get some help."

My wound seemed to have stopped bleeding and only hurt when I breathed in or out. Some time after midnight we arrived in Syosset and I stopped at a closed Esso station with a pay phone next to it. I dialed information for a newly listed number of someone I knew would do me a favor.

Dave Sands' groggy voice answered. "Hello?"

"Dave, it's me, Tommy. I need a favor."

"Tommy, it's the middle of the night."

"Yeah I know, but I got a sick puppy here needs some urgent care."

There was a pause, a woman's voice in the background and then the muffled sound of Dave's hand over the phone while he made up some kind of excuse to his wife as to what was going on. I'm sure he knew I was up to no good, but I was betting on some kind of old friend loyalty to come through just this once for old times' sake.

"What do you need?"

"I've got two guys bleeding who need medical attention."

I looked over at the Ford and out at the empty dark streets of Syosset and felt the cold of winter tearing at my field jacket and thought about the bullet lodged in my shoulder and wondered if Sal was still alive.

"Where are you?"

"On my way to your office. I'll be there in five minutes."

I found the Village Animal Clinic to be on a dead-end street on the edge of town. A small parking lot was between the clinic, which was a one-story brick building, and a residence that had the name "Sands" on the mailbox. I had to have Dave help me get Sal out of the car and into an operating room inside. The room was painted — ceiling, walls and trim — with the stark white hi-gloss paint that I had sold to Dave not long before.

Sal was conscious but not all that lucid, lying on his back on a short stainless steel table with his legs bent at the knees hanging over the end. Dave lifted up Sal's shirt and looked under the blood-soaked dish towel. He looked over at me sitting in a chair against the wall. He shook his head in a not too promising manner.

He took a step toward me and said, "What about you?"

"I'm fine for now. Just fix him up so I can get a few answers out of him."

"Jesus, Tommy. He needs more than what I can do here. He needs a blood transfusion. He needs surgery—"

"What *can* you do? It's important."

He went into some cabinets and closets and in a few minutes had a bottle of some kind of fluid going right into Sal's arm. After another minute Sal opened his eyes and looked around the room, trying to focus on his surroundings. I stepped up to his side.

"Sal, we made it, buddy."

He looked up at me with a thin smile on his pale lips. "Made what?"

"We're safe," I nodded toward Dave. "The doc here is going to get us all fixed up."

He made no attempt to look over at Dave. He said, "That's swell." But there was no weight to the words.

"Look, Sal where would Fiori be keeping my, uh, friend — you know, the girl, Dottie?"

The sides of his eyes in his big face revealed a small knowing smile. "You mean your girlfriend?"

"Yeah. Yeah, my girlfriend."

The affirmation took a little of the edge off my anguish for a second and replaced it with resolve. A calm vision of my hands around the throat of Vito Fiori brought some momentary, quiet relief.

Sal's eyes slowly closed again; his chest rose as he drew in a deep breath. As he exhaled I shook his shoulder and he opened his eyes again. "Where, Sal?" I whispered close to his ear.

"Warehouse in Jamaica," he said, barely audible.

"Queens?"

"Yeah. I'm thirsty. Can I get some water?"

I looked at Dave, who closed his eyes halfway and shook his head.

"Yeah, hold on, Sal, I'll get you some."

I pulled Dave off to the side. "Can you take out the bullet so he can have some water?"

"Look," he said. "There's no bullet to take out. It went right through him. He's bleeding internally. He's probably not going to last the night. If you give him a drink, he'll go faster."

I took out my pack of Luckies, lit one up, walked back to Sal and offered him the smoke. He took as deep a drag as he could. As he exhaled he said, "How 'bout that drink?"

"Sure. First tell me about the warehouse. What street in Jamaica?"

"Tuckerton. Near the train station."

"I know that area. You mean the auto wrecking place?"

"Yeah, it's called J&J Auto Salvage. There's a tin building with an office upstairs. That's where they'll have her." He reached up feebly with his hand, trying to touch my arm. "Bring plenty of guns."

Sands came up and handed me a glass of water. I lifted Sal's head a bit and held the glass to his lips while he drank a good gulp. I stepped back to a sink that was against the wall and smoked the rest of my cigarette. After running the water in the sink to douse the butt I looked over at Sal, who was quiet but still breathing. Dave motioned me over to talk to him.

"Look," he said. "What're we going to do with..." He looked at Sal. "You know, after..."

"I'll take care of it." I hadn't really given any thought for that contingency. "By the way, what did you tell your wife was going on?"

"Your dog was hit by a car. Now what about you? What's your medical issue?"

I took off my jacket and shirt and dishrag to expose the angry red hole in my chest that was about the size of a quarter. Dave sat me back down in the chair up against the wall and brought a bright lamp over and took a closer look. He then got out some shiny tools and put them on a tray next to him on a small table on wheels.

"This is going to hurt," he said. "I'm guessing the bullet is lodged in your scapula. It's going to take a little tugging to remove it."

"Just make it quick."

He did. And it hurt like hell.

He stitched up the hole, put some bandages over it and told me not to let it get wet. For some reason I thought that that was the most useless piece of medical advice I had ever heard. I almost laughed but stopped when I looked over at Sal, who was totally motionless; the only movement around him was the slow trickle of blood dripping off the table and pooling up on the linoleum floor.

"Damn," I said. I went up close to Sal's face, studied how quickly the hue of life leaves the skin. In a matter of seconds what little pink had been there was replaced with the pasty dull oatmeal pallor of death.

"He a friend of yours?"

"Yeah." Someone who saves your life, what do you call that person? Friend didn't seem like enough.

"Yeah," I said again. "I gotta get him out of here."

"What are you going to do?"

Well, that was the question, wasn't it? I had three or four objectives but not a single plan or strategy to reach any of them. Half-baked wouldn't even be close. Hell, I didn't even have the oven preheated.

"Is there anything else I can do for you?" Dave asked.

I looked at the blood all around the room and began to realize that I had dragged Dave deep enough into my nefarious affairs and he had more than paid off any debt that he imagined he'd owed me.

"Look, Dave..." I looked at the clock on the wall; it was two thirty. I thought of a quick trip I needed to make while it was still dark. "I can't let you be any more involved, you've done plenty. Just help me put Sal here in my car, and I'll be on my way."

He nodded eagerly and the two of us struggled getting Sal's body outside and into the trunk of the Ford. I looked back toward the building and said, "Sorry about the mess."

Dave took a step closer to me, put his hand on my good shoulder. "Just—" He struggled for the next word but it wouldn't come.

"Yeah, I'll be fine." I got into my car, moving stiffly. "Thanks."

"Sure."

SEVENTEEN

With the bank heist having gone terribly wrong, not to mention that Vito's son Tony was dead, I knew I couldn't count on just going to Vito Fiori and collecting Dottie like I was picking up my dry cleaning. I would have to rescue her, and that was the only pressing thought on my mind other than staying clear of the fuzz or falling into the hands of Fiori's gang. But there had to be a plan, and I had to come up with it without the counsel of my friend and partner Mitch O'Neill. The disposing of Sal's body was obviously the first thing I had to prioritize. But wouldn't O'Neill have used it somehow to our advantage? It seemed like an opportunity I should be able to use to bring some heat, or at least send a message, to someone. And I didn't want to just dump him like so much litter on the side of the road. No, Sal deserved to have a decent send-off to attach some purpose to his death.

I got to Oyster Bay close to three am. I turned off my headlights and pulled into Irene McKenna's driveway. I could see the two Corvettes parked side by side up near the front door of the house, which brought on a wave of stale nostalgia like that nauseous feeling you get in your stomach when you bang your knee. Sal's Lincoln was parked in front of the garage, so I backed the Ford by the side of the garage out of view of the house and quietly and agonizingly slowly got Sal's body out of the trunk with one arm, dragged it over to his car and put him on the floor in the backseat, covering him up with the bloody blanket from the farmhouse. Then I grappled with the two duffle bags and managed to get them out of the trunk — and with every move I made, no matter which part of my body was involved, it caused pain in my shoulder. But at least I was not getting the bandages wet, as per doctor's orders.

After removing two packs of hundreds for myself, I crept up the driveway, with the bags, toward the house and the two Vettes. The owners of both cars had left the keys right in the ignitions, like two people would do if they felt safely protected by a gangster security guard on the property, but who was in fact not coming back to his post because he was lying dead in a pool of blood in a farmhouse in upstate New York.

I put one bag in Frank Smith's trunk and one in Irene's, and placed Allen's automatic under Irene's passenger seat, then quietly walked back down the driveway, started up the Ford and drove away. As I drove slowly and more or less aimlessly through the streets of Syosset, a seed of a plan was sprouting, like a weed in the crack of a sidewalk reaching for daylight. It involved mostly creating an overall state of confusion for Fiori and his mob. Unexplainable events, lies on top of colossal lies, one outlandish scenario after another were to be the order of the day. I'd have Vito Fiori believing anything and nothing.

I got started by heading northwest out of town to Northern Boulevard and then west toward Manhasset. On the bridge over the water inlet near Mott Cove I stopped and pulled over to the rail. The road and the early morning air were empty and cold. I got out of the car and opened the back door on the passenger side. I painfully pulled out the backseat cushion, which was red and sticky with the blood of Sal Buetti. The seat popped out easy, since it was not bolted down, and I wrestled it over the rail and let it drop into the water about fifty feet below. I heard the splash and could just make out the seat slowly sinking to the muddy bottom.

I needed some rest and headed to my place. I turned on the car radio and listened to Jack Lazare play a few requests on his show, *The Milkman's Matinee*. After Glenn Miller's version of "Stardust" was over, the news came on with the usual local, state and national troubles rattled off, followed by a weather report of more snow due later today. There was no mention of the upstate heist — neither the robbery itself nor the bloodshed at the farmhouse — so I figured, one, the mother and daughter hadn't found a way to break out of the basement yet and, two, Fiori and his pals hadn't heard anything about the mayhem, and it should be safe for me to go home and get some shut-eye.

I walked into my apartment and shut the door on the sunlight that had just pierced the predawn's dull gray dimness. I got to the couch and lay down on my side facing the door and put my gun under the cushion. I thought of Dottie and prayed for sleep and hoped I would wake refreshed and wished for no more pain and ached for a clear mind and yearned for a purposeful path in life — and, as always happens without your knowing exactly when, I fell asleep.

***

In a few hours the sound of someone groaning woke me up. The sun was coming through the icicles that hung from the roof in front of my living room window, and as I made a move to get up off the couch a stabbing pain traveled from my shoulder to my mouth and I realized the groan that woke me was my own. The agony in my chest was surprised by my sudden move, and like a coiled snake it sprang out and bit me. I moved around the apartment slowly for about a half hour, washing up, shaving, frying some eggs and drinking coffee. After a handful of aspirin, the pain was somewhat manageable, so I slipped on my shoulder holster, put two extra clips of ammo in my pocket, went out to the Ford and headed to Queens.

Somewhere in Mineola I pulled into an Esso station, told the kid to fill it up to the neck with hi-test and went to the phone booth on the outside wall of the station, where I called the NY state troopers and told them where to find Laura and Gwen Dearborn. Then I made a call to the Great Neck Police Department and told them where they could find some of the money from the Arnold's Bakery robbery. I wanted it so that by the time I got to Queens and came into contact with any of the Fiori family, there would be a lot of moving parts to Operation Chaos. The plan, such as it was, had a few objectives. The first and most important one of course was to free Dottie from her punk captors. From there it would get a little more fluid.

Jamaica, Queens is known for one thing. It's where commuters coming out of NYC change trains to go to different parts of Long Island. Change at Jamaica — they should write a song. I made my way to Tuckerton Avenue, where Sal said I should be able to find Dottie. I circled around J&J Auto Salvage, which took up a whole square block. A twenty-foot-high fence with barbed wire on top surrounded the lot and the two-storied tin building that was at one end of the yard. I rolled up slowly to the front gate. It was around noon and about half a dozen workers from the yard were coming out through the gate and heading toward the diner on the corner of the next block. I drove in through the gate and backed the car up in front of a trailer with a sign over the door that said "Office." I stepped out of my car and looked around.

The lot was about five acres of tormented steel. There were rows and rows of defiled automobiles, some missing large sections, like hoods, rooftops and fenders, and each one no doubt keeping horrific tales of human tragedy within its contorted metal. Beyond the rows of cars, like distant mountains, were hills of usable parts — a thirty-foot-high pile of transmissions, a low knoll of batteries, rear axles and differentials stacked like some kind of inside-out barbells. And under all of this was a floor of mixed dirt, oil, gas and all manner of fluids that run through the veins of the American motor vehicle. Despite the multicolor collection in the rows of cars, the overall color of the place was a dull rusty hue like the color of dried blood or a dead worm you'd come across on a sidewalk. There was a faint odor of burning rubber in the air, which was tempered by the sweet smell of the grease beneath my feet.

I stepped up on the short stack of wooden pallets at the door of the trailer and let myself in out of the cold, only to find the air inside the trailer to be too warm. The space inside was about six feet wide and twenty feet long. Three of the walls were taken up with metal shelving overstocked with car radios. At the end of the room there was a desk with a man sitting behind it who appeared to have nothing to do all day but be distracted from the magazine in front of him by strangers entering his hot little world.

He was younger than me by a few years, shorter, and had a face peppered with blackheads. His thin moustache and slick hair matched the black in his eyes, and the annoyed tilt in his head made him the type of guy I could tie in a knot should I get a whim. He looked me up and down, glanced at the clock on the wall behind him and slowly lowered the magazine to the desktop.

"Can I help you?" he said. But help was a concept this guy was never taught back at the school for chumps. His delivery was part Brooklyn, part Spanish, and all insolence. I could tell right away that he was using his job as a mob front man for a pair of balls. If he were in Congress, he'd be the first voting to send someone else to war.

"Yeah, I need a backseat for a '51 Ford."

He waved his hand in the general direction of the northern hemisphere and said, "Yeah, there's one out there somewhere. Help yourself."

I went back outside to the refreshing near-freezing air and zigzagged through the rows of cars, heading toward the big tin building. I found the '51 Ford about halfway to the warehouse, struggled getting the backseat out and then dragged it with my one good arm back to my car. I put it in the Ford and then stuck my head in the trailer door to tell the loafer at the desk that I was going back to get a side mirror. He didn't bother to lower the magazine and just grunted.

The two-and-a-half-storied corrugated tin warehouse was situated halfway down the side fence of the lot, with the front of the building facing inside the lot. I walked past the two open roll-up doors, where men inside were cutting up cars with blowtorches. On the far side of the building was a steel stairway going diagonally up the side of the wall to a door on the second floor, and parked right at the bottom of the stairs was the two-tone Pontiac. My breathing quickened and there was a pounding behind my temples. I took a deep breath, exhaled and relaxed every muscle in my body. After two light steps up the stairs I stopped to turn and survey the landscape in my view. Nothing moving. I went up to the landing at the door and checked the doorknob. Locked. It was a steel door with no window, and I pounded on it hard four times with my fist, waited three seconds and pounded five more times harder still, then took out my gun.

I stood behind the door as it opened outward, and when a man of my size and twice my age stepped out onto the landing, I put my rod in his ribs and said softly, "Inside."

On the other side of the door was a hall that went for about twenty feet, with two doors on either side. I had the guy turn around so I could pat him down and took a pistol from his shoulder holster and stuck it in my waistband. I kept my hand on the back of his collar and pushed him up against the wall.

"What's your name?" I said.

"Huh?"

"Your name. What's your name?"

"Dean."

"Okay, Dean. How many other greaseballs are here?"

When he didn't answer, I shoved my gun harder into his ribs. "I'll plug you right here, Dean, so help me. You know how love can make a man do crazy things."

He pushed some air between his front teeth. "You'll never make it out of here."

"Don't be too sure. Now who else is here?"

I pulled back on his collar and slammed his head into the plaster wall, making a dent and flaking off some paint.

"All right. It's just me and Eddy. And the girl."

"Where is he?"

He nodded toward one of the doors.

"Call Eddy out here."

He hesitated, so I pulled on his collar. He cleared his throat, said, "Eddy, come out here a minute."

I heard a chair scrape across the floor and footsteps approach the door. As Eddy started to pull the door inward I put my forearm against Dean's back and pushed him in through the door, crashing him into Eddy, who fell over backwards, landing on his backside, which was considerable while Dean's momentum carried him skipping over Eddy's sprawled-out body and into a card table in the center of the room, bringing a game of pinochle to an end. Eddy's first move of course was to reach for his piece.

"Don't do it, Eddy," I said.

But he did, so I put a bullet in his knee, which caused him to let go of his weapon in mid-draw, and the gun went sliding across the floor, stopping at the feet of Dean, who instinctively bent down to pick it up, but by the time he got his finger inside the trigger guard I already had a bead on him, and when he raised the gun in my direction I dispatched another slug into yet another knee. Neither hood let out any cries of pain, which impressed me, but they did both roll from side to side on the floor holding their knees, looking like some kind of off-off-Broadway modern dance.

"You crazy son of a bitch!" Dean said.

I walked over to him and kicked the gun away from him and then picked it up, a .38 revolver. I went over to Eddy, who had managed to lift his large frame onto one of the chairs at the card table and was holding his bloody knee with both hands, which was doing nothing to stem the bleeding. I got up behind him and wrapped my left arm around his neck in a choke hold and pressed the .38 hard up against his temple.

"Where's the girl?"

A half second too long went by, so I squeezed his throat and pulled back the hammer.

"She's in the next room, goddamnit," he said, trying to tilt his head to the left toward a door to an adjoining room. I backed my way to the door, keeping the gun leveled between the two men, reached behind me and knocked on the door.

"Dottie."

A muffled sound came from the other side. As I opened the door, the sight of Dottie sitting on a metal-framed bed with her feet on the floor, her hands tied to the headboard and a rag tight across her mouth brought a mix of relief, elation and anger. Holding the gun on Eddy and Dean, I kept my eyes on Dottie for the three steps it took me to get to her. I got the gag off her mouth and held her head close to my chest.

"You okay?" I said.

She nodded affirmative, but the red in her eyes suggested I might have to wait a while for the truth to come out. Meanwhile I put Dean's .38 on the bed and got her untied.

"Did they hurt you?"

She shook her head no. "They just talk tough," she said. She looked down at the gun. "What's going on, Tom? How are you mixed up with these guys?"

There was not enough time right then to either explain the truth or to fabricate a fable. I went for a postponement.

"Let's just get ourselves out of here for now. I'll explain things later. Okay?"

She nodded.

"Good."

Back in the room with the two bleeding mobsters I found Eddy still sitting on his chair, and Dean had managed to crawl to a small table in the back of the room, where he was on the phone with someone.

"Is that Vito?" I said.

"Yeah," he said and held the phone out to me. "He wants to talk to you."

"Tell him I'll be at White Castle tonight at six. We can talk then."

As Dean was relaying the message I held Dottie by the arm and we made our way out of the room. At the steel door to the outside I turned back and watched the door we had just come out of for a moment. I saw the doorknob turning and pushed Dottie outside just as Eddy limped into the hall with a shotgun pointed vaguely in my direction. He got off a shot that went high and to my right by inches, putting a perforated circle in the upper part of the door. Before he could see through the smoke to get another shot at me I put a tight three-bullet pattern in the middle of his chest. He met the floor without much grace, and I went outside, grabbed Dottie and we ran down the stairs.

There were big flakes of snow falling through the gray air of Queens and landing on the black, greasy ground of the junkyard, disappearing instantly as if they never existed. We snaked our way through the rows of cars and then made a dash through the open space from the building to the trailer. The yard was quiet except for our footsteps sucking out of the mud grime as we ran to the Ford. At the car I opened the passenger door for Dottie and realized I was still carrying the two guns of Eddy and Dean. I tossed them on the floor in front of Dottie.

"Push these under the seat," I said.

As I rounded the trunk of the Ford between the car and the trailer, the office weasel opened the door and stood in the doorway with a pistol in his hand hanging down at his side.

"Where do you think you're going?" he said.

I didn't know if he just wanted me to pay for the backseat, or if he had gotten a phone call from Dean upstairs with orders to keep me there. Either way I had to think fast.

"I've got to get my wallet in the car," I said and took a step toward the driver-side door.

"You're not going anywhere," he said and raised the gun, pointing it directly at my head.

Suddenly there was a crack, and Weasel grabbed his shoulder and fell backward onto the floor inside the trailer. Not knowing exactly what happened I took advantage and darted into the car, started the engine, put it in gear and gunned it. The speedometer said thirty mph but we were only moving at about three, the rear wheels spinning and shooting greasy mud all up against the trailer wall. The air inside the car was thick with the smell of gun smoke and when I looked over at Dottie, she was rolling up the window with her right hand and holding Eddy's smoking .38 in her left. When we made it through the gate I said, "Didn't know you were a lefty."

"I am now, I guess." She looked down at the gun contemplatively, as if going over the last few moments in her mind.

"Ever shoot a gun before?"

"No," she said, looking passively out the window. "And I'm not sure I ever will again."

"Don't worry. You just winged him."

"Oh, it's not that. Up in that room there he was the guy who brought food up to us — a real creep he was. He said things to me that weren't very nice." She looked down at the gun again. "He deserved a shot in the arm. It's just—" She took in a deep breath and exhaled like she was hoping words would come back out but fell silent for the next two blocks.

"You're not sure what you've gotten yourself into with me," I said, trying to give her an out.

"No. I know what I've gotten into with you. I don't know what you've gotten *your*self into."

I felt her eyes on the side of my face.

"I mean, gangsters, guns? I always knew you were up to something shady in your off time, but—"

"What do you mean, shady?"

"I don't know. No one at the hardware store really knows what you do outside of work."

I gave her a sharp look.

"Yes, Tom, we talk about you at the store. We all know about your family history with the place. Everyone likes you, Tom. But no one really knows you. No one but me, that is. But you seem to be so secretive about something."

We stopped for a red light. I watched the snow come down in front of us and then turned to face Dottie, who was beautiful at that moment.

"But in case you haven't guessed," she said. "I'm in love with you too much to care what that something is."

My eyebrows went toward each other with a question between them.

"Hell, Tom, I shot a man for you." She sounded both accomplished and contrite.

My face went into a deep look of gratitude, while she smiled wryly.

"Okay, look, I will explain everything to you, but not right now. First we have to get you to someplace safe where those mobsters can't get a hold of you. Do you have somewhere where you can go for a night?"

She bit her lower lip. "My friend in the Village. Patty."

The light changed to green and I made a turn toward the train station. I had her write down Patty's phone number on a pad I had in the glove box and told her I would call her by tomorrow night, Sunday. It would be tight but I would have to get the mob issue off my back by then so I could get back to work on Monday and be looking as normal as the pitcher striking out.

As I pulled up to the curb I asked, "Do you have any money?"

She shook her head no, so from a pocket in my field jacket I took out one of the packs of hundreds and peeled one off and handed it to her. She stared at the pack as if it were on fire.

"Like I said, I'll explain everything tomorrow."

She looked at me as if resigned to a direct order from someone just one rank above her.

"Be careful," she said.

We kissed, and then she was off to catch a train into Manhattan.

EIGHTEEN

I've found that criminals in general and mobsters in particular have certain rules. Some rules they keep, some they bend and some they regard as plain nonexistent if their hide is in jeopardy. They pride themselves on the so-called "honor among thieves" creed and will keep their word as long as it suits the individual who's giving it. Break any of the rules and you may find yourself dead or at the top of the food chain, depending on the loyalty of some of your cohorts. And loyalty too is no sure thing. But the one quality that remains strong and steady among crooks, is greed. Money has a power over them like a drug, and they will do just about anything to hold on to what they have and scheme like a back room full of aldermen to get more. So, with greed at the center of the web of confusion that I was hoping to get Vito Fiori caught up in, I drove out toward Great Neck to a diner I knew on Old Mill Road that had some excellent meatloaf.

With the snow still falling and slowing down traffic, it was late afternoon already when I started mixing my peas into my mashed potatoes. A slice of cherry pie, coffee and a cigarette later, I was on the road for my meeting at White Castle on Northern Boulevard. I wanted to get there early before any of Fiori's men, who would be trying to get there earlier than me.

Driving in the snow can make for some tense moments, and being slowed down and possibly not getting to the meeting early enough revved my anxiety level up near the red line. But as I neared the entrance to the restaurant I told myself that snowy conditions had never kept me from fighting off any foe in the past, and with a few deep breaths my game plan came to me and became as obvious as the take sign on a 3 and 0 count. The White Castle parking lot was full of course. In this neighborhood it was a popular spot for fine dining on a Saturday night. With the snow and cold, few people were eating in their cars, most patrons opting for the warm ambience of Formica tables and plastic chairs inside the joint. I rolled into a parking spot carefully eyeing each car for members of Fiori's clan. There was no sign of them, so I parked and went inside to the noise of the crowd and the smell of onions frying. I ordered a few hamburgers and found a stool at the counter near the front window, where I had the entrance and exit of the parking lot in my line of sight. The place was crowded, with hardly a table or stool to be had, and I felt relatively safe, figuring gangsters don't like to bump people off with too many witnesses around or with people getting caught in the crossfire, making for bad press.

Twenty minutes and four hamburgers later, the long, black Caddy Fleetwood came gliding through the entrance and parked in a spot near the very back of the lot. Four men got out of the car and walked toward the restaurant's front door. One of the men was hobbling along with the aid of crutches. As they walked past my car they recognized it and took a quick look at the driver-side window, saw I wasn't behind the wheel and continued toward the front door. As they walked past the front of the building I recognized Vito Fiori, and the limping man as Dean from the junkyard warehouse. The other two men were nondescript middle-aged thugs with black watch caps and walked with a menacing gait. When I tapped on the window they all four stopped and looked at my face. Vito Fiori said something to the two in watch caps, and they nodded and remained outside while Fiori and Dean came inside and walked toward me.

As the two men approached me, a nearby table became available and I nodded toward it and we all went to sit down. Dean hopped around with his crutches and winced his way into a chair. Fiori unbuttoned his overcoat, took out a handkerchief, dusted off the seat, sat down slightly sideways to the table, crossed his legs and rested his Homburg on his knee. He looked at Dean and jerked his head toward the service area. "Get me a coffee," he said.

Dean took a little longer getting up than he did sitting down and hobbled his way over on to the line for ordering.

Fiori slowly scanned the space over my left shoulder and then my right and said, "You've damaged two of my employees." Then he made direct eye contact with me. "One of them permanently."

The icy stare was held for effect, and it was working. This was a dangerous man who could make awful events take place with the mere wave of his hand. These next few minutes were going to set in motion certain actions that would hold my very life in the balance. I had to bluff just enough manly bravery and mix it with a respect that would not be detected as phony.

"I was only trying to take back something that belonged to me. Something that I valued very highly."

Dean came back and placed the paper cup of coffee in front of his boss and with some more hopping around sat himself down.

"And to achieve my goal," I continued, turning toward Dean and glancing down at his knee, "I really didn't want to shed any blood, but I was met with some resistance and I took appropriate action to accomplish my mission." I paused and then added, "And really, Fiori, why didn't your guys just turn over the girl like you said you would? I mean, I did the heist, you got your money. That was the deal, wasn't it?"

Fiori stopped mid sip of coffee with puzzlement engraved on his smooth face. "What do you mean, I got my money?"

I tried to look as puzzled as he. "The money that Sal brought you last night. How do you think I knew where to come for Dottie? Sal told me to go to J&J after I dropped him off with the dough."

Fiori looked over at Dean, who shrugged his shoulders.

I tried to put a concerned look on my face and sincerity in my voice as I said, "You mean Sal hasn't told you about what happened up there in Ravena?"

"No. I haven't seen Sal. What happened?"

"Well you should really hear it from Sal."

"Tell me what happened." He was not going to say it again.

With great focus not to speak of Sal in the past tense, I laid out my bullshit. "Well, it seems your mastermind, Allen, had a plan of his own concerning the proceeds from the bank. I was upstairs in the house when I heard a loud argument going on downstairs in the dining room. On my way down, all of a sudden there was a shootout and by the time I got to the room the only one left standing was Sal."

I could see Fiori going through the roster of men on the job and when he got to the most important member, his eyes widened and he looked at me for answers.

"I'm sorry," I said. "But Sal couldn't get his gun out fast enough before Allen had already killed my partner, O'Neill, and, uh, your son Tony. Sal did get in the last shot, at Allen."

I gave him a moment before adding, "That's probably why Sal hasn't turned up yet. He feels real bad about not being able to protect Tony."

I looked over at Dean, who was rubbing his wounded knee.

He spoke up to Fiori hesitantly. "I told you, boss, nobody liked Allen."

"But listen," I said. "Don't be too hard on Sal, he did his best. I actually like the guy. He's a good man."

Fiori blinked his way sober. "Yeah, well where the hell is he?"

"I don't know. The last I saw him is when I dropped him and the money off at your brother's place in Oyster Bay. Maybe he's still out there, for all I know."

"Oh I'll find him all right, you can be sure. Meanwhile, speaking of my brother, Enzo wants his share of the bakery job dough."

And there it was, my theory of greed over all other emotions. Money separated Vito from his grieving like a ref breaking up a clinch.

"Well yeah, about that. I figure you can have O'Neill's share."

I let that hang in the air between us for a moment.

"And just how do I go about getting that?"

"Well, you could have just asked him for it. But since your guy, Allen, killed him, that might be a little tough."

He sat back in his plastic chair and sipped his coffee, taking me in, weighing out options and most likely thinking about killing me, and observing the activity in the room around him. He looked as if he couldn't believe he was in such a place.

"But I'll tell you what I can do," I said.

Vito looked over at Dean, said, "This should be good."

"Yeah, maybe he's gonna pay for Eddy's funeral."

"Yeah, or maybe I'm going to give you your gun back if you promise to play nice and never let a stranger take it away from you again."

Dean squirmed slightly, working his jaw muscles. Vito put a palm toward him, said, "Relax."

He nodded his chin up at me. "So what's your offer?"

"I think I know where you can get your hands on a hundred sixty thousand."

"I'm listening."

"Well, like I tried to explain to your brother up in Attica, we only took three hundred forty thousand from that job, and the bakery said it was a half mil. I think your brother-in-law, what's his name, Vic Gaudiello, has the missing money or knows where it is."

"And what makes you think that?"

"Call it a hunch. Why don't you just make a phone call and ask the guy? What could it hurt?"

Fiori looked at Dean and jerked his head toward the window. "Go call Vic. Tell him I want to see him. And tell Johnny to come in here."

Dean groaned his way to a standing position and with his crutches, gimped his way to a phone booth just outside the door. In a minute Johnny, one of the watch cap boys, came in.

"Take Freddy with you and go out to Oyster Bay and see if Sal's there. And poke around see what else is goin' on with that broad and the new boyfriend. Call back to the phone outside pronto."

"Sure, boss."

Johnny and Freddy drove away in the Caddy and then Dean came back inside. He didn't bother to sit down before he started speaking to Fiori.

"Vic's been pinched," he said.

"What?" Fiori almost raised his voice but brought in his emotion with a slight grimace around the cheekbones.

"His wife — I mean your sister — says the FBI came to the house, found some money 'n took him away."

Something started to slowly surface on Fiori's mug, like steam on a mirror, while he tried to hide his anger.

"I guess you weren't the only one with that hunch," he said to me.

I couldn't tell if there was a subtext to his statement, so I played it dumb. "Yeah, I'm sorry I couldn't get it to you sooner. But anyway you'll have the haul from the bank upstate. I'm not even going to ask you for a cut. All I want is to get out of your business."

By the time Dean had gotten himself back into his chair, Fiori looked deep into his cup of coffee. He handed Dean the empty cup. "Get me another."

When Dean came back with the coffee Vito told him to wait outside at the pay phone for Johnny's call. I figured the two torpedoes in the Caddy getting to Oyster Bay, investigating the situation and then calling back should take about twenty minutes. That was the time I had left to make sure Fiori couldn't come at me with any reason to do me bodily harm. And the only way I could think to play that was for innocent small talk.

"We never got a chance to count the cash from upstate," I said. "But I'm sure it was well over a million."

Fiori leveled his gray eyes at me. "There's more to life than money."

That wasn't the type of small talk I was looking for. Could he have been the one mobster with a heart? Was he human after all? Had I made a colossal misjudgment? I had to come back fast and make a connection.

"I know what you mean. I mean, I haven't lost anyone as close as a son, and I don't for a minute mean to suggest that I know what that's like. But I've lost some very good friends, brothers of mine, in that fucked-up mess of a war in Korea."

He was silent, staring straight into his coffee, not a wrinkle on his face. I thought it safe to press. "That's why, Vito, I was as aggressive as I was to save my girlfriend. She's someone I care for a lot. It's what we do as humans when we love someone. We go to great lengths to protect them. I'm sure that's what you were thinking when you put your trust in Sal to look after Tony. And from all I've seen, he was the right man to have on the job. It's just that, sometimes bastards mess up our best-laid plans. Sometimes we just can't see things coming." I looked as close as I could without staring to see if anything was getting through, but I was like Superman trying to see through lead. Nothing doing. But I didn't get a stop sign either. "And I'll say it again. In the car ride all the way home, Sal was feeling really bad about what happened."

"Bad enough to skip out on me?" Fiori said without bitterness but more with hope that it was not true.

"Never. He's a loyal soldier."

"Yeah, he is," he said almost wistfully.

"But tell me. Did Sal say anything, or if he was going anywhere else, when you left him in Oyster Bay?"

"Just that he was going to check in on Irene."

Fiori was gazing out the window and checking his watch. I was hoping I was getting through.

"He's got quite a protective thing for Irene, Sal does," I said.

"Yeah, I don't know why. What happened between you and her anyway? Heard the two of you were an item."

"I think she found out I was involved in criminal activity," I said, holding back that his kid, Tony, was to blame. "Guess she lost her taste for crooks."

That brought a momentary frown, and then he went right back to stone. Outside the window the pay phone rang and Dean hopped over, picked it up and did a lot of listening. He shook his head no twice, then nodded yes, hung up and came inside. He came up to Fiori and, bending at the waist while holding on to the tops of his crutches, whispered in his ear. At one point in whatever Dean had to say, Fiori drew his eyes to me and held them there until Dean finished saying what he had to relay.

"Okay, Wait outside.

Dean disappeared.

For the first time all night Fiori turned in his chair and faced me squarely. He leaned in slightly toward me with unblinking eyes connected tightly to mine as if by piano wire. I felt my palms get wet and my mouth get dry, but my balls were intact and I gave him a shrug that said, *what?*

"Sal is dead," he said, showing less emotion than a bar of soap.

I put out my *What?* verbally, with a force bordering on tears.

"What? How? Where? What happened?"

"It looks like Irene and the boyfriend. They were planning on taking a powder with Enzo's dough."

I wasn't sure what he meant by Enzo's and gave him a bewildered look.

"The boys found they were planning a little trip. They had two tickets to Mexico and a suitcase full of money that Enzo had stashed away over there. Might even have gotten away with it too except they got greedy. Sal must have caught them in the act, so they iced him and figured they'd take the bank loot too."

He paused to look at my face, which I hoped was not beaming.

"Greed," he said. "People never learn."

"Yeah."

But what I was thinking was that those two, Irene and Frank, really deserved my frame-up. She must have had her eye on that money in the garage for a long time and was just waiting for the right sucker to come along to help her steal it. And that just took away any trace of guilt I may have had for putting them on the hook.

"I'm still not sure what to do about you though, Decker. You killed one of my men. And you're involved in my son's death somehow."

"Me?" I said with as much contempt as I could put in one word. "I'm the only one here who has kept his word. I

222

risk life and limb, you get bags of money, and I get my girlfriend back. It was supposed to be a simple transaction. I can't help it if one of *your* guys decides to change plans midway and gets people killed up there in Ravena. I can't help it if Irene tries to break out of the imprisonment you got her in — "

"She's no prisoner," he said, cutting me off.

"What do you mean?"

"I mean she's living there because she wants to live there. And she'll keep living there."

"Even after this?"

He nodded. An explanation was coming to me.

"She's got something on you guys."

"You might say that."

"So if something were to happen to her, people would go to jail."

"And worse."

"So," I said, and stopped. I didn't want to know any more, and anyway it was time to throw the switch to full-throttle muddled.

"But anyway I'm the least of your problems. You got that whole Vic-holding-out-on-you thing going on."

This got the first facial reaction out of Fiori I had seen all night. He rolled his eyes like a man very tired of having to put up with the mundane.

"All right," he said. "You're off the hook for right now. We'll keep our eyes on you though."

"Okay," I said and started to get up.

"But don't bother going back to work at that store tomorrow."

I stopped and stared at him.

"The place is going to be under new management."

When I kept staring, he said, "Yeah, we're going to own it. It'll be more profitable and a, uh, cleaner deal for us than any alternative *arrangement* with the boyfriend."

I nodded in peculiar agreement but said, "Look, Vito, I'm fine with not going back there but, I have to go back to work for a while just to look normal in case the coppers come around, which I'm pretty sure they will."

He took a deep reluctant breath and said "Okay," and I got up and left with a hearty feeling of being, at least, not dead.

I made my phone call to Dottie short and as sweet as possible. "Get on a train, I'll be at the station."

In an hour, I saw her coming down from the platform in a very fast walk. She got to the car, and we were in a hug kissing before the door closed.

"I love you," I said.

"I know."

"It's over."

"Is it, Tom?" she said and looked at me not with suspicion but something else. "Or is it just beginning?"

"It?"

"Us."

"Yes. It's beginning."

She drew away from me to take me into her full gaze.

"But *us* has to change a bit."

I gestured in agreement and pulled the Ford away from the curb.

"My place?"

She nodded.

On the drive out to Syosset I spoke about myself more truthfully than I ever had. I leveled with her about the bank robbing and my honorable motives, which she brushed off as so much rationalizing.

"I really don't care *why* you do it. The fact is that you do it. You're a bank robber." She looked at me with a twisted smile that she was trying to conceal. "I don't particularly like it, but that's who I've gotten myself involved with. I don't like the gun part. I don't like the fact that you may get caught and go to jail. Then where does that leave me?"

She wasn't asking the question for me to answer but rather as if weighing pros and cons.

"I'll tell you where it leaves me. It leaves me needing a new boyfriend."

If that was meant to provoke, it did. But I had no response, and my shoulder started to hurt. I looked over at her and shrugged with a wince.

"You know, you're kinda cute when you're in pain," she said and laughed. "In fact, I do find this whole bank robber thing pretty sexy."

"Really?"

"Yeah, I can live with it a while. But I'm going to have to fix you, like girlfriends do."

"You can try."

"Oh I'll try all right."

She reached down under her seat, retrieved Dean's gun and held it in the palms of her two hands as if it were made of liquid about to slip through her fingers.

"Oh crap," I said, seeing the gun. "We've got to get rid of that and the other one too."

Dottie said she knew where there was a nearby sump close to her place, where she wanted to stop for a change of clothes anyway. We made the stop without going into Duke's and left quickly. On the Jericho Turnpike somewhere just outside Westbury we came to the sump, where I pulled off to the side of the road and waited till there were no cars. I threw the guns one at a time over the ten-foot fence like grenades. They both landed right in the middle of the water with a quiet splash and sunk probably twenty-five feet to the bottom. Never to be found.

NINETEEN

To set up the appearance of a routine Monday morning at work, we arrived a few minutes early. Dottie went straight to her register and blended in to the store with the rakes and brooms. When I walked into the paint department my routine got off to a bewildering start. Standing there were Dean, leaning on a cane, Freddy in his uniform watch cap, and Frank Smith behind the counter. I actually wasn't too surprised to see Dean and Freddy, but Frank stood out in the room as if a spotlight were on him.

He was wearing an apron.

I looked at the three individuals one at a time, ending up with Frank.

"Frank, what's going on?" I said with a twitch toward Dean and Freddy, giving the impression that these were two strangers to me.

"You're being let go," Frank said. "There's going to be a change in — "

Dean cut him off, said, "We're reconstruction, reconstruct—"

"We're restructuring," Frank said. He pointed at the two mobsters and said, "These are my new, uhh, partners. Dean—" He waited for Dean to supply his last name.

"Martin," Dean said, and nodding toward Freddy added, "And this is Freddy Lewis."

Dean was at least quick on his foot. I gave a blank stare between the comedy duo, no hands were extended, and the room became quiet, until Dean moved toward the store's rear exit door with great effort, looking at me between every painful step, each grimace laced with daggers.

"Yeah," he said as he walked. "So Frank there will be your replacement. We figure two weeks should be enough time for you to show him how to mix paint."

Seeing Frank in an apron about to take over my job was a sight too good to be true, but I had to maintain a look of shock and dismay after having just lost my job, after all. I could only hope that the frown command was overriding the grin command from my brain and was being carried out by my face.

Dean and Freddy left, and when the door closed behind them I kept my gaze on the door for a moment to gather my thoughts and rein in the elation from seeing Frank Smith in such a position. I tightened my lips to suppress a crooked smile and faced Frank squarely.

"Well," I said. "I don't know what circumstances have brought about such a development, but here's how you mix paint."

Frank wasn't about to take this without a fight and said, "So, you and Dottie a no-show on Thursday and Friday. Mind explaining that."

"Fuck you, Frank."

Man, that felt good. And I knew there was nothing he could do about it. So then I went through some basic points about pigments and how to turn on the main mixer, while Frank looked at me with a look of stunned disbelief. He was a man quite out of his element and began to shake and look disconnected from reality. His face went soft, the skin drained of his usual year-round tan, and his eyes seemed to sink an inch into his skull. He licked his lips, not wetting them, and tried to speak.

"I need a..." he said. "I'm getting some coffee."

But before he could leave the department, the booming voice of Billy Connolly entered the room about five steps ahead of Billy himself. Brother Ned's sullen face and skinny body followed in Billy's wake, like a dinghy behind an aircraft carrier.

"Tommy me boy!" Billy said as he stretched out his meaty hand for me to shake. I grabbed as much hand as I could, managing at least to get my thumb over the top.

"Billy," I said. "What can I do for you?"

He took a double take at Frank but didn't say anything about the apron. Ned looked upon Frank with as much regard as he would a cigar store Indian and handed me a list of paint colors to mix up. Frank at that moment seemed to shrink within his clothes, and I suddenly felt a momentary touch of pity for the creep. I nodded to him and said, "Just watch for now. This is how it's done."

As I worked on the gallons of paint, Ned drifted off into the aisles to get some sundries off the shelves and Billy settled into small talk about the weather. Suddenly he turned to Frank.

"So, Frank, is the Christmas party on for this week, then?"

Frank, as if just awakened by a hypnotist, shook his head and said, "Oh, uhh, yeah, yeah, it's on." His face twisted in deep thought. "It's tomorrow night at the Legion Hall."

"Tomorrow's Christmas Eve," Billy said with some worry. "I've gotta be home, put that damn tree up, or there'll be hell to pay with the missus."

He gave me a wink and said, "Tommy me boy, you'll have to do the drinkin' for the two of us."

I grinned and nodded, but since I was soon to be an ex-employee, I felt no need, let alone desire, to go to the party. I put their paint on the shaker and in the middle of chatting with Billy, I noticed three men in dark suits coming in the front door of the store. They didn't look like any of Fiori's men, but they didn't look like they were coming in for nuts and bolts either. They went to Dottie at her register and I saw her point over to the paint department. As they got closer I recognized one of the men as a Syosset cop. He was in fact the arresting officer when I was nabbed breaking into Big Bob's Guns and Ammo back before the Marine Corps. They stepped into the department, and the Syosset cop came right up to me with a dishonest smile on his face and the smell of cigar coming off his overcoat.

"Decker, right?" he said. He pushed his brown fedora to the back of his balding head. He knew me of course — me, the Connolly brothers and just about everyone else in the store and in the town for that matter.

"Yeah."

"Yeah, I never forget a face. You still look just like your mug shot." He flashed a smile, revealing tobacco-brown teeth. "I'm Detective Browning, Syosset Police Department," he said all official like, letting me know that he had come up through the ranks since our last encounter and was nobody's fool. "And these two gentlemen are FBI Agents Gleason and Jenkins. They have some questions for you."

Jenkins came over to me and said, "Why don't you grab your coat and we'll go downtown for a talk."

I looked over at Gleason, the taller, older and obviously the lead man of the two, who stood in the middle of the room like a lighthouse, scanning the entire environment around him without moving a muscle. He had sharp features and bright blue eyes but there was nothing behind them. Since he was devoid of body language, the only way to get a read on his thoughts or feelings was going to be by way of his words, and there were precious few of them so far. His partner, Jenkins, was a man you could tell would never rise to the level of Gleason. He had a chip on his shoulder that would weigh him down throughout his career. He was a sidekick, tag-along, a mere accoutrement of Gleason's, and I paid as much attention to him as I did to the color of his cuff links.

Cops take a lot of things for granted and have many preconceived ideas. They think that once someone commits a crime he is a criminal forever, which may or may not be true, but you can't assume that of every offender. In my case it was true I had committed a crime and I was still committing crimes but they didn't know that, and so a person can get indignant.

"I really don't feel like going anywhere. You can ask me questions right here. I have nothing to hide."

"Look, Decker," Browning said, just itching for a confrontation.

"It's okay, Browning," Agent Gleason said calmly. "We can ask Mr. Decker some preliminary questions here." He looked at me, his face still blank, but his voice went into the please-and-thank-you of the classic good cop. "There may not be any need to take him downtown if we are satisfied with his answers. Does that seem fair to you, Mr. Decker?"

These guys wouldn't have known fair if they had it in cuffs.

"Sure."

A look passed between all three cops. Jenkins and Browning didn't like it but they backed off for the moment. Gleason glanced at Billy, who was watching the situation unfold as if it were very entertaining. Frank, looking less and less in control of the store or anything else, was trying to drift out from behind the counter and was clearly trying to make a break for it.

"Hold on, Frank," Browning said. "We may need you here."

Something triggered Frank to reach back and get a hold of his blue-blooded bag of tricks, and he managed to pull out some indignation of his own.

"What's this all about, Browning?"

"We'll ask the questions here," Jenkins said.

Frank retreated behind the counter.

"So, Mr. Decker," Gleason said. "Do you know a Mitchell O'Neill?"

Everyone in the room, including all three cops, already knew the answer to this.

"Yeah, I'll probably be having a drink with him after work today."

"I doubt that," Jenkins said with a short, knowing little snort-laugh that everyone in the room except Gleason took notice of.

"Can you account for your whereabouts this past Friday the twentieth?" Gleason said.

I felt all eyes on me and had to control the blood flow to my face. I really hadn't any time to make up an alibi; Sal died before he could supply me with one. I probably could have cooked one up with Dottie but perhaps some strain of moral chivalry kept that from happening. I was drawing a blank and could hear the blood roaring through my brain like a flood, ripping any creative thoughts by the roots and washing them out to sea. Seconds passed, my pause was about to turn suspicious, and then I heard the lilting voice of Billy Connolly.

"Hell, I can answer that for you, Agent Gleason. Tommy was working with me and Ned over in Lindenhurst."

I could practically hear all the eyes move off me and land on Billy. But before Gleason could ask him anything, Frank suddenly came alive again.

"So that's where you were."

I gave Frank a glare and said, "I didn't want you to know I was moonlighting, Frank, and give you another reason to fire me."

"Another?" Gleason said.

"Seems I'm being let go. Something about restructuring, whatever that is." I looked over at Frank with as much malice as I could get away with without actually slugging the guy. "You'll have to ask Frank about it."

Gleason gave Frank a look, and I watched him squirm.

"We're tightening our belts," Frank said. "Some people had to be cut from the budget. It was strictly business."

Gleason seemed satisfied for the moment and turned his attention again to Billy.

"He was with you all day there in Lindenhurst?"

"From eight in the morning to around five thirty, six maybe."

"Did anyone else see you there? The home owners?"

"The house is a summer home. The owners live in Manhattan. My brother, Ned, was with us of course. You can ask him."

"Where is this brother?"

Billy pointed over Gleason's shoulder to Ned, who was just returning with his arms loaded with cleaning materials, scrub brush, soap and a bucket filled with other items. Ned stopped and took in the scene, his eyes darting from one personality to another, trying to size up the situation.

"Ned," Billy said. "I was just telling these FBI agents about the job in Lindenhurst where Tommy was helping us out on Friday."

Gleason put it to Ned directly. "Decker was with you guys all day on Friday?"

Ned's jaw went slack and his eyes narrowed some. He was known to be unpredictable and go in directions unknown from any given set of coordinates. Even Billy looked like he had just tossed the dice across the table. Ned looked at me for what seemed like a week, all the while hiding what was behind his eyes, before finally speaking.

"He wasn't all that much help. But, yeah, he was with us all day Friday. Why?"

Feeling my balls back in their proper place, I followed Ned. "Yeah. What's this all about anyway? What happened on Friday? And what's Mitch O'Neill got to do with it, or with me?"

Gleason started for the front door. "It's an ongoing investigation," he said.

Jenkins, following Gleason, stopped in front of me and tapped on the counter with the knuckle of his middle finger.

"We'll be in touch if we have any further questions," he said, then shrugged and moved on.

Next was Browning, who pulled his hat off the back of his head, adjusting the brim to an inch above his furry eyebrows.

"Don't leave town," he said in black and white.

"Actually, Detective, I'm going to have to leave town to look for another job. I mean, I don't want to look like I'm not gainfully employed."

Browning took the brothers into his gaze. "Why don't you just work with these boys here," he said with a little more than a pinch of sarcasm.

Ned blew air between his tight lips. "Like I said, he wasn't that much help."

Browning frowned at Ned and held his hand out to me. "Gimme your home phone number."

I wrote it down, handed it to him, and he was on his way. I tracked him with my eyes until he was out the door with the other two. Frank said he was going for that coffee now and left the department. The Connollys' paint had stopped shaking and I brought the cans to the counter.

"Thanks, boys. I owe you."

Billy waved me off. "You didn't kill anyone, did you?"

I had to think for a moment, and I answered the question honestly. "No one who didn't deserve it."

"Then all you owe me," Billy said, extending his bear-like hand, "is the story of how you got your medal in Korea."

I got a better grip on his paw this time and matched as best I could the squeeze I was getting.

"You got it."

"But some other time," Ned said. "Billy, we gotta go."

I held on to Billy's hand, keeping him from moving. "Just tell me, guys. Why'd you stick your necks out for me?"

Billy looked at Ned, who lifted his shoulders to meet his ears. Billy said, "Because we're vets. We don't stop lookin' out for each other just because we're not on the battlefield anymore."

And with a wink and a broad smile on his round face, Billy made me feel safe. Even though in many ways we were still on the battlefield, but for that moment I was covered by someone I could count on no matter what.

"And besides," Ned said. "That candy-ass Browning? Four F. While the rest of us were scattered round the world for Uncle Sam."

He grabbed two of the four gallons of paint from the counter. "And now he's a cop." He said, and mimed spitting on the floor.

Billy picked up the remaining two gallons. "Stay out of trouble, Tommy me boy."

And they left.

A few minutes later, Dottie appeared, and my stomach went back to eighth grade and filled itself up with butterflies. She came around the counter, strolled up close to me and grabbed a handful of apron at my chest to pull me down to her face, which was serious with intent.

"What was the big meeting?"

She released her grip on the apron and stepped back to lean on the counter, assuming a position of *Don't give me any bullshit.*

Honesty was new to me, but I gave it my best shot. "Nothing to worry about. I don't think I'm going to jail."

"*This* time," Dottie said.

That was true enough and if I were going to try to create a relationship here, I was going to have to give some thought to a career change.

"Yeah," I said. "This time."

But time was on my side for the moment. I thought of the free time I had coming up, not to mention the hundred thirty grand I had hidden away at my apartment. And then I thought of a way I could sort things out, with Dottie's help.

"How would you like to move into the city with me and go to that radio school?"

She didn't move her position an inch, kept her face expressionless. Slowly she stood up straight and tilted her head into a question mark, her eyelids lowered to half-mast. I raced through my mind, second-guessing myself. Did I overreach? Was she not that kind of girl? Did I even deserve her love and any subsequent happiness in my life? She took a step toward me and I felt redness in my face, trepidation in my heart.

"Can we live in the Village?"